I0565472

Outcasts of Essex

Jane Hulse

OPEN
BOOKS

Published by Open Books

Copyright © 2025 by Jane Hulse

All rights reserved. No part of this book may be reproduced, scanned, or distributed in any printed or electronic form without permission except in the case of brief quotations embodied in critical articles and reviews.

Interior design by Siva Ram Maganti

Cover image © Shutterstock AI Generator
shutterstock.com/g/ai-image-generator

To my husband, Steve Chawkins, for his boundless love, patience, good humor and sound editing.

CHAPTER 1

It's all Elisabeth Foster's fault: Elisabeth and her big belly.

If she weren't about to explode with child, I wouldn't be chilled to the bone, trudging through wet snow to a dreary shack on the other side of town.

Of course, Mother, in her quest for sainthood, is the one who ordered me on this march. It's my bad luck to be the daughter of the only midwife for miles. No doubt she's already at the birthing bed with herbs, tinctures, and appropriate scripture for balky births and hysterical mothers-to-be.

Worse yet, she's anointed me her apprentice, at her side for births, bee stings, bowel disorders and conditions too foul to even mention. I've tried to tell her a hundred times that I don't have the stomach for catching newborns. The sight of blood leaves me queasy or worse, puking my innards out. But she insists it's God's will. Obviously, God didn't consult me.

My life has been a disaster since Father printed his latest edition of the *Essex Journal.* He called the patriots "a pack of rabid dogs" for denouncing the King and his abysmal rules. Is it any wonder that nearly everyone in Essex—and probably most of New Hampshire— hates him, and now me too? Father, a loyalist, would die for the King, or so he says. I wouldn't go that far, but he's hardly ever wrong about anything, at least anything he admits.

Finally, I see the Fosters' tiny log cabin. At least it will be warm, and I can thaw out my frozen feet. But I walk into what surely is the most miserable home in Essex. Barely a stick of furniture. The floor is dirt and the place smells of wet dog. Rain plinks into buckets in the one drab room.

"What kept you, child?" Mother asks, her eyes never leaving the small bed where Elisabeth lay huddled under a ragged quilt. *I'm not a child, I'm 15, old enough to know my own mind!*

"One of the hens escaped again. Had to go round her up," I say. The truth is I overslept—a mortal sin in Mother's view. Lately she's a bundle of nerves, nagging Father daily to give up the newspaper before the rebels, the so-called "patriots," drive us out of town.

I greet Elisabeth with a cheery "good morn," which she barely acknowledges. Only 18, she looks scared to death, pale and scrawny but for the colossal bump under her quilt.

"Sarah, fetch a damp cloth for poor Elisabeth's brow."

Poor Elisabeth? My feet are numb, and Mother is already barking orders. I want to scream. But she looks like she's been up for days. Her blond hair, usually so tidy under a cap, is loose, with thick strands hanging down over her face. She keeps biting her lip, a sign this isn't an easy birth.

"I'm going to die. I know it, Mrs. Barrett," whimpers puffy-eyed Elisabeth. Sweat drenches her forehead. "God is punishing me."

"Hush up now, my dear." Mother can wrap a command in a blanket of tenderness for the likes of Elisabeth, but not for me. It's "Sarah, fetch this," or "Sarah, wash that."

I know exactly what Elisabeth has done. She let John Foster seduce her before they were properly wed five months ago. According to Mother, John was slow to marry a pregnant Elisabeth until her father stepped in and threatened a taste of his whip. Knowing all the local gossip is the only advantage to being the midwife's daughter. Of course, Mother swears me to secrecy, although it's no secret the Fosters' little bundle is arriving months early.

I press the cloth to Elisabeth's forehead. "There, this will help," I say, putting on my most soothing voice. But water drizzles down her face and onto her bedclothes.

"Just leave me be!" Elisabeth barks.

I jump back, nearly falling over. "Why must *I* be here?" I whisper to Mother.

"Shhh! Poor soul has no womenfolk in Essex."

I'm a prisoner. Sleet pounds the roof. Wind rattles the windows. The walls close in. Worse yet, the room stinks of motherwort, black cohosh and shepherd's purse—Mother's herbal concoctions for sluggish births.

When she isn't tending Elisabeth's every whim, she frets.

"I hear the smallpox has descended on Boston," she says. "That deadly scourge will be here in no time."

Soon Elisabeth lets out a shriek that pulverizes my brain. "The pains are fierce ... they're coming faster."

"I feel the child's head," Mother says, reaching under the quilt. "Sarah, come here and give me your hand."

"No, please Mother." Suddenly, I feel hot and dizzy. I can't force myself to feel or look at the source of Elisabeth's screams. Nor can I summon the excitement Mother always has at these moments. I feel the morning's porridge rising in my throat.

"Push, Elisabeth!" Mother commands. "Push like it's the devil himself fighting to come out."

Elisabeth's face contorts into a grimace that makes me look away.

"Watch closely, Sarah. Once you've birthed your own, it'll be easier."

Birthed my own? What is she thinking?

"I don't plan to marry, Mother." I didn't intend to blurt it out, but there it is.

"What nonsense! Of course you will. Now come here and give me a hand."

It's not nonsense. I've got bigger plans than having babies. Besides, I'm not as fetching as my best friend Emma. My face is long and thin. My red hair, a mess of curls that won't behave. Emma has mountainous breasts that she flaunts whenever she can. Mine are the size of two fried eggs.

Even worse, Emma has doomed even the least prospect of my marrying. "Sarah," she told me, "You're too headstrong. Boys don't warm to that."

"Sarah, pay heed!" Mother's voice jars me back to the awful reality.

Elisabeth's rigid body produces one last push and the baby shoots out, covered in white muck and splotches of blood. I struggle to keep my balance.

"Elisabeth, you have a fine son! What will you name him?" Mother beams.

"John Edgar, after my husband." Elisabeth whispers.

Naturally, I think. Name him after the irresponsible lout who got you into this mess.

Mother wipes the squalling infant clean and wraps him in a fresh blanket. Then she pauses for a moment and closes her eyes.

I know what's coming. I've heard it a thousand times before.

"Our God in heaven, thank you for giving us another soul," Mother intones, just as she does with all her babies. "May you bless John Edgar Foster with good health and a strong spirit."

The familiar words calm me. Mother loves babies, probably because she's lost so many of her own. Two from influenza just weeks after birth, and the twins to scarlet fever before their third birthday. Now it's just me and my older brother Seth.

"Sarah, put the kettle on," Mother says. "I can do with a cup of tea."

I smile. Mother knows full well that the colonists are refusing to drink tea from England just to show King George they won't be bossed around by the mighty British Empire.

"No one will tell me I can't have my tea," Mother says, removing the precious stash she keeps hidden in her medical bag. I love this tiny, wicked part of her.

By the time I leave, it's nearly dusk and Mother is asleep in the rocking chair, her Bible in her lap. She'll likely spend the rest of the night tending Elisabeth and the baby, though it seems to me they can manage just fine without her.

The air is clear, but the chill returns and I wrap my cloak tight around me. When I approach the Essex green on my way home, I see a crowd under the giant elm tree. How odd, at this time of day when everyone is settling in for the evening.

As I move closer, I hear loud voices and see something hanging from a limb. It looks like a person, a man. A man with a big-brimmed hat, like Father's, hanging by the neck from a rope. Heart pounding, I run toward the crowd, then stop abruptly.

They're laughing. Now I can see it's a straw dummy made to look just like Father with his white clay pipe and long black coat. This can't be happening. I shut my eyes and breathe deeply, willing the ghastly image to disappear.

Then the shouts begin. "Traitor! Scoundrel! Crawl back to England and take your bloody newspaper with you." Leading them on is Abner Rollins, the burly blacksmith who hates Father and makes no bones about it.

"We don't need a Tory-loving swine telling us what to think," the blacksmith's voice booms.

Then a higher-pitched voice pipes up. "Tar and feather him— that'll send a message." It's Jed Rollins, the lamebrain smithy's son.

The crowd, dozens strong, shouts: "Traitor! Traitor!" The chant becomes a roar and the whole grisly scene seems unreal. As darkness closes in, the towering pines around the green look like witches, leaning in and cackling. I want to run home, get away from it all, but I can't take my eyes off the macabre spectacle.

Then Jed takes a torch to the grinning dummy, and the crowd howls. The effigy bursts into flames and lights the sky. Then it shrivels up and falls to the ground in a pile of ash. I can't move.

As if on cue, Jed spots me. "Tell your father this is just the beginning," he shouts as the crowd roars. I back away and walk as fast as I can, hoping that no one can see my tears.

CHAPTER 2

IN THE GROWING DARKNESS, I'm desperate to find Father. I can barely make out the road and slip on a patch of ice. Panicked and out of breath, I stagger to my feet and forge ahead. I imagine the worst. Father wasn't at the green, and his print shop is dark.

When Mother finds out about this latest threat, she'll come unhinged, insisting we sail back to England before we're all slaughtered in our beds. I hate admitting it, but maybe she's right. When people threaten to hang you, it might be sensible to pack up and leave. Maybe Father will finally shut down the *Essex Journal*. His rants aren't changing anyone's mind. Tonight's drama warns of worse to come.

As I stumble on in the dark, it seems as if our house is a hundred miles from the green, not the mile that I walk nearly every day. Past Emma's brick manse, with its eight—yes, eight—fireplaces, as she reminds me all the time. Finally I see our place, puny by comparison. The light in the window gives me hope I'll find Father, or at least Seth.

I explode through the heavy oak front door, and see Father at the table by the hearth, quill pen in hand and a mess of papers before him. He's running his fingers through his unruly dark hair.

"Thank God you're here," I gasp. I try to tell him about the terrible mock-hanging in the green, but the words come tumbling out topsy-turvy.

"Sarah, I know all about it," he says, drawing on his pipe as if musing over his next commentary for the newspaper. "I was at the tavern with Jud Bascomb, and he warned me they were up to something."

"It was awful," I burst out. "The figure hanging from the tree looked just like you. I thought it *was* you at first."

"But it wasn't me, child. Now sit down and calm yourself," he says as he turns back to his writing.

Easy for him to say after his usual dram of rum at the tavern. I feel like I've just stared down death. A little comfort is all I need. As Mother says at least twice daily: Is that asking too much?

He doesn't seem the least bit troubled by a mob bent on destroying him. As I think about it, I wonder if he's actually pleased by the attention.

"I suppose you won't shut down the *Journal*," I ask, knowing the answer.

Finally, he puts down his pen and looks at me for the first time. "Of course not. And we're not running back to London. I'll keep warning those ignoramuses they're asking for retaliation if they keep provoking the King with their pathetic tantrums."

Father doesn't suffer fools. I know that only too well.

"But they could hang you for real next time," I say, barely above a whisper.

"No, they won't. They're bluffing, and I'll not be scared into keeping silent or, even worse, pretending to join their nasty little cause."

Not another lecture. I hate it when he blusters on and on, as if he's getting paid by the word. Seth comes in with an armload of wood and throws a log on the fire. I hang my cloak on the peg by the door and warm my hands over the flames.

Father was more fun before all the ruckus over the British. He'd play endless games of chess with Seth and me. He'd break out his fiddle after dinner and raise a chuckle out of Mother with his silly love ballads.

Now he just confounds me. Didn't the townspeople just send a clear signal that he's a dead man? Yet, he sits here calm as can be telling me he won't back down. In fact, he seems even more determined about his mission to set everyone straight. It's courageous but it's also, I fear to say, insane.

That's absolutely how Mother will see it. "When Mother finds out—"

"You let me worry about that. I'll not be badgered by anyone."

Seth, silent all this time, rolls his eyes. He moves in closer to Father and takes a seat. I bite my lip. Seth tends to blurt out whatever is on his mind, no matter the consequences.

"What if the patriots are right, Father, and breaking from your precious King is the smarter path?"

Over his spectacles, Father regards him as if he were vermin. The silence is thunderous. Finally, he clears his throat and employs the precise diction and quiet voice that in our house allows no argument.

"Now leave me be, both of you," he says.

Jed is true to his word: The mock hanging was just the beginning. Two days later I find a bloody pig's head on the doorstep of the print shop when I bring Father his pipe tobacco. Wrapped in a copy of the *Essex Journal*, it's crawling with maggots and stinks to high heaven. It's bloody and gruesome, but I don't even stumble. A ladylike intake of breath is all, combined with a silent wish to give even worse to the miscreants who pulled this disgusting little prank.

"Thank the Lord it's you who came upon it," Father says, lifting the gory head with his ink-stained hands. "Your mother would be hysterical by now."

I'm pleased with Father's praise. "I know who put it there," I say, relaying Jed's threat of additional terror.

"The boy's father put him up to it, no doubt," Father says. "The man doesn't have the sense of an ass."

Samuel, Father's apprentice, rushes over to see the spectacle. Tall and pleasing enough to look at, he doesn't even notice me.

"What do you intend to do about it, Mr. Barrett?" he asks, his straight sandy hair falling over his blue eyes.

"Do about it, boy?" Father's voice is booming now. "I'll let the readers of the *Essex Journal* know that it will take more than a dead pig—we'll call it *porcus mortuus*—to reverse my loyalty to the King."

"That's a fine one, sir," Samuel says with awe, still ignoring me.

"Boy, clean the type and mix up a new batch of ink. We've work to do. Sarah, you'd best go home and help your mother. You'll just be in the way here."

"Despite your good intentions," Samuel adds with a hint of a smile.

He grabs his leather apron from the hook and heads for the printing press that takes up most of the shop's space. It vexes me that he pays me little mind, and even more that he and Father seem to get on so well.

If he cares to know, I can set type just as fast as he can, and Father knows it. I learned before I was 10, much to Mother's dismay. And I could write if Father gave me a chance. But ever since Samuel arrived, I've been relegated to tiresome women's work. I'd go insane if it weren't for my diary. I'd write more—much more—if paper weren't so precious. I'd write a novel, maybe even two. Yes, someday I'll do just that.

I take my time walking home. I'm in no mood to be at Mother's beck and call. I can just hear her now: "That pile of mending won't mend itself, Sarah." I put off that drudgery this morning by pointing out the need for more needles from Mr. Bascomb's store. Not exactly the truth.

The store is the only place in Essex where anything of note ever happens. Mr. Bascomb usually has a fire blazing, and people linger and chat about everything, though these days it's all about the loathsome British and how cleverly they can make our lives more miserable.

When I walk in, all the chatter stops. I'm sure they were buzzing about their perennial source of amusement, indignation, outrage, and frustration: Father. By now, I expect he's gotten his office stoop cleaned of pig's blood and again mounted the Union Jack outside his shop—a flag that's been torn down by the town drunks more than once.

I ignore the snub and give Mr. Bascomb an especially hearty "Good morning."

"What is it you're needing today, Sarah?" he asks. It's hard not to stare at him because his face is so pock-marked from the smallpox epidemic that struck Essex 10 years ago, killing more than a dozen of us.

"Sewing needles," I say.

"Let me think, where did I put them?" It's no wonder he can't lay his hand on them right away. The place is jammed with everything imaginable—oak barrels filled with coffee, sugar, molasses, rum, flour, along with chaotic heaps of buttons, bolts of linen, glassware, lanterns, even playing cards.

I hear the rat-a-tat-tat of a drum coming from the green, a stone's throw from the store.

"What's happening now?" I ask.

"The militia, preparing for battle against the redcoats," he says. "They want to be ready if the fighting comes here." Mr. Bascomb is always careful not to say which side he favors. I like that about him; it shows he's a smart merchant.

Ordinarily, I'd linger to look over the new ribbons or the peppermint candies or peek at the latest novel from England, but I'm anxious to see what's happening on the green. I rush outside, along with everyone else, and see a ragtag band, about two dozen young men from town, trying to march in unison. Not a uniform in the bunch, but the muskets on their shoulders look real enough. A small crowd is watching.

Until now, the tiff with the British seemed so far away, just a silly stir over tea and taxes. The thought of musket balls whizzing through the air in boring Essex makes my heart race. This will surely set Father off.

As I watch, one of the marchers breaks step. It's Jed Rollins and he's swaggering toward me.

"Well, if it isn't Sarah Barrett come to mock us."

"Not so," I say with as much disinterest as I can muster.

Now the marchers encircle me, closing in on their prey.

"Did your father send you down here to spy on us?" Jed snickers. "If that pig's head wasn't enough, we've got something even worse for bloody Tories like him."

I feel my face burning red with rage. "Maybe he's right. Did you stop to think of that?"

The men roar. I command myself not to cry.

"Enough, men! Eyes forward, step smartly," a voice orders. It's Thomas Jordan, my friend Emma's older brother.

I walk away, careful to keep my head up despite my humiliation. I'm not a hateful person but I despise Jed and wish he'd march off the edge of a cliff.

I'm so deep in vengeful thoughts I nearly mow down Seth. He's supposed to be chopping firewood, at least according to Father's orders this morning.

"Where are you going, Seth? Isn't that Father's musket?"

"It's none of your concern."

As I grab his arm, he yanks it away. "If you *have* to know, I'm joining the militia."

"Have you lost your mind? You know what Father would do if—"

"I don't care. I want to fight. I'm 17 and I know what I want." Seth's dark eyes narrow, and I can see he's made up his mind.

"Father will kill you."

"I'm not afraid of him."

I try to reason. "What makes you think they'll take you, with Father so cozy with the British?"

"I'm not him! He's an old fool with ridiculous opinions."

"Seth! If he heard you…"

"Go ahead. Tell him. I don't care," he yells as he brushes past me.

As I walk home, dread settles over me like a toothache. As a boy, Seth crossed Father at every opportunity and suffered the strap on his backside for it. But he's never gone this far. If he thinks *I'll* tell Father, he's crazy.

CHAPTER 3

THWACK! I JOLT UPRIGHT in bed, heart pounding. The angry, grunting pigs march in formation, closing in on me. In my hand, the bloody axe; at my feet the headless sow, still wriggling. Slowly I open my eyes. No pigs. No axe. Gasping for breath, I scan the bedroom in the morning sunlight.

Thwack! There it is again. Gradually, my muddled brain sorts it out. Seth is chopping wood. Relief is but a flicker. As I slide off the bed, I see my diary, still open to the final line of last night's passage.

"I'm so scared for Seth, but I'll never tell him, the bloody idiot."

At least Seth had the good sense not to tell Father about joining the militia last night. Still quietly seething about the pig's head, Father spent half the evening scribbling his next blast at "those damnable rebels." Mother read scripture to settle her nerves, though I can't see that it does any good.

It's pointless to go back to sleep. I'm still rattled from the nightmare, though the details are slipping away. The cold sets me to shivering, and for half a minute I burrow under the quilt.

Thwack! There is no escaping that loathsome noise. I drag myself out of bed and pull my stays on over my white shift. I lace it up tight, then loosen the bothersome thing a couple of inches. Mother wouldn't approve, but I suppose trying to be comfortable is just another of my failings. The woolen petticoat is itchy but warm. Hurrying, I slip on my faded blue dress and apron.

I bound down the narrow staircase and open the front door as Seth's axe plunges down with a crash, scattering wood chips about the yard. He's sweating and his dark, curly hair has come loose from its leather tie at the back of his neck. He's handsome all right, in an irksome way.

"Where's Father?" I ask.

"In town." He leans his axe against a stump. "And no, I haven't told him yet, if that's what you've come running out here for. I'll tell him tonight."

"No! Don't be a half-wit."

Seth snorts. "Don't meddle in my affairs. Seems you overslept… again. You're lucky Mother rose early and went to the Fosters'."

I fire back: "You're lucky Father isn't here to see the scrawny pile of wood you've chopped this morning."

We both have the good sense not to snitch on each other. We never have. We share other secrets too, like the cave we found as children and vowed never to reveal to anyone. I know he and Emma exchange long, hot kisses behind the woodshed whenever they get the chance. I'll keep that to myself unless he riles me way too much. Even then, I'm not sure I'd turn against my best friend.

Seth's bow leans against a tree, the arrows in a leather quiver on the ground. The temptation is too great. I pick it up, slip an arrow in place, and draw back the taut string.

"Now I see what you've been up to this morning, Seth." I aim at the target, a bale of hay 20 yards away with a spot of red fabric affixed to the center with a rusty horseshoe nail.

The arrow whizzes through the air, striking just an inch from the red dot. I swell with pride. Let him try to beat that!

"Don't play with that," Seth says, grabbing the bow. "It's strictly for hunting."

"You're just prickly because I'm a better shot." He doesn't know that I practice when no one is home. But that isn't the source of his foul mood. "Was Father still worked up this morning?" I ask gently.

"Worse than ever," he grumbles. "He publishes these attacks on good men, and then he's offended when they leave a pig's head on the doorstep."

"What they did was …was…" I search for a word Daniel Defoe

13

would have used in *Robinson Crusoe*. "Savage! It was savage!"

"Don't get fancy, missy. It's just a swine."

"It's a threat!"

"Good! Maybe it'll convince him to back the patriots and the militia, not that swine of a King."

"You know he won't do that."

He glowers at me. "I should be training with the other militiamen instead of wasting my time talking to you."

He turns back to the wood pile, and I go inside realizing that I'm the one who'll get stuck with all his chores when he's gone. I already work just as hard as he does, even if he doesn't notice. I milk the cow, feed the hogs and chickens and sheep, cook the food *he* happily eats, and spin the wool for *his* clothes. All of it is sheer drudgery, especially when I'd sooner be setting my pen to paper to write some bold, adventurous tale that could proudly stand beside Defoe, Swift, and all the rest.

Inside, I stoke the fire and warm up the porridge Father left in the iron pot by the hearth. After gulping down a few spoonfuls, I gather bread, cheese and the last of the stew to bring to Mother at the Fosters' place. It's a good excuse to escape this tedium and see what's going on in town.

———

I know every inch of the muddy, rutted road—the stone fences that line the way, the occasional farmhouse, the bare maple and elm trees that are just beginning to show some greenery. In another month or so, a leafy canopy will shade the whole road. I can't wait for summer, when Emma and I pick piles of blueberries and raspberries, stuffing our mouths as we go along. Though lately, Emma seems more interested in Seth than anything else.

Emma's father and brothers are patriots, or rebels, as Father prefers to call them. Mr. Jordan goes around telling everyone it's high time to take up arms against the British before they tax us to death. Luckily, Emma doesn't give a fig about all that. She's more interested in procreation, and especially those amorous bouts of passion that precede it by some nine months. She pesters me for every womanly detail whenever I accompany Mother on her rounds.

As I come upon Emma's stately home, I see her hanging wash on the line and she asks if I'm heading for the Fosters'.

"Did you see the birth this time?" Emma's eyes are wide. "Did Elisabeth scream? What about the blood?"

I roll my eyes. "Really, Emma."

"I hope your mother's fee is better than that goat cheese she got last time. It stunk to hell and back."

"Won't be much. The Fosters have barely a stick of furniture. Maybe a skinny chicken."

"Enough about the Fosters. Are you going to see Samuel today?" Emma grins at me like a fool.

I feel my face heat up to a bright red scald, and I can't do anything about it. Why did I tell Emma about Samuel? She's been plaguing me with questions ever since.

"Even if he's about, he and Father will be debating one thing or another," I say as if I couldn't care less. "Whenever they talk, I might as well be invisible."

"Bake him a pie," Emma suggests.

"Are you crazy? Maybe I should wash his shirts and darn his socks too." It galls me but I suspect he'd take more notice if I were more like Emma—flirty, jolly, bosomy, her blond hair always just so.

"He's not as handsome as Seth," Emma feels compelled to add. "Seth has those wicked brown eyes."

She sighs so loud it leaves little room to wonder what she and my brother do when they manage to steal a few minutes alone. On the other hand, there's little need to wonder, as Emma has all but told me. I have no such details to relate about my own exploits, as I haven't had any, but I can't let on to her. With her superior knowledge on the matter, she'd lord it over me.

"Aren't you the least bit curious about Samuel?" she asks as if there's something wrong with me.

"I have more important things to think about."

"Well, go tend to your important things. See if I care." She dismisses me with a flick of her hand.

I turn back to the road and resume my traipsing toward Mother with my basket of food. If Emma knew the truth, she'd hound me to death. As it happens, thinking about Samuel occupies a good deal of my time, though all I know of him is that he's 17, bookish, and didn't take to farming. And, I have to say, he looks comely in an ink-stained apron.

As I walk into the center of Essex, I hope I'll run into him doing some errand for Father. Of course, I can't think of a single thing to say that doesn't sound simple-minded. Alas, there's no sight of his lanky frame. A teamster rolls by with a load of lumber. In front of the general store, Mr. Bascomb unloads barrels of molasses from a wagon. And poor old Mr. Butterfield, drunk as usual in his stained brown coat, is headed to the tavern.

Nearing the blacksmith's shop, I hear loud footsteps and turn, hoping it's Samuel. But no, it's the despicable Jed.

"Sarah Barrett!" he says in a condescending tone. "Was that hog's head enough to change your father's tune?"

My sarcastic answer, "Well, what do you think?" is drowned out by a thunderous noise, a horse galloping toward the green at a furious pace. No one has blown into town at such a flat-out roar since the Indian scare two years ago. The rider pulls hard on the reins and halts in front of the Essex Tavern. Both rider and horse are panting wildly.

"I have news!" the man yells between gasps. He slides down and his knees buckle as he hits the ground. "Been riding since yesterday afternoon and I have a terrible thirst."

"What's the news, young man?" someone shouts.

"The British attacked our militias in Lexington and Concord. They were after our munitions. We gave 'em hell, but they killed near 50 of our men before we sent 'em packing back to Boston."

I can hardly take it all in. The fighting is little more than a day's ride from Essex. As the commotion around the rider grows, people pour into the street, and someone gives the dust-covered man a mug of ale that he downs in a gulp.

I cringe when I see Father at the edge of the crowd pushing his way in. *Please, not another rant. Not here, not now.*

"Who fired first?" he asks the rider.

"The redcoats. But they say we did, those lying bastards."

"Sarah, give the man some food," he yells. "He must have a fearsome hunger."

Relieved that he's not on another rampage, I gape at the rider, trying to make sense of his words. *Fifty dead?*

"Sarah, for God's sake!" Father's patience is limited.

I dig into my basket and shove a hunk of bread at him from the plate I was saving for Mother. He chomps into it like an animal. His horse's wild eyes seem to be glaring at me. *What he must have been through!* Blood trickles from the horse's ribs where spurs ripped away the flesh.

I feel a hand on my shoulder gently pushing me aside. It's silver-haired Silas Spooner, the owner of the tavern, making his way to the front of the crowd. "We have no choice now but to fight," he says.

"That's what I've come to tell you," the rider pants. "The militias all over New England are gathering in Boston. They need every patriot who can load a gun. Surely you have men ready to help."

"Certainly we do," Mr. Spooner says.

"I'll go," someone yells from the back.

That voice. That irritating voice, so smug. Jed Rollins, of course.

"Not so fast, boy," Mr. Spooner says. "Spread the word: We'll meet here tomorrow at daybreak. Pack food for yourselves and be sure your wills are in order. And men, don't forget to kiss your wives goodbye. God help us!"

Wills? I freeze. Seth thinks this is some grand adventure. The very thought that he could die hasn't entered his head.

The crowd starts to leave, but Father is holding up his hand. I fear the rant about to come.

"Wait, men," he shouts. "Don't join the fight. The redcoats will outnumber you. They'll slaughter you. Our men, *our boys*, will come home wounded if they come home at all."

The crowd pays him no mind. I look away, embarrassed. Father, so proud, so wise, so smart about everything—and now, just an annoying mosquito pricking the flanks of a behemoth lumbering off to war.

Abner Rollins grabs Father's arm. "Mind what you print, my friend, or it'll be your blood spilt next."

CHAPTER 4

April 20, 1775

Dear Diary: I'm sure Seth is set on joining the rebels. He told Emma all about it, and she gushed about how brave he was. Now she's hurrying to finish the sweater she's been knitting him for weeks. She told me she and Seth kissed for five minutes and she even let him touch her breasts.

I'VE NEVER SEEN ESSEX, the very definition of boredom, so alive. The news about the battles in Concord and Lexington is only a few hours old, and it's all everyone is talking about. But I'm stuck at home roasting a chicken for dinner. Mother's orders.

I turn the spit, paying little heed to the bird. I can't get the image of the wild-eyed horse out of my head. "Mother, you should have seen the poor creature, bleeding and panting. And the rider, he was near dead from exhaustion."

"A fool's errand, if you ask me."

Mother has a way of sucking the excitement out of any spectacle. Father gets enthralled just watching the stars, but Mother looks up and sees only what the weather holds for tomorrow. She'd rather spend hours tending her herb garden, preparing all kinds of concoctions for every ailment you can imagine. She even keeps a journal of all her preparations and all the latest medical news she can find.

She would be hysterical if she knew about Seth's plan. If he had a pinch of common sense, he'd drop the whole subject. But I know he won't. Not now. All the talk in town has only stirred him up more. I think his bluster is a pathetic attempt to dazzle Emma with his manliness.

"I knew we should have stayed in London," Mother says.

Not London again! I certainly have no memory of it, though I was born there in 1759—the year after Halley's famous comet chose to revisit us, as Father likes to point out. Nor do I recall what must have been a harrowing trip across the ocean. Essex has been home for the last 14 years. London sounds all too proper, especially if Mother wants to go back there.

"We'd have peace and quiet in London. We'd have fine linen, go to the theater, even the opera. We'd be…"

Miserable, I want to shout. "I'll fetch more water for the potatoes," I say before she finishes her thought.

It's a flimsy excuse to go outside for a few blessed minutes of privacy. A chance to think about Samuel and what he's doing this very minute. He's revealed little about himself since he came down the road from Gilroy a month ago, and that only makes him more mysterious. His meager belongings include a book, which intrigued me until I discovered it was a battered old volume of legal cases and ordinances. He sleeps in the back room of the print shop, and usually eats his meals there too, but maybe today Father will bring him to dinner.

Back inside, I add a little water to the boiling potatoes. Seth comes in from the field, smelling of smoke from burning brush. A familiar dread passes over me. As he hangs his coat on the peg by the door, I sidle up to him and whisper, "Don't do it! Don't tell him!"

He grunts. For all I care, he can take a cannonball in the gut.

Minutes later Father strides in—without Samuel.

"The whole town is in an uproar!" he exclaims. "The meetinghouse was packed. The tavern closed, so did the sawmill and the tannery. The only person doing any work is the cobbler and he had a half dozen men lined up to get their shoes patched before they march to Boston in the morning."

I glance at Seth. He looks agitated, biting his lip.

"Come to the table, Benjamin," Mother says. "Set all that business aside while we give thanks and eat."

"Of course I'll have to write about this lawless idiocy," he says, ignoring her as he takes his seat at the head of the table.

"No!" Mother seldom raises her voice, especially to him. "Do you want a hanging too? Must you rile them more?"

"Yes, Mary, I must."

"Don't you owe us a little peace of mind?"

"I owe you only my great and good conscience, and that's exactly what I'd expect from each of you," he says, staring in turn at each of us as if we were suspects in some horrid crime.

Mother scowls at him. "We'll discuss this later, Benjamin." I can tell by her voice she won't let it drop. Dinner will be joyless.

Then Seth clears his throat, and I fear a certain hell is about to come. I catch his eye and shake my head, but he plunges in anyway.

"Father, Emma's brother says the militia can whip the British troops. They'll have help from the other colonies."

"No chance of that," Father murmurs. "British have five times the military might."

I kick Seth under the table to shut him up, but his face is already bursting with anger. There's no pulling back.

"Father, I'm going to Boston with the militia tomorrow."

There it is, like a bomb exploding in the middle of our chicken. Mother moans. I nearly choke.

"I know what I'm doing." Seth's jaw is set. I've never seen such determination in his eyes, and I'm scared. Father takes a deep breath before launching in.

"No! I'll not have *my* son bearing arms against the King."

"Even after Lexington and Concord?" Seth digs himself in deeper. Will he ever learn?

"Never mind Lexington and Concord. We have laws."

"Maybe you're wrong, Father, and the others are right."

I want to cover my ears.

"No, I'm not wrong. Plenty of other men in town feel as I do."

"Only those scared of the King," Seth mutters.

Oh, dear God! I half expect Father to lunge across the table and strangle him. Is he trying to provoke a fight he can't possibly win? *Seth, stop, please!*

"You foolish boy! Have you forgotten we're here through the good graces of the King?"

"I know the Crown pays you to print the royal newspaper and all their legal announcements," Seth says. "At least the rebels have the guts to act on their beliefs. They're not swayed by money."

In ominous silence, Father rises.

"Such insolence! I'll not have it in my house." He slaps Seth so hard that his chair topples over.

"How dare you suggest my beliefs are tainted by money! Even if I weren't a royal printer, I would still be loyal to my country."

I've never seen Father so enraged. It terrifies me. I'm worried for Seth, who's crumpled in pain on the floor.

"Stop it, both of you!" Mother shrieks.

Seth, fuming like a riled-up bull, pulls himself up. Father's face is full of confusion and anguish, as if he can't believe what he's just done. Nor can I. Mother looks horrified.

The sound of horses outside finally breaks the silence. "I'll see to it." I jump up, eager to get away.

Outside, Abner Rollins and his repulsive son Jed rein their horses to a stop. *What are they doing here?* Bringing up the rear is the blacksmith's brother and town jailer, Ezra Rollins. This is surely trouble.

Abner is brisk with orders: "Get your pa for me, Miss."

"I'm right here," Father yells, pushing me aside. "What do you want?"

The blacksmith swings his leg over the horse and drops to the ground. He's solid muscle. His dark, whiskery face makes him look sinister.

"We're enlisting men to march to Boston. We've got near 30 signed up in Essex. Are you with us? You and your boy?"

I gulp. Could he have chosen a worse moment?

"We want no part of any rebellion. Now get out of here."

As usual, the blacksmith has come equipped with lethal taunts. "Are you Barretts going to let others do what you don't have the courage to do? Shall we form a brigade especially for cowards?"

"I said leave, and don't set foot on my property again!" Father turns to go back inside. "Come along, Sarah."

"Maybe he's a Quaker and don't believe in fighting." It's Jed's mocking voice.

"How dare you!" I yell.

"He's no Quaker, son," the blacksmith says, stepping closer to the doorway. "He doesn't have the stomach to go. He'd rather hide behind that rag of a newspaper and pretend everything the King wants is fine and dandy."

Father whirls around and gets in his big, red face.

"I'll not be part of your treason, and you're a damned fool if you think you're above the law."

I can't believe this is Father speaking, as if he's ready to take on the world with his bare hands. I'm scared to death.

"To hell with your fancy words!" The towering blacksmith balls up his fists and lands a blow square on Father's nose. Blood sprays everywhere. Another blow catches him in the stomach, and he doubles over, groaning.

"Give him a good drubbing, Abner," his brother yells.

I can't bear to see this animal beating Father to death. Where's Seth? I look about frantically for a rock, a log, anything to stop it. The blacksmith, no doubt weighing in at more than 200 sweating pounds, is on top of Father now, pounding his head on the ground. I grab a hoe leaning against the house and swing it above my head, leveling it hard on his back. He screams, jumps up, and lunges toward me.

A man's voice behind me is cool and even: "Stop or I'll blow your head off." Seth is in the doorway aiming Father's rifle at the blacksmith.

Then a single shot cracks the air and Mother screams.

Seth tips backward against the door. I think he's reeling from the gun's kick—but something is wrong.

He slumps to the ground and a red stain quickly spreads over his white shirt.

It makes no sense. I look first to the blacksmith, then to Jed, whose gun is still aimed at Seth.

I scream in disbelief. "You shot him?"

CHAPTER 5

I'M DIZZY WITH CONFUSION. It can't be Seth's blood that's soaking his shirt, streaming onto the doorway.

Mother kneels beside him. "Oh Seth, my sweet boy! What have they done to you?"

Father's face is frozen in horror.

"Seth's brown eyes flicker. His breathing is raspy. Mother springs into action as if one of her births has gone horribly wrong. She rips open Seth's shirt and a torrent of blood gushes from the torn flesh in his stomach.

My head is spinning, my legs wobble, my hands feel tingly. I feel faint and grab the doorway to steady myself.

Mother's voice breaks through the chaos in my head. "Sarah! Take off your petticoat."

"What?"

"Now!"

Too upset to be embarrassed, I reach under my skirts and yank it off. Mother rips it apart and stuffs a wad into the wound to stop the blood. Another wave of nausea, but I steel myself to ride it through. *Please God,* I pray silently. *If you're there, please stop the bleeding.*

"'Tis very bad," Mother says. Calm and methodical: Even now, she gently lifts his wrist to check his pulse.

I can't take my eyes off Seth's face. Surely he'll awaken any second and demand I fix him a slice of bread and jam.

Behind me, the blacksmith is berating his son. "Look what you done, boy! Now quit blubbering and fetch the doctor!"

Father cradles Seth's head and issues a pathetic command, as if he were ordering him to cut more firewood: "Seth! Open your eyes!"

Meanwhile, I harangue Mother. "He'll be all right, won't he? You can fix it, can't you?" I'm desperate for some assurance. Please, please let me hear, *"He'll be fine. Don't worry, Sarah."* Anything that says it's not as awful as it looks. But she doesn't answer, and the blood is trickling down the front steps.

Suddenly Seth opens his eyes and looks straight at me. With great effort, he tries to speak. His lips move but nothing comes out.

"What is it, Seth?" I whisper, close to his face. His eyes flutter shut again.

I hear the creak of leather as Abner Rollins mounts his great black horse.

"Get down!" Father bellows, grabbing the gun at Seth's side. "You're not going anywhere. Sarah, run as fast as you can and get Sheriff Willard."

"No need for the sheriff, I'll just—"

Father levels his rifle at the stunned blacksmith. "Sarah, go now."

I can't move. I can't leave Seth. It's like I'm tethered to his arm. "But Father—"

"Do as I say! Go!"

Slowly I rise and take one last look at Seth.

I locate Sheriff Willard at the jail, with Mr. Butterfield retching in his cell after his customary drunken rampage at the tavern. We return in the sheriff's wagon to find the doctor in Mother and Father's bedroom, where Seth lay still. A scream forms in my throat. Then I see a flicker of movement in his jaw. He's alive!

At his side, Dr. Obadiah Davis pulls his suturing needles from his black leather medical bag. "I need room to work, so I must ask all of you to leave at once." His voice cracks with uncertainty and his face reddens. He can't be much older than Seth. *What kind of God listens to our prayers only to send this boy doctor who knows less than I do about saving someone?*

"I'll not leave," Mother protests. "I'm his mother. I can help you."

"Madam, I don't need your help. This is no place for a woman."

"This is the only place for a mother." She doesn't budge.

I would have cheered if I could have. I don't like this so-called doctor with his beady eyes and garlic breath. Mother has vexed him on more than a few occasions when he's arrived at the birthing bed only to find that she already has things well in hand.

"Very well, Mrs. Barrett," he says. "Everyone else kindly leave."

Reluctantly, I walk out with Father. "He'll pull through, won't he?" I ask. "Father?"

His eyes are bloodshot, his face swollen and bruised from the fight. He paces by the bedroom door.

"He's in God's hands now," he says. In all my life, I have never heard him admit that any earthly task was beyond our capabilities. Seth is in the boy doctor's hands, and if that bungler can't fix him up, then what good is a doctor? A sickening dread settles over me: Seth might die. I might never see him, talk with him, argue with him again. I feel sweat trickling down my neck. I must get some air.

Outside, Jed is sitting on the stump where Seth usually splits logs. His face is buried in his hands. Little whimpers hiccup from his slumped body. He seems so small, not the swaggering bully anymore.

He looks up at me and I look away. I can't bear the sight of his pimply face. I hate him, hate everything about him, his wispy mustache, his squinty black eyes.

"I had to shoot, Sarah," he whines. "Seth was fixin' to shoot my Pa for sure. I had to defend myself and Pa. That's what the sheriff says." He nods toward the barn where Sheriff Willard and Jed's father talk amid swigs from a jug.

I'm disgusted with all of them. Where is Jed's apology? He can't muster a simple *I'm sorry*. He hasn't even asked about Seth's condition.

"Don't you even care to know if my brother is alive?"

"Is he?" Jed whispers.

"He's alive, and you better wish you were dead when he comes after you. If you and your father hadn't barged in here, none of this would have happened."

Jed suddenly jumps up, all weepy traces gone. "Maybe you shouldn't have come after him with the hoe. You're as much to blame as—"

Then Father's voice explodes across the yard. "Boy, you'd best pray hard that my son lives." He's standing in the doorway, the rifle in his hands.

I freeze, my eyes riveted on the gun. This cannot be happening. Again.

Father slowly raises it to his shoulder, aiming straight at Jed whose mouth is wide open in shock.

"Please s-s-s-sir, I'm s-s-s-sorry…I had no choice." I can see his jaw trembling. A foul puddle is suddenly gathering at his boot.

I squeeze my eyes shut, bracing for the gunfire. Father is a madman.

"Put down that gun, Benjamin," the sheriff yells.

"I'm not going to shoot the boy," Father says, lowering the gun. "What good would that do? I'd sooner shoot his father, but he's not worth wasting the powder on."

I finally let out the breath I've been holding.

Mr. Rollins rushes to Jed, who's trying to hide his soiled pants with his hat.

"You're all right. Get ahold of yourself, boy." His face taut with anger, he turns to Father. "We were just doing our job out here. The militia needs men. If you had just agreed—"

"You're saying *I* brought this on?" Father says incredulously. "My son is clinging to life in there."

"You're the one who'll pay for turning your back on the cause. The Committee of Safety will see to that."

"This is no business for that bunch of outlaws," Father says. "This is for the law."

The sheriff steps between them, shoving each man back with his beefy hands.

I can't listen. I keep hearing what Jed said. It was *my* fault. My mind shoots back to the moment I grabbed the hoe. If I hadn't… maybe Jed is right. A wave of guilt crashes over me.

They're still yelling when I hear Mother's sharp voice. "Stop it! Stop it!" She's bounding down the steps in Father's direction, her skirts flying. "Shame on you! Shame!"

The sheriff speaks first, taking off his hat. "I'm sorry, ma'am. I'll finish up quickly, then I'll be gone."

He looks from the blacksmith to Father. "Well, there isn't any dispute that Jed Rollins shot the boy. There will be a hearing, but I can tell you right now it was self-defense." He turns to the blacksmith and his son. "You boys go home now."

"Home?" I blurt out. "My brother didn't suffer a black eye; he was shot. He could be bleeding to death. Why isn't someone going to jail? Father, do something."

"If that boy dies, someone will hang for murder," Father says, his voice quavering. "We did nothing to provoke this."

The sheriff stays calm, but barely. "Nor did they. They were here doing a service for the cause. And you, Benjamin Barrett, apparently have more important things to do than fight beside your countrymen. Go write that in your damned Tory newspaper!"

It's nearly an hour before Dr. Davis emerges from the bedroom. Emma is here now, and she holds onto my hand so tight it hurts. She's been a weepy mess the whole time. I'm too mad to weep. I want Jed behind bars, rats gnawing at him in the dark.

"There's nothing more I can do," the boy doctor says. "The wound is massive. I fear he won't last the hour."

"No!" I scream. "You're a doctor, for God's sake. Act like one." Everyone looks at me as if I've gone crazy. I don't care.

The doctor's lip is trembling, and he looks to be on the verge of tears. "No, there's nothing more to be done. I extracted the musket ball and closed the wound. Best come in and say your goodbyes."

Mother collapses in father's arms. Emma sobs. I race into the bedroom. That bumbling doctor has to be wrong.

Seth's eyes are open, and his lips are moving. A bolt of excitement rushes through me. I lower my face close to his. "What is it, Seth?

27

What are you trying to say?"

Seth moans and his eyes dart back and forth. "For God's sake, shoot! Stinkin' redcoats! We can take 'em!"

"It's the delirium talking," Mother, now at my side, says. Father leans back against the wall, his face in his hands.

"Mother, do something! Please!"

She takes my hand. "Let him be."

Desperate, I whisper, "Wake up, Seth. Please!"

He turns his head toward me, a faint smile on his lips.

"You're a fine shot with that bow and arrow," he says. Then he's gone.

CHAPTER 6

April 23, 1775

Dear Diary,

I know Seth is dead, but it feels like he'll walk in here any second with an armload of wood. Mother hasn't stopped crying, but I can't, no matter how much I try. I'd rather not go to the funeral tomorrow. I don't want to remember him cold and alone in a splintery box. I don't see that funerals do any good for anybody. People come just to watch us sob and carry on, and the dearly departed don't care.

THE CHURCH BELLS ARE still ringing when I follow Mother and Father up the granite steps into the meetinghouse. I decided to go, but only as a comfort to them. Father calls me his rock, which pleases me. Mother needs me more than ever. Both seem to be holding on by a thread.

Emma, her mother, and her two sisters are already seated in the Jordan family pew. Emma manages a wobbly smile. Even Emma, perpetually jolly Emma, is torn up in the proper way. Why can't I be at least equally and obviously distressed?

I sit down next to Mother, who wears a black mourning dress borrowed from Mrs. Jordan. I make do with a faded black gown I've outgrown and an itchy black ribbon around my neck. Father wears a black armband, same as the other men.

I finally allow myself to look at the plain pine coffin before the pulpit. The only decoration is the tasseled strip of black satin that drapes the closed lid. I imagine what Seth would think if he could see all this weepy fuss and formality. He'd likely offer up a rousing toast to his own health.

The meetinghouse is only half full. "Where is everybody?" I whisper to Father.

"Gone off to fight. Even Jed and his pals."

At least I don't have to face them. I'd rather have a tooth yanked out than let them see me cry.

The big oak door creaks open, and Samuel, in his good clothes, slips into a back-row seat. My heart races and my face heats up. I hunker down, hoping nobody notices.

Short, stout Rev. Ichabod Evans huffs his way up the five steps to the pulpit. He wipes his forehead with a handkerchief and clears his throat, a signal for all to be quiet. Suddenly I feel trapped and panicky and wish I could escape.

"Seth Barrett was a fine young man whom the Lord has chosen to take from us before his time." As the pastor gushes, I think about how today would have gone had he not been shot—or joined up with the rebels. He'd have cleared and burned brush to make way for the spring corn. No doubt he'd have tried to play some obnoxious trick on me. I can't even count his lame attempts to lock me in the privy! And he might have called on Emma in hopes she'd consent to more than a kiss. Knowing Emma, I doubt he'd have to ask twice.

"It is not our place to question God's plan, but we must heed the meaning of Seth's passing. Perhaps God sacrificed our dear boy to show us the folly in our conflicts with the Crown."

What? What is he going on about? Why isn't he tearing into Jed? If anyone deserves fire and brimstone, it's him. And what about the sheriff who stood by and did nothing? Why isn't he preaching about justice, whether mortal or divine—where was justice on that terrible day?

Rev. Evans takes a deep breath and plunges ahead. "Perhaps God is warning us to put down our weapons and mend fences with the King, before we suffer more senseless deaths."

Why is he pushing all this muck about the Crown? Especially since Seth hated the almighty British.

"Father—"

"Hush!"

I hate being hushed.

People murmur uncomfortably, but Rev. Evans is just getting started. "God is telling us we've chosen the wrong path. 'Tis not too late to make peace. As Matthew 5:9 tells us, 'Blessed are the peacemakers, for they will be called the children of God.'"

Has he lost his mind? This crowd is in no mood for peace talk. Is he agitating for a riot?

The final straw is when he calls on the whole congregation to pray for King George and the royal family.

A clatter erupts as Silas Spooner takes his wife by the arm and hustles her out, shaking his head in disgust. Then Horace and Maude Button leave in a huff too.

No one ever walks out of church before the pastor's last word. It's not only rude but tempting the wrath of God, if you believe that sort of thing. Rev. Evans has the good sense to quit his blathering before the whole place empties out.

"Now I would like to call on our pallbearers to carry Seth's coffin to its final resting place," he says. "Let us all rise as Seth makes one last journey."

I watch as Father, Mr. Bascomb and three others clumsily lift the coffin to their shoulders and teeter down the aisle. Father, his face grim, looks straight ahead. I doubt that Rev. Evans understands the rage that awaits him outside.

The congregation is abuzz as parishioners file out. Mrs. Jordan's shrill voice tops them all: "He should preach freedom, not cowardice!"

I want to scream: *"My brother is dead! Does that mean nothing to you?"*

I follow Mother and Father to the back of the hall, where I spot Samuel in the corner fidgeting with his tricorn hat. It's as if he's waiting for me.

Desperate for a little comfort, I walk right up to him, imagining his arms around my shoulders, drawing me close.

"Oh, Sarah, there you are."

"Hello, Samuel."

"Rev. Evans is fearless, speaking up for peace with this crowd. He took your father's latest editorial to heart."

His political viewpoint isn't the comfort I'd hoped for.

"Who cares about all that now," I blurt out. "My brother is dead!"

Samuel looks at me dumbfounded. I storm away, embarrassed by my outburst and mad at him for being an insensitive clod. I can't say or do anything right. I wish I could burrow into a hole and hide there for a month.

Desperate for a moment of privacy, I spot the entrance to the bell tower and dart through the door behind the altar. The narrow, dusty stairs creak as I scramble up, dragging my skirts. I don't care.

I sit on the top step, inches from the huge brass bell that rings for services, and I contemplate the mess of my life. I ache for Seth—to tease me or dare me to do something foolish like climb out on the roof. And now Samuel thinks I'm an idiot.

"Sarah? Sarah!" Mother's voice. How I wish I could ignore it. But I know I can't and head down the stairs.

"Where have you been?" Mother's eyes are red from crying. "I've been looking—oh, never mind. Come outside. Now."

Mother can muster the tenderest compassion and affection for pained women with their swollen bellies. She pours her love upon the babies. As usual, I'm just a bother.

Bitterly, I follow everyone outside to the burial grounds. Mr. Bascomb has just finished digging a hole for the coffin.

"We couldn't do it any earlier," I hear him tell Father. "Ground's still frozen."

Suddenly I shiver. *What if Seth isn't really dead? What if he cries out for help tonight and no one hears?* I try to shake the image from my mind. I know he's dead. Of course he is. What's wrong with me?

Emma breaks from her mother and sisters and rushes over to me. "I didn't say goodbye to him," she cries, grabbing my hands.

"Nobody did," I remind her. In her typically dramatic way, Emma sounds like she's the only one grieving for Seth. But she's so upset, I can't help but feel bad for her. "Can you keep a secret, Emma?"

"Of course."

"I slipped something into the coffin when no one was looking."

"Like a keepsake?"

"Sort of. You know those worn pages from *Fanny Hill* that the boys were passing around? I found them under Seth's mattress and slid them in the folds of the coffin lining. Mother would faint dead away if she knew."

"Sarah, you are sinful," Emma whispers, stifling a laugh.

I move closer to Emma and lower my voice even more. "I put something else in for you."

"What?"

"My sampler."

A smile breaks across Emma's face. "You mean *my* sampler? The one you told your mother you stitched? You, who can't thread a needle without drawing blood!"

I nod. "It'll be our secret."

It's a momentary respite. The men are lowering the coffin onto stout ropes for its descent, and part of me aches to scream. Most everyone has left, still in a lather about Rev. Evans who acts as if he hasn't just infuriated his entire flock.

He gathers us in. In a solemn voice, with none of the passion he'd shown before, he recites the 23rd Psalm. "The Lord is my shepherd; I shall not want...."

I close my eyes, just like everyone else, but I wonder: Where was the Lord the day Seth died?

———

Hours later at home, I help carry pies, cakes, and puddings to the table, thankful I have something to do rather than talk to neighbors. Why is it when something awful happens, people go into a baking frenzy? Neighbors pour in with offerings of gingerbread, shortbread cookies, custard pie. Even my favorite, bread pudding. But I can't choke down any of it.

They stand around in their mourning clothes, sip rum and offer their condolences. I wish they'd all go home and leave us be. They aren't even talking about Seth. Even Emma blathers on about the custard pie. Finally I can't hold it in any more.

"Emma, nobody gives a fig about your pie!" Her face crumples, and I wish I'd kept my mouth shut. The mourners look at me with pity.

"I'm sorry," I mutter. I don't know if Emma even heard my apology, but it echoes in my head. I grab a plate of cookies to offer the guests, who seem ravenous despite the circumstances.

The guilt creeps up on me, just like this morning when I first awoke. It's *my* fault Seth died, and Jed said as much. If I hadn't swung the hoe, the blacksmith wouldn't have lunged toward me. And Seth wouldn't have raised his gun. And Jed wouldn't have fired. I see it over and over, clear as day. It was definitely my fault.

Mrs. Jordan's loud voice jolts me back to my senses. "My husband and son set out for Boston yesterday with the others, leaving me here to run the farm. And me, with a child due soon."

"Good men, they are," says Silas Spooner, the tavern owner.

The door opens and in walks Rev. Evans. The room goes quiet, except for the crackling in the fireplace. Mr. Spooner steps right in front of him, blocking his path to the dessert-laden table.

"How dare you show your face here after that disgraceful display at Seth's funeral." Mr. Spooner towers over the rotund Rev. Evans, but the pastor doesn't seem flummoxed.

"And what part of my service did you find so distasteful?" he says, knowing the answer full well.

"We are laying down our lives to be free of the bloody King, and you call for peace and then have the gall to ask us to pray for the King's health." Mr. Spooner is an inch from the pastor's face.

All eyes are on the pastor.

"As an Anglican clergyman, I serve the Church of England," the pastor slowly explains, as if to a not-very-bright child. "I've sworn an oath to the leader of the church, our King, and that's where my loyalty lies. And if you had any sense that's where yours should lie as well."

Mr. Spooner is breathing hard and fast, his jaw clenched. "You, sir, are a disgrace to the noble cause we're all fighting for."

"Not all of us," Rev. Evans counters.

"I'd watch my back, if I were you," Mr. Spooner says. "No telling what a righteous mob will do."

"Amen!" Mrs. Jordan says, and a few nod in agreement. "We need more men like Seth to take up arms."

Father is clearly riled. He downs his glass in one gulp and plants himself before the ever-irritating Mrs. Jordan.

"Madam, I can assure you that no matter how many good men and boys march to Boston, some will not return. I would not wish that on any wife or mother."

I want to cheer. Father always knows exactly what to say. Mrs. Jordan is so stunned she dribbles pudding down the front of her dress.

I wait for someone to yell, "Yes, old Barrett knows his stuff!" No one does. I open my mouth and draw a breath, but Mother shoots me such a horrific look that I swallow the words.

"I must be going," a rattled Mrs. Jordan finally announces. "Mary, you let me know if you need anything."

"Thank you kindly," Mother says. "And you be sure to drink the herbal compound I gave you. It will give you and the baby strength."

"And God give you strength, my dear," she says, glaring at Father as she hauls her pudding-stained bosom out the door.

CHAPTER 7

June 18, 1775

Dear Diary,

*Seth has been dead only two months, but all traces of him are
gone from the house. I salvaged his bow and arrows, or they
would be gone too. Mother's way of grieving is to work herself
to death, and me as well. Father is ragged from running the
newspaper and the farm. He drinks rum every night until he
falls asleep at the table with pen in hand. I never see Samuel.
Tomorrow I'll present my brilliant plan to Father.*

BREAKFAST IS DISMAL AS usual. Mother frets about burning the
oatmeal and the day's work looming ahead. Two newborns await
her—rather, our—attention. Father is mostly silent and tries his best
to still his trembling hands.

"Benjamin, we're getting low on firewood," Mother says.

"I know, Mary," he says wearily. "I can't afford to hire an extra
hand. And I need Samuel to help me print the newspaper."

"You can't do it all," she says. Usually this leads to her daily
plea to shut down the *Essex Journal*, as if it were as easy as closing
the barn door.

This seems like the perfect moment to come to Father's rescue
and effect my own deliverance from Mother's circle of hell.

"Father, I can help you."

He looks at me with surprise, as if I've just uttered some wise proverb in Chinese.

"What?"

"I can help with the newspaper. I can set type with Samuel. I know how. We can run the press."

"No." He dismisses the idea without any thought.

That only makes me push harder. "Why not?"

"It's no place for a young lady," he says.

"I won't hear of it," Mother snaps.

That alone invigorates me. "I can do everything, Father, even make the ink. Everything except write the editorials, of course. You're the only one who can do that." Blatant flattery, but I'm desperate.

"I said no."

"I'll be there every day before sunup." The likelihood of that is zero, but I keep it to myself.

"Enough, Sarah!" he explodes. "Have it your way. Now don't bother me anymore, either of you."

A week later I open the heavy oak door to the print shop, and the stink of black lamp soot, tree sap, and linseed oil greet me. Samuel is mixing up another batch of ink. The smell used to nearly gag me. But now it's really no worse than Mother's cabbage stew.

"I have it," I say, taking Father's latest essay out from under my cloak. I smooth out the wrinkles and lay it on the desk. Father's handwriting is unmistakable, with its bold strokes and underlined words.

"Another rant," I say, just so Samuel will know I read it, every word. Seth's death has convinced Father more than ever that the rebels' cause is sheer insanity.

Samuel leans over to read the title and his blond hair falls in his face. "*Criminals, Not Patriots.*" He lets out a slow breath. "They're going to string him up for real when they read this." His eyes continue down the page. "He calls the Committee of Safety a band of outlaws."

"Well, they are," I say. "They let Seth's murderer go free!"

"It wasn't exactly murder. It was an accident. You know that, Sarah."

"How can you call it an accident when Jed aimed right at him! People can't go around shooting other people. That's ... that's anarchy."

Samuel looks stunned and amused that a word like that has flown out of *my* mouth. Let him be surprised. I have plenty more words. After all, I dive into the London newspapers as soon as they hit the print shop.

A little twitch of a smile crosses Samuel's face. "I wouldn't quite call it *anarchy*."

"Call it what you want." His condescending tone annoys me. Worse than that, he's set my mind to thinking about Seth's death. Does Samuel think I'm to blame for this "accident" too? I won't ask him—I couldn't bear it if he does.

For hours we set type, taking one tiny metal letter at a time from the drawers and fitting them into a form. It's a mind-numbing, neck-twisting feat, especially as the letters are upside down and backwards. My hands and back ache, and I'm tired and hungry. But I won't rest until Samuel does. I won't have him call me a weakling.

I concentrate on Father's high-flying denunciation, which will convince no one. Only a few people in town agree with him, and they're afraid to say so. The others despise him, but they can't wait to see what he prints every week. They despise me too. Emma was invited to see Abigail Spooner's new harpsichord. Not me. Emma was asked to the Bates's house after church for coffee. Not me.

I doubt Emma even thinks about Seth anymore. She jabbers on about the militia, a regular sight in Essex now. She's out gawking whenever the ragtag groups of men and boys, weighted down by their muskets, bayonets and bulging knapsacks, trudge through town on their way to Boston.

Emma thinks I've lost my mind. "Working at the print shop? Boring!" she told me last Sunday at church. Then she smiled in her sly, know-it-all way. "This is about Samuel, isn't it?"

"No!" I insisted. "Well, maybe." I'm not even sure myself. I can't dismiss the excitement I feel when I see him, even though he vexes me most of the time. I know as much about printing as he does, probably more. But he's always right there, ready to show me how to set type faster or tell me to slow down and make fewer mistakes.

I study his tall, thin frame and the way he keeps his back perfectly straight as he works. Will he ever take a break? Finally, he stops to study the mass of metal pieces that will become the front page. At the top is the article from the *Connecticut Courant* about the thousands of British troops descending on Boston to put down the rebellion. Next to it is Father's editorial calling the rebels "foolhardy."

"There's no telling how far the town will go this time," Samuel says. "They're losing patience with him."

"Are you saying we shouldn't print it? You're not afraid, are you?"

"Of course not… but we're losing subscribers and advertisers. Old Spooner pulled his ad for the tavern this week."

"But we have three new ads." I point to the Irish linens a widow is selling, a farm for sale, and the search by the town for a new schoolteacher.

"I don't want to scare you, Sarah, but did you hear what they did to that New York publisher for backing the British?"

"No."

"They ransacked his house and burned down his press. He fled for his life."

I shudder. I've never pictured Father in any real danger, at least nothing he couldn't fend off with his clever words. Could he be wrong? I never used to think so.

With a mighty push Samuel cranks the press to life, and I shove my worries aside. He eases the inked drum over each dampened sheet of paper, a job I could do equally well. Instead, I'm relegated to hanging up each sheet to dry without tearing it. Before long it looks like rows of clothesline with papers hanging over most of the shop.

I manage to keep up with him, which pleases me. Last week I was too slow, and he gave me an earful. I could have given him an earful right back, but I held my tongue.

"I'll fetch a load of wood out back for the fire, then we'll clean up," he says. My eyes follow him out the back door. There's something about him that bothers me. In the weeks we've worked together I've peppered him with questions. I learned little, except that he reads whatever he can find, especially ancient law books that would put me to sleep.

The front door creaks open, and I expect to see Father walking in to make sure we haven't made a mess of things. But it's the silver-haired tavernkeeper, Silas Spooner, and behind him, Abner Rollins, just back from the fighting. The sight of the hulking blacksmith rattles me, and I struggle to stay calm.

"How may I help you?" I ask. "An advertisement?"

Mr. Spooner starts to speak but the blacksmith pushes him aside. "We want to see what lies your father is printing this week."

"Well, you can't," I say, steeling myself. "My father doesn't allow it. You can read it tomorrow like everyone else."

"Abner, let me handle this," Mr. Spooner says. He gives me a forced smile that makes me wary. "Look, the Committee of Safety won't allow propaganda in favor of the redcoats. That just hurts the cause we're all fighting for."

"Not all of us," I say. My boldness comes out of nowhere, except maybe the hatred I have for Jed and his father.

"You'll regret this," Mr. Spooner says, still smiling. "The town's had enough of your father's contemptuous words. Just show us—"

"No!" I glance at the back door. Where is Samuel?

The smithy fixes his black eyes on me. "You wouldn't want something to happen to your Pa would you? There's no telling what people will do when they're stirred up."

"Are you threatening us?" I glare at him.

"Just stating a fact." He moves in closer, as if testing my boldness.

"While your Pa is printing this tripe about how we should all get along with the lousy British, good men like my son are fighting on the battlefield."

"Your good son killed my brother."

"Abner, we're wasting our time here," Mr. Spooner says. But the blacksmith elbows him aside and comes so close I can smell the stink of stale ale.

"Let's have a look at those papers hanging up," he says.

"No!" I thrust my arms out to block his way, but he shoves me aside. "Samuel!" I scream. "Samuel!"

Mr. Spooner tries to pull him back. "You drunken fool."

"Leave me be, old man," he yells.

Samuel finally bursts through the back door with an armload of wood.

"Get away from her!" The wood crashes to the floor, and he grabs a hefty log. "Get back!"

The blacksmith doesn't budge. "I'm not leaving here until I get a look at those papers," he says. "If it's more sympathy for the bloody Tories, we'll build a bonfire to get rid of the whole lot."

"No! You can't do that!" I scream.

"Let's all settle down," Mr. Spooner says, as if he can make it right with a broad smile and the smooth tone of his voice. "Now young man, under the law the Committee of Safety gives us the authority to put down subversive behavior. Show us the papers and there will be no more trouble."

Mr. Spooner takes a step toward the papers and Samuel blocks his way. "You know full well you need an order signed by a magistrate to barge in here and take these papers."

"No, we don't. The Committee of Safety is all the law we need."

"You're wrong," Samuel says. "Under statute 285 of the Act for the Impartial Administration of Justice, you proceed with this and you're looking at jail for assault, robbery and destruction of property. If you don't believe me, go check with the magistrate."

I'm pleasantly stunned. This is Samuel, sounding every bit like a real lawyer.

"Don't listen to him. He's just a boy, a cocky one at that," the blacksmith grumbles.

Mr. Spooner looks perplexed. He stares at Samuel for several seconds before he speaks. "Abner, let's go."

"No!" the blacksmith snarls. "What's the matter with you?"

But Mr. Spooner is already at the door. "Come along, we're not done with them."

As the blacksmith turns to leave, he glowers at me. "You better learn your place, Missy."

When the door closes, Samuel bars it. "Are you all right, Sarah?"

"Yes, of course." But I can't keep up this charade. My hands are shaking, and my legs feel wobbly. "No, not really. Is that true, all those legal things you said?"

"Maybe," he says with a sly grin.

I look at him with new respect.

"You're shivering, Sarah." He takes off his jacket and puts it over my shoulders. I breathe in deeply, inhaling the manly smell of leather. He puts his hand on my shoulder. "Would you like me to walk you home?"

I start to say I don't need a bloody chaperone. But something stops me. "I'd like that." And I mean it.

CHAPTER 8

June 19, 1775

Dear Diary,

Samuel wanted to kiss me on the way home tonight. I'm sure of it. But he didn't... didn't even hold my hand. Now I keep wondering what his lips feel like. I can't tell Mother anything about the threat from crazy Abner Rollins. She'd ban me from the newspaper. Father would hunt him down with his gun.

It's barely morning when I race off for the print shop, certain that Samuel lay in a pool of blood. I dreamed that the blacksmith had returned with a knife, and it was terrifying.

If Samuel is unscathed, he's already distributed the newspaper to Bascomb's general store and other spots around town. No doubt everyone's in an uproar over Father's latest pronouncements. Mr. Spooner and the blacksmith may already be there with a court order to shut it down, not to mention somehow shutting up Father for good.

I'm out of breath when I reach the green. All of a sudden, the meetinghouse bells clang so loud that a flock of pigeons take wing from a giant elm on the grassy common. It's Thursday, not Sunday: No call for church bells. Young Ann Brewster rushes out of the cobbler shop with a baby in one arm and a pair of shoes in the other. "Is it the British come to attack us?" she yells at me.

"No, that's two bells." Now I'm certain it's about Samuel and the print shop, and fear grips my chest. As people gather, I look all about for him but to no avail.

After the clanging finally stops, Silas Spooner climbs onto the meetinghouse steps and raises his hands for silence.

"I have news of the gravest kind," he says. The knot in my chest grows tighter. Where is Samuel?

"A messenger arrived this morning from Boston," he pauses, looking about uncomfortably. "As you know, our brave Essex men joined others to prepare for battle with—"

"Get on with it," yells Mrs. Brewster. "My husband was one of them."

"There's been a fierce battle in Charlestown, near the Boston Harbor. The redcoats attacked and took our ground, a place called Bunker Hill." He pauses again. "We lost more than a hundred good men, four from Essex."

"Merciful God!" Mrs. Brewster exclaims. "Is John safe and sound?"

Clearly uncomfortable, Mr. Spooner looks down at his papers. "Essex can be proud of the sacrifices our men have given to this noble cause."

"I don't care about your noble cause," Mrs. Brewster yells as her baby starts to wail. "Just tell me plain and simple. Is he dead?"

Mr. Spooner finally looks straight at her and after an interminable silence, he says with a quivering voice, "Yes, my dear, I'm so sorry."

"No!" she shrieks.

I want to comfort her, just as Mother would. I put my arm on her shoulder, but she shoves me aside and marches right up to Mr. Spooner's face.

"Look what your noble war has done. My John would still be here to run the farm. Now I must carry on by myself with barely enough food, and another baby on the way. Is your precious war worth all that? Well, is it?"

Clearly addled, Mr. Spooner clears his throat.

"Yes, but—"

"What about my boy, Thomas?" It's Emma's father, pushing his way to the front of the crowd.

"He's not on the list of dead," Mr. Spooner says. "Could have been wounded. Hundreds were."

"Good God, Silas, just tell us who died," a man in the crowd shouts.

Mr. Spooner looks as though he might cry. "Someone will need to tell Martha Ames her husband and son both took fire and died on the field." I gasp along with everyone else.

"And the fourth man?" It's Abner Rollins, his voice loud and gruff.

"I'm sorry, Abner. They say Jed died immediately."

The blacksmith stands rigid as a board, "No! Tell me it's a mistake. Show me the damn list."

Mr. Spooner hands it over. "I wish it weren't so, my friend."

The blacksmith crumples the paper, then collapses. His chest heaves with big, choking sobs.

I can't believe it either. I study the man I've reviled so the last two months. For a moment I'm glad he feels such pain. *Now you know what it's like.* But as I watch, I start to pity him. And I'm ashamed that I wished for Jed to die in some painfully gruesome way.

Mr. Spooner helps him to his feet. "Jed gave his soul for his country. You can be proud of that, Abner."

"Amen," Emma's father shouts. "What about the wounded? Where's that list?"

"I have it—be patient," Mr. Spooner says, unfolding another paper with trembling hands.

Mr. Jordan snatches it from his hands and peruses it quickly calling out names. "Baker, Davis, Fuller, Hill, Johnson." Then he stops suddenly. "Jordan, Thomas Jordan. Leg wound…may require amputation."

"I'm sorry," Mr. Spooner says.

"Amputation? That's a death sentence," Mr. Jordan says.

"Some of them make it," Mr. Spooner says without any visible conviction.

"Most of them don't—we both know that."

Instantly I think of Emma. First Seth, now Tom. She'll be devastated.

A jolt of sadness overcomes me as I think of the last time I saw Tom. He'd put a stop to Jed's taunting when the militia was training. I never thanked him.

Mr. Jordan looks shaken as people encourage him not to give up hope. I approach, hoping I can somehow do better than the others.

"I'll be praying for Tom," I say, realizing immediately how empty that sounds, especially coming from me. "If there's anything I can do…"

He gives me a weak smile. "Perhaps there is, my dear. Maybe you can talk some sense into your father."

Before I can answer, Mr. Spooner pipes up. "The British paid a steep price at Bunker Hill," he tells the crowd. "We killed more than 200 of theirs. Wounded a thousand. Let's show our support for the militias and press on for victory."

The crowd soon breaks up, and I head across the green to the print shop, still reeling from the news about Jed. And Tom too. Mr. Jordan's final words keep echoing in my head. He thinks I might have some sway over Father? Preposterous!

"Sarah, wait!" It's Samuel. I'd forgotten all about him.

"Did you hear about Jed?" I ask.

"Yes. I guess you don't have to worry about that bully anymore."

His callousness takes me aback. "I didn't actually wish him dead."

"Yes, of course," he says, sounding unconvinced. "And the others?"

"I knew the Ames boy a little," I tell him. "He and Seth hunted pheasant together last fall. Now they're both dead, and Jed too. How can that be?"

"It's war, Sarah," he says as off-handedly as if he were talking about an approaching cold spell. "Spooner paid me a visit early this morning. Said he would make sure we receive no more paper shipments from Boston."

"He can't do that," I say. "Wait until Father—"

"He says paper is just like tea. If it comes from England, it's banned by the Committee of Safety."

"We'll have to make newsprint out of rags," I say. "That takes forever. Father won't stand for this."

"I have something to show you," he whispers. He reaches in his knapsack and pulls out a dark flintlock pistol. "Rev. Evans gave it to me. Said I had to be prepared if Abner comes after me."

I stare at it, wanting to hold it, wanting to feel my finger on the trigger. But Samuel puts it away quickly.

"If Abner wants to test me, let him try," he says. "I'd love it if he did."

CHAPTER 9

MOTHER IS IN AN extraordinarily happy mood tonight as she sets three places for supper. She hasn't quoted scripture all day. I even caught her humming a tune.

"That's a fine-looking pie, Sarah," she chirps.

Something isn't right. I burned the piecrust as usual. I've been so worried she'd talk Father into fleeing with the other loyalists that the pie was the last thing on my mind. Maybe she's trying to jolly me up before she casually mentions that my life in America is over.

But she continues to chatter. "I visited Emma's mother this afternoon. Her labor has started, and I expect she'll give birth by the morning. We'll go see her after supper."

"Mother, you don't need me to go too. Mrs. Jordan's birthed so many babies she can do it standing on her head."

"Sarah!"

Still, she indulges a slight giggle. Something is definitely wrong. Mother never giggles.

When Father joins us at the table, I catch the two of them exchanging a sly smile. He even gives her shoulder a tender pat. I don't know what it means, but it's better than the gloom that has hung over the house since Seth died.

During grace, Mother breaks into a huge grin. "And thank you Lord, for blessing us with another child."

I nearly choke on my cider. "A baby? You're having a baby?"

They both laugh, the first gush of happiness I've seen in an eternity.

Then it hits me: There will be no leaving Essex, at least for a long while. Mother would have to be insane to undertake an ocean crossing. That means we'll be staying in Essex—and I'll see Samuel as usual tomorrow at the print shop.

"That's wonderful, Mother." Of course, she can't possibly know just how wonderful, and I mean to keep it that way.

"And what news did Rev. Evans have today when you stopped by for his sermon, Sarah?" Father asks.

"The pox has taken Mary Bradley's husband, and two others are down with it as well."

Mother stops ladling the soup into our bowls. "That's dreadful news," she says, setting the kettle down with a jolt. "The last time the pox swept through it brought total misery. Some of those who didn't die were wishing they had."

I don't remember the pox, but every Sunday in church I see the hideous scars it left on poor old Mrs. Simpson's face. Mother, Father, Seth and I were all spared, but that was before Mother made it her mission—her God-given mission—to treat anyone and everyone. Sometimes I wonder if I'm really her daughter because, in addition to all our other differences, I don't feel that way in the least.

"I'll be needed more than ever now that Dr. Davis is leaving soon for Massachusetts to aid the rebels," she says.

"I hope you're not planning on treating any smallpox patients," Father says. "You must think of the baby." *What about me? What am I—cold porridge? What if she contracts it and gives it to me?*

"I can't ignore someone suffering, regardless of their politics," Mother says.

"I know, but your family comes first," he says.

They stare at each other for what seems like a minute. It's obvious neither will give in. Father takes his usual tack: He changes the subject—his way of stifling more discussion.

"Now Sarah, did the reverend give you his next sermon for the *Journal*?"

"It's his usual appeal to the Almighty for peace. He also warned that people who flee the rebels won't be any closer to God if they head for Quebec or London, or God knows where."

"This family is not leaving," Father says calmly.

Mother opens her mouth but, mercifully, there's a pounding on the door and Emma bursts in.

"Please, Mrs. Barrett, come quickly. It's my mother. It's the baby. Something's not right. Please hurry."

Mother grabs her battered satchel of herbs, tinctures, and medicinal aids. "Sarah, I'll need your help."

———————————

Emma's house is twice as big and twice as nice as our house. Flowery blue wallpaper covers the long hall and stairway up to the five bedrooms. No one else in Essex has wallpaper imported all the way from Philadelphia, Emma brags.

We follow her up the stairs with its shiny mahogany banister. Mrs. Jordan lies still on a sheet soaked in sweat. Her eyes are closed, and her face is ashen. She looks dead, but suddenly she sucks in a shallow breath and cries out in pain.

Emma's older sister, Martha, jumps up from the bedside. "Emma, what have you done?"

"I brought Mrs. Barrett to help Mother."

"You foolish girl! You know what Father said!"

"I don't care," Emma says. "She needs help now."

Mother flashes her don't-worry-about-a-thing smile at Martha, a smile that just barely hides her impatience. "What's the trouble? I helped your mother through her last labor."

"Father wants the doctor this time," Martha says. "He's gone to fetch him."

I can't imagine any mother-to-be relieved to see Obadiah Davis, the pompous boy-doctor with the garlicky breath.

"Why the doctor this time?" Mother's voice is full of suspicion.

"Not for me to say, Mrs. Barrett," Martha says.

I don't need anyone to tell me why—it's our loyalty to the King that's turned the Jordans and everyone else in town against us.

"At least, let me have a look," Mother insists. "Perhaps I can comfort her."

"It's all right, Martha," Mrs. Jordan whispers. "I'm glad she's here."

Mother puts her hand on Mrs. Jordan's damp forehead and speaks softly. "Shall we do this, Hannah?"

"No use, I'm going to die. The child too."

"We'll let the Lord decide that, my dear."

I watch her with envy: Her touch so soothing, her voice strong and sure. For a second, I wish it were me on the bed, Mother stroking my forehead.

Mrs. Jordan closes her eyes. If she dies, can Mother save the baby? The room is stifling. I wish I were anywhere but here.

"Sarah, bring me some cool water and cloths."

Thank God! I can leave. Emma and I stride out to the well with a bucket.

"Is she going to die?" Emma asks tentatively. "You're almost a midwife. You know all about these things."

"I don't know *anything* about these things," I say. Even Emma assumes I'm destined to follow my mother. I regret my harsh tone right away. She's scared, but I can't tell her that her mother is as close to death as anyone I've ever seen.

"Mother won't let anything happen to her."

I hope my words sound convincing. I half believe it myself. Mother seldom bungles a birth, or for that matter, anything else. She's always right, righteous, and in command.

When we return to the bedroom, Mother is moving her hand slowly over Mrs. Jordan's big belly. Gone is the look of confidence, replaced by the deep worry lines that crease her face when things aren't going well.

"What is it, Mother?" I ask.

"A breech."

Emma looks puzzled and scared.

"It's when the baby—"

"I know what it is, Sarah. The head should come out first, but it's upside down. And stuck."

That's exactly what it is, and it could end disastrously. "Don't worry," I murmur.

"The only way I know is to try to turn the child around," Mother says. "But it may be too late."

"No, you shouldn't do that," Martha says, grabbing her arm. She turns to Emma, eyes angry. "Look what you've done. Father will punish you good for this, and I hope he throws you out."

Mother clears her throat. "We'll let Mrs. Jordan decide. Sarah, fetch the rum from my bag. It will help with the pain."

"I won't be a party to this," Martha says, flouncing out the door.

Mother slowly spoons the rum into Mrs. Jordan's mouth. After several minutes, she opens her eyes.

"All right, let's begin. May God be with us."

I have more faith in Mother than God right now. God has failed me lately. But Mother somehow always comes through.

I hear the front door opening and then footsteps on the stairs. Mr. Jordan suddenly barges in, followed by a frightened-looking Dr. Davis.

"Why is this woman here?" Mr. Jordan yells, shoving a finger in Mother's direction.

"I'm here because your wife could die without swift attention," she tells him.

"The doctor will judge how sick she is. Now, step aside and let him do his job," he orders.

I know Mother won't take the doctor's intrusion kindly. For his part, he looks utterly despairing that she has beaten him to the birthing bed once again.

A low moan comes from Mrs. Jordan.

"Daniel?"

He gently takes her hand. "I've brought the doctor. He'll know what to do. You rest easy."

"But I don't want the doctor, I want Mary Barrett."

"Now Hannah, I thought we decided to call for the doctor when the time was right."

"I'm afraid." She lowers her voice. "And it doesn't seem right… proper." It's clear she's embarrassed that a man, no less the bumbling Dr. Davis, should be present and even touch such a private place. It's always been women's work.

Mr. Jordan looks unsure. "But Hannah, Dr. Davis surely knows all there is to know about delivering babies. He's had schooling. Obviously, he's far better suited to help you than this . . . well, there's no trusting her!"

I was right! He didn't have to call her a Tory to express his hatred for her.

"You don't deserve my mother!" The words shoot out before I have time to think.

He looks at me, clearly stunned. "Why, you rude little heathen!"

He steps closer to Mother, towering over her. "After this, you'll be lucky to find any work at all. We don't want any traitors here. Go, and take your ill-bred daughter with you."

"Don't be a fool," Mother says in a sure, steady voice. "But if you prefer Dr. Davis, I'll take my leave. Sarah, get my bag."

"But Mother…" How she can keep calm strains belief.

"Don't go," Mrs. Jordan screams.

Mother takes her hand. "Dr. Davis will take care of you. I'm sure he knows how to turn the baby so it will have safe passage."

I see the sudden fear in the doctor's beady little eyes.

"It's a breech?" His cheeks burn crimson, and he wipes his forehead. "Uh, uh . . . perhaps Mrs. Barrett would like to assist me?"

I will myself not to smile.

"For God's sake, Daniel, say yes," Mrs. Jordan pleads.

He's silent, stone-faced. Does he care more about politics than his wife?

"As you wish, my dear. But this isn't the end of it," he finally says, glaring at Mother as he leaves.

The doctor opens his black bag and takes out a metal contraption that looks like a medieval torture instrument.

"What's that?" I ask.

"Forceps. I can pull the baby out with these. They're from England, and they're something a midwife wouldn't know anything about." He holds them in the air, clasping and unclasping them.

I picture a gruesome scene with the baby coming out in pieces. "Mother, you can't let him use that."

She's horrified but stays calm. "I think I can turn the baby around

52

with my hands. I've done it before. Let me try."

"I certainly can handle this myself, but if you insist..." the doctor says.

He knows he's in way too deep. Mother moves in closer to Mrs. Jordan and massages her belly. "Now calm yourself." She positions her hands, feeling the shape of the baby. "This may pain you." In one swift, smooth move, Mother tries to shift the baby's position.

Mrs. Jordan screams.

"Did it work?" I ask.

"No." Mother's brow is damp with sweat. With the second attempt, Mrs. Jordan cries out again.

A trickle of sweat emerges from under Mother's cap and slides down her face.

"Here," I say, dabbing her forehead. She simply cannot fail, not now. It's as if all womanhood is resting on her shoulders.

Dr. Davis grows impatient. "She'll die if we don't get that baby out." He picks up the forceps.

"Mother!"

She blocks his skinny arm like a seasoned fighter. "You cannot go in and pull the child out limb by limb. They'll both die."

I feel light-headed and grab onto the bed frame. "Mother, try once more. Please."

She positions her hands on the big belly and gently rocks.

Mrs. Jordan suddenly gasps and opens her eyes wide.

Mother looks up, smiling. "Bless the Lord. It's turned. Now we can let nature do her work."

CHAPTER 10

THE NEXT MORNING DR. Davis appears at the door before we've even cleared away the breakfast dishes.

"What brings you here so early?" Mother says as if she's greeting a dear friend, not the imposter who claims to know everything about doctoring. His face is broken out in red blotches and his hands fidget.

"I'm leaving for Boston this morning to serve General Washington. They're sorely in need of surgeons, and I can't stand by and not help." The words come out haltingly and with great effort.

"You don't think the town of Essex has more need of your services?" Mother asks with mock earnestness.

"That's why I've stopped to see you Mrs. Barrett. You were of great assistance to me with Mrs. Jordan's birth last night." *Assistance? Mother did everything. He was merely in the way.*

"So, you've come to thank me," Mother says.

"Well, yes." These two words come out as if pried by forceps. "Also, Essex will be without a doctor while I'm gone. Of course, you're not a doctor but I thought perhaps you could take care of the sick and injured until I return."

"So, you think this babbling, uneducated woman is capable of taking over your duties?" Mother says, stifling a smile.

"I think you'll have to do," he says. "There's no one else."

"Well, I'll certainly do my best to fill your shoes—big though they are." Mother can be such fun.

Then she turns serious. "What about the smallpox? You know about the latest cases in Essex?"

"No, I don't." His eyes are shifty. I can tell he's lying. Little wonder he's anxious to leave town. "Not much we can do for the unlucky wretches who contract it. They'll either make it, or they won't," he says with all the compassion of a snail.

"We can inoculate them *before* they get it," Mother says.

"No, we can't!" He looks as if Mother has suggested robbing the church collection plate. "You know very well, Mrs. Barrett, the town council won't allow it."

"Why not?" I ask, bracing for the worst.

"Inoculation is a dangerous, harebrained scheme that violates God's will and man's laws," he says, spitting out the words as if they were pox-laden themselves. "It could cause a massive epidemic."

"Not if it's done correctly," Mother asserts. "It can save lives and reduce hideous scarring among the survivors."

I fear another lecture coming on. Mother has told me all about inoculation. More than once. It's the most nauseating, disgusting ordeal I can imagine. First, they make a small cut on your arm. Then, they gather the revolting pus from some poor, pox-stricken soul and rub it into the gash. By some miracle, if you suffer only a light case, it protects you from ever getting it again.

"I've read of Dr. Boylston's work so many years ago in Boston," Mother says, drawing a surprised look from the doctor.

"Hogwash! No competent doctor would risk his patients' lives, not to mention his own good reputation."

Mother is unstoppable. "Their reputations? Even as we argue, doctors in Boston, Philadelphia and other places are doing it with some success."

By now, the boy-doctor looks like he'd prefer inoculation to spending another five minutes with Mother. Still, he persists.

"You must know, then, that some of their patients die horrible deaths anyway, as if they were subjects in some grotesque experiment. And if they ignore the isolation order, the pox will spread far and wide, and it'll do what the plague did when it killed a quarter of London a century ago. Is that what you want?"

"I'd sooner suffer a light case of the pox than risk getting a severe case the way you seem to believe God intended," Mother says. "That's a death sentence."

"I still say it's a reckless idea. That's why some towns have banned inoculation and fined those who are crazy enough to do it."

I'm still wallowing in the thought of someone else's pus in my body as the doctor opens the front door to leave.

"If you're wise, you'll forget all about it," he calls out. "Good day to you both."

Not only does Mother *not* forget about it, but it's all she talks about at supper.

"Benjamin, imagine if we could stomp out the pox, once and for all," she gushes as she dishes up the cornbread and hash.

It seems the boy-doctor's point about inoculation being a diabolical mission has made no impression on her at all. That's more than strange, as Mother ordinarily pays great heed to the wrath of God. I like this new side of her.

Father isn't having any of it. "Too risky. Too experimental."

"It's not new—it's been used for centuries in places like Africa and China," Mother says. "I've read about it in *your* newspapers."

"Then you should know it's been a bitter controversy here and elsewhere for decades."

They yatter on, then suddenly Mother gets up from the table and looms over Father with a knife and fork still in her hand. "The idea of the earth revolving around the sun was once controversial too," she says. "Even as I try to argue some sense into your stubborn head, doctors in Boston are doing inoculations and saving lives."

"And how would you know that?"

"I was treating Adam Skinner's boil when his son returned home from the fighting. He said the pox was rampant there, and inoculation was all the talk.

"Then you probably know that General Washington has banned it for the troops," Father says with sickening smugness.

"I fear the worst here in Essex," Mother sighs. "Someone must care for these poor sick souls."

"It doesn't have to be you," Father says. "You'll soon have a baby to worry about. I'll not have you bring the pox into our home."

———————

I knew Mother wouldn't take kindly to being told no. The next morning over oatmeal and cider she looks straight at Father and delivers the news.

"I've given it a lot of thought and I've decided to inoculate myself with the pox. God willing, I'll have a mild case of it, and then I can tend the sick."

Father starts to open his mouth.

"Don't try to convince me otherwise, Benjamin. Save your arguments. I've made up my mind."

I can't believe this is *my* mother, defying Father outright instead of cloaking her intent with some Bible verse or, as she does sometimes, saying nothing at all but going very much the way she wants.

"How could you even consider putting Sarah and me at risk, not to mention our unborn child?" Father spouts. "I said 'no' and I meant it," he asserts, signaling the matter is closed.

"I'm hoping that you and Sarah will inoculate as well," Mother says, dropping yet another bomb.

"Are you mad, woman!" he yells. "You know that inoculation means we quarantine for a month while we're ailing and contagious. I can't afford to be holed up and not working."

I want to scream, *What about me?* Is anyone going to ask what I want to do? Not that I have the faintest idea.

"I know you'll come to your senses, Mary," he says, rising from the table abruptly. "I'm heading out to the field."

"It's raining, Father," I say.

"I don't care!" he says slamming the door.

Mother turns to me. "I still intend to do it. It's worth the risk."

"What about the town council?"

"They don't have to know just yet," she says clearing the dishes from the table.

Then she looks straight at me, and I know what's coming. I've been dreading it.

"As my apprentice, Sarah, I'd be much obliged if I could inoculate you too." After a long pause, she adds, "then you could help me treat the pox sufferers."

"Mother, I don't want to do it," I stammer. "I can't do it."

"You *can't?*"

How can I tell her all the reasons why this is a terrible idea. First, I don't want a knife ripping my flesh, even for a good cause. And the sight of someone else's pus will send me to my knees puking. Perhaps the worst of all, being cooped up with Mother for an entire month—no walks with Emma, no sight of Samuel—would make me crazy.

I tell her the only thing I figure she'll accept.

"I'm afraid. I don't have your strong constitution, Mother."

She can't hide her disappointment at the notion that her only daughter isn't willing to risk a horrible death or even modest disfigurement. Her eyes, so hopeful, are sad. It's yet another of my failings.

But then she surprises me, as she so often does these days. In a voice warmer than the morning's oatmeal and sweeter than a drop of honey, she comforts me.

"Child, I won't make you."

CHAPTER 11

"You made the right decision," Samuel tells me. I'm huddled over a sea of lead as I set the type for an article about King George's latest call for more taxes. "Too risky. You could die."

"Maybe, but Mother says inoculation has been used in Africa for centuries," I say.

"And you trust witch doctors in Africa more than our learned doctors here? Have you ever heard of science?" His sarcasm annoys me.

"Samuel, you can't deny the pox is spreading all around us here," I say. "Two new cases from the tannery, and God knows where others will crop up. We should print something about it—let people know. Perhaps Mother has the right idea."

"You sound like you've changed your mind about your mother's disgusting experiment," he says.

"No, I haven't. But inoculation does seem the saner course." I would rather die than admit to him I'm too scared to shove foul pus into a fresh wound on my arm.

"I'm relieved," he says, smiling. "Saves me having to worry about you."

I'm so pleased by his caring that I nearly drop a handful of type.

"At least your face will be spared the ugly scars," he says.

I think he means well, but it rubs me the wrong way. "So you'd sooner have me risk death from getting the pox the natural way, than see my pock-marked face."

"No, that's not it at all," he says. "You're twisting my words." He wipes the sweat from his face. "I merely meant you have a pretty face... that I fancy."

We both blush. The compliment, however hard I had to work for it, pleases me immensely, and I finish setting the type with shaky hands. I tally the advertisements, noting the new one for a physician to replace Dr. Davis. They'll be hard pressed to find one while the fighting continues. I'm just about to pen an announcement about the next town council meeting when Father walks in.

"Come to make sure we haven't made a mess of everything?" I say to him, hoping he's over his spat with Mother.

"I'm still the editor and publisher of this newspaper, young lady," he says gruffly.

Samuel, never missing a chance to curry favor with the boss, floats the suggestion I made 30 seconds earlier as if it were his own: "Sir, might I suggest we print an item in the *Essex Journal* about all the new pox cases?"

"A fine idea, my boy," Father says, and I want to scream. "People need to be warned it's here. The sick must quarantine themselves or it will spread faster."

"I'll write something straightaway," Samuel says, obviously pleased with himself.

I'm beginning to doubt the sincerity of his so-called compliment.

"And sir, how do you feel about inoculation? Sarah and I were just discussing it."

"Bad idea," Father says. "Sarah knows where I stand. Inoculation could trigger a huge epidemic, far worse than if we let the scourge occur naturally."

I can't stand Father's certainty on something he couldn't possibly know for sure. "Fewer people would die if everyone were both isolated *and* inoculated," I blurt out. "That's what Mother says."

Father's face goes stern. "Your mother is wrong. That's why I won't have her jab herself with pus and invite the bloody disease into my home. And Sarah, I forbid you from doing the same."

Samuel practically hugs him. "Well-spoken, sir. I agree. Better to take our chances with Mother Nature."

I look from one to the other and suddenly my path is clear. My fear of pus, knives, blood, and death are still there—but my hesitation is gone.

———————

I find Mother at Mr. Bascomb's store, buying armloads of supplies—flour, molasses, cheese, candles, rice, thread. I have an inkling why, but Mrs. Bascomb is perplexed.

"Are you expecting the militia to take quarter at your house?" she says, half-joking.

"They won't find a warm welcome from me," Mother says, gathering up her purchases. "Sarah, give me a hand."

Mrs. Bascomb lowers her voice. "I heard about your run-in with that hothead Daniel Jordan at the birthing bed. He's spreading the word, warning folks not to seek your services unless they want to be branded Tory lovers."

"He can't do that, Mother," I say. "You saved Mrs. Jordan and the baby."

"He's a fool," she says.

Mrs. Bascomb says nothing but nods ever so slightly.

As soon as we're out the door, I confront Mother. "I need to talk with you."

"What is it, child?"

I stifle the urge to remind her I'm hardly a child. "Are you going to inoculate yourself, even though Father is against it?"

"Yes. It's my decision." Arms loaded with bundles, we walk in silence. A wagon piled high with hay rumbles by us.

"I'll do it too," I finally burst out. I expect her to be thrilled, but she turns to me with a serious face.

"You do know you could die? Dr. Boylston said it's inevitable a few won't make it."

"Yes, I know." I'm still fired up by the thrill of doing something that will infuriate both Father and Samuel.

"Then I'm pleased and very proud of you."

I savor each word.

Later that day, before Father returns, Mother and I are traipsing through drizzle to the cobbler's house. A big red flag hangs from a pole by the front door—the usual warning sign to stay away. I bang on the door, and it's a full five minutes before a pale Peter Haskell cracks it open.

"Didn't you see the flag? Go away," he rasps.

"Don't be frightened, Peter," Mother says, as if she's treating one of her mothers. "We know what we're doing." I push on the door, and he doesn't resist. Inside, a blazing fire pops and crackles. It's sweltering, yet he's wrapped in an old blanket, shivering and pale. His face is swollen and speckled with pus-filled bumps. I wasn't prepared for this, and I almost change my mind.

"Wife and children are staying with the neighbors while I ward off this damnable disease," he says with difficulty. "Pustules in my mouth," he gestures. "Can't eat or drink."

I'm ready to leave, but not Mother.

"I'll make a tea that will help you," she says. "But first I must ask a favor."

Minutes later she's puncturing a pustule on his face, capturing the pus on a rag, and dabbing the yellow, smelly glob into a small cut she's made with a kitchen knife on her wrist. Then she bandages it.

"Your turn Sarah," she says. Now I'm almost certain I want no part of this nauseating procedure. I feel my breakfast rising. The gentlest discouragement from her—"you needn't do this, my dear, if you're frightened"—and I would be gone.

"This may be the bravest thing you've ever done," she says. "I could not be prouder."

There's no turning back—I'm trapped. I hold my arm to keep it from shaking as Mother makes a little slit in my skin. Blood bubbles up and I look away, forcing myself to think about blueberries, butterflies, snowflakes—anything but Peter Haskell's disgusting pus entering my body.

When it's over, Mother brews some willow tea and spoons it gently to his swollen lips. I'm desperate to leave, but she lingers to give him a hog balm for the pustules.

Finally, we're walking back home in the drizzle, and I wonder if I've lost my mind. Father will be furious with both of us, but I'm strangely exhilarated.

At the house Mother gives me a big piece of red cloth and I hang it on a tree branch by the door. When Father arrives, his reaction is immediate.

"So you've done it," he yells from outside. "You deliberately disobeyed me. And I suppose you cajoled Sarah into it too."

"She didn't cajole me," I yell back through a crack in the door. "I made up my own mind."

"As did I, Benjamin," Mother adds from inside.

"It's also about *our* son, or have you forgotten that?" Father shouts, backing down from the steps into the yard.

"Son? Now you're certain I'll birth a boy?"

Anyone passing by would have thought we were all crazed, and maybe we were.

"You leave me no choice but to board with Samuel at the print shop until it's safe to return. Then we'll deal with your disobedience."

Disobedience? At this moment, there's no one on earth I despise more than Father. As for Samuel, he'll probably take his cues from Father and think me a wild and wicked child. Would it even occur to him to praise my bravery and independence?

CHAPTER 12

July 2, 1775

Dear Diary,

Emma thinks I'm the bravest girl in New Hampshire for letting Mother inoculate me. She told me so in a letter she slipped under the door. I can't bring myself to tell her how close I came to backing out. Let her think me the martyr. It's the first time she's been impressed by anything I've done. Of course she had to remind me that I might end up with pox scars all over my face, which would dim my marriage prospects.

A WEEK GOES BY without a hint of illness in either me or Mother. I fear her grand experiment has failed, but she says be patient. Easy for her. She can busy herself with chores for hours without complaint. I have scrubbed, churned, sewn, and baked everything in sight. Even the privy is spotless, smelling of cedar and soap. I think I'll lose my mind. When Mother isn't knee-deep in some worthy project, she's reading the Bible aloud. If she thinks I'm not listening, she reads louder until I think my head will explode.

Being confined to the house and yard is torture. No gossiping with Emma, no time at the newspaper office, and, especially, no Samuel, though he can so irk me. When I have a scrap of free time, I squirrel away with my diary or reread *Robinson Crusoe* and daydream about writing my own novel—something about a young woman who does something impossibly courageous.

I decide to pour out my frustration in a letter to Emma.

Dear Emma, you may think me brave but right now I'm bored to death.

I use up two pieces of paper confiding my vast misery. When I'm done, I fold it and write Emma's name on the outside. How to get it to her, I haven't figured out. It doesn't matter, because Mother sees it on the table and erupts.

"Don't you realize Emma could get the pox simply by touching the paper you've written on?"

"Mother, I don't have a trace of disease. How can I possibly infect anyone?"

"You could still be contagious," she says. "When we've recovered, we'll need to smoke all our clothes and bedding to rid them of the disease."

She's the Duchess of Drama, but I don't make a fuss and toss the letter in the fire.

The next morning I wake up with a headache so bad I can't think straight. I'm hot, then shivering, and the thought of food sets off waves of nausea.

"Must be the pox," Mother says, feeling not a bit of it herself.

She was up at dawn kneading two loaves of bread that are rising on the table right now. I can barely lift my head off the pillow.

In a matter of hours, a rash covers my entire body. Mother is delighted.

"It's working," she says. "And so far, it seems a light case, just as they predicted."

How she can determine that is a mystery. I ache from head to toe. I've puked so many times she finally puts two basins next to my bed. Even though it's summer I can't get warm, so I wrap myself in my heavy coat and two quilts.

Three days of agony pass before Mother finally comes down with a slight fever and a rash. But she never takes to her bed. She brings me broth and bread with grape jam that I can't keep down, and she changes my bedclothes when I sweat up a small lake.

After a week, the fever lifts, but I'm so weak all I can do is lie in bed. I was thin to begin with, and now I'm boney. Today Mother is making a pot of chicken soup, and the house fills with the smell of carrots and onions and thyme. She brings me a steaming bowl on a tray, along with cornbread and honey. I choke down a swallow or two just to please her, but that's all I can manage.

"You won't get your strength back until you can eat something," she says, clearly worried.

She starts sewing a new patchwork quilt from a wool cloak I've outgrown and Seth's old shirts. When she works on the pieces at my bedside, I'm surprisingly pleased with her company.

She tells me familiar old stories about growing up in London. My grandfather, Augustus Bingham, was a doctor, a graduate of the Royal College of Physicians, and Mother was always underfoot in his offices.

"We weren't as well off as the rich who filled their mansions with upholstered furniture and fine dishes," she recalled. "But we were moneyed enough for me to go to school. My father opened an infirmary for the poor, and I helped him when I was old enough."

"And Father? How did you meet him?" I ask.

"He was working at the *London Messenger*, and I stopped by to purchase an advertisement for my mother. She was looking for a new maid. Your father looked over what I'd written and liked it.

"Nicely done!" he said.

"I thought he was merely complimenting my handwriting. But no."

"You've spelled 'accommodation' correctly," he said. "And you've not mixed up 'who' and 'whom,' in the manner so common today."

"I was flattered. He didn't think me just a pretty face," Mother says.

It makes me laugh, and that makes my head hurt. I miss Father so, but I don't miss his rants.

Each day I feel stronger. Neither of us is covered head to toe in pus-filled sores, as we'd feared. I'm troubled by only a smattering, and within a week they've scabbed over and fallen off. Emma needn't worry about my marriage prospects.

Finally, Mother deems us both fit for the company of others. I feel like celebrating, now that I'm no longer a prisoner.

Mother is elated. After all, we've recovered, and her experiment seems to be a success. When Father returns, she's quick to point that out.

"Either you were lucky, or God had a hand in it," he says. I think he's so relieved we both survived that he's shelved his lecture about our "disobedience."

Mother stirs a kettle of steaming potato soup. "Would you reconsider an inoculation now, Benjamin?"

"No! I'm too busy."

"But Father, now that I'm well I can help Samuel again," I offer. I've not seen him for three weeks, and he's all I've been thinking about.

I feel my cheeks reddening in a rush of excitement as we all sit down for supper. I'll see Samuel soon! I keep my face down, so they won't notice.

Mother passes a plate of brown bread she made especially for Father's return. Despite being pregnant and just over the pox, she seems more energetic than ever.

"I was at the Bascombs' store this morning buying molasses," she gushes. "They were mighty pleased that Sarah and I survived the pox with so little discomfort."

Little discomfort! For days, I left the better part of myself in a basin.

"Now Mrs. Bascomb wants the inoculation too," she says, with a big smile.

Father scowls. "I suppose you said, 'Yes, there's nothing I'd love to do more than infect you with pus and send you vomiting to the very shadow of death's door.'"

I pray that Mother doesn't want my assistance on this mission.

"How can I turn down a plea for help?" she asks.

"I thought Mrs. Bascomb had more sense," Father says, tearing into a chunk of his bread.

The degree to which Mrs. Bascomb is sane or insane hangs silently for a minute before Mother turns toward me. "Of course, I'll need your help, Sarah. Mrs. Bascomb specifically requested it, as will others."

Suddenly, I imagine endless retching—though I can't tell whether it's Mrs. Bascomb or me.

"Absolutely not. I need her at the newspaper now that this fool war is barreling ahead," Father says. "The boy can't do it all."

Of course, I'd pick the *Journal* and Samuel over the pox-laden interiors of Essex's finer homes, but no one asks me.

"Sarah, you'd best get an early start tomorrow," Father says. "We have much to do for the next issue."

For Father, it's all settled. Mother and the smallpox be damned. He pushes off from the table and heads for bed. He doesn't see the look of defeat on her face.

———

Samuel is cleaning the ink roller with horse piss when I stroll into the print shop. I'm so glad to be there that the usual stink is like the first lilac of spring. Predictably the comely apprentice sides with Father on the question of inoculation.

"So you whipped the smallpox," he says with a big smile. "Lady Luck was on your side."

"It wasn't luck," I insist, as I straighten a pile of papers. "It was the inoculation. Mother was right. And in case you didn't know, I was sick as a dog."

"Yes, I figured," he says. "You look pale and thin—but not in a bad way." Then, as if to make things better he says, "I missed you while you were gone."

"Did you miss me, or my labors?"

"I missed your cheerful disposition and your eagerness to follow my direction without complaint," he says.

"You're a bad liar."

We work silently for a few minutes, and I sneak glances at him. I like the way he constantly flicks his long blond hair out of his eyes. He's humming a tune that I can't quite make out, but it makes me feel warm and cozy.

"Did you hear Alan Hopkins came back from Bunker Hill with a broken leg and the pox?" he says. "He was the last one the doc treated before he left Essex."

So Mother and I were right: the boy doctor knew there was pox here and fled from it. What a coward!

"And I heard about two more cases this morning," he says.

I start setting type for a new advertisement. A farmer is offering a reward for the return of his runaway slave, Thomas, "a chatty fellow with a gimpy leg." It makes me wonder if slave ownership—so widespread in the colonies—will ever fall into disfavor as it is in England. They've even let a couple of Negro men vote.

I tell Samuel about Mother inoculating Mrs. Bascomb and anyone else who wants it.

"That's a risky business," he says.

"Oh, she insists we're both immune now."

"That's not what I mean," he says, coming closer to face me. "The rebels are bolder by the day when it comes to harassing those of us who don't agree with them."

"What do you mean?"

"Now they say they have the right to take our guns, our businesses, our freedoms," he says. "If one person dies from this so-called inoculation, they'll just use it as an excuse to come after your family."

"You're exaggerating. You can't stand it that Mother has succeeded at the unthinkable. You're as bad as Father."

Samuel rolls his eyes. "I try to tell you something that might help, and you turn it against me. You confound me, Sarah." He pulls out a drawer of type and says over his shoulder, "I'm going to set type about the King's latest pledge. If you care to know, he says he'll free slaves who quit their rebel masters and take up arms with the British. And, no, I do not need your help."

I bite my tongue. *Why can I never say the right thing?*

After an hour, he's still setting type, struggling to finish. Beads of sweat dampen his brow, and I hear him muttering.

"Want my help now?" I offer none too sweetly.

"No! Thank you."

About that point he spills the type he's already set, scattering pieces of metal all over the floor. He looks like he's ready to walk out and never come back. I soften.

"Samuel, why don't you have a cup of tea and let me finish that?

You've been at it quite a stretch."

I wait for him to say that he doesn't need so-called help from a rank beginner, but it never comes.

He looks at me tentatively. "I'd be grateful. Thank you, Sarah."

I'm wondering if something's wrong—or very right.

CHAPTER 13

Aug. 15, 1775

Dear Diary,

Mrs. Bascomb has recovered from the pox and sings Mother's praises. Now she's gone all the time, either inoculating willing sufferers or tending them when they're mired with fever, chills and the awful rash. Interestingly, it doesn't bother them that she's a loyalist when she's cleaning up their puke. Samuel nearly kissed me today. Our noses were practically touching as we sorted type. I've given him every opportunity, but still he holds back. What am I doing wrong?

"YOUR MOTHER WASN'T IN church this morning," Emma says, catching up to me as I walk home after struggling to stay awake through the two-hour sermon on salvation. My back hurts from the straight-back wooden pews that would torture Satan himself.

"No, she's tending the Petersons and their four-year-old," I say.

"The pox?"

"Yes. The parents are over the worst of it, but little Polly is quite sick."

"What if she doesn't get better?" Emma asks.

"She will!" I didn't mean to sound so shrill, but Emma has a way of needling me when I can least tolerate it. The truth is I'm worried about Polly—the first of Mother's patients to fare badly after the inoculation.

"Someone's prickly today!" Emma says. "I only said—"

"Emma, if anyone can save Polly, it's Mother."

"*Save* Polly? Is she that sick?"

"If you must know, her fever is so high she's just moaning when she's not unconscious. Mother is at her wit's end."

We walk in blessed silence for several minutes. I see scads of blueberries ripe for the picking, but not today. I'm not in the mood.

"Father won't allow us to get the inoculation," Emma finally says. "He says it's wrong to play God, and more to the point, it could kill us."

"Probably because my loyalist mother is the one doing it. If it were someone else—"

"No, that's not it, I swear," she says. We both know she's lying.

When we finally arrive at Emma's house, she gives me a sly look. "Has Samuel kissed you yet?"

"That is not your business!"

"I guess he hasn't. That's why you're crabby."

The next morning, daylight is just peeking through my bedroom window when I hear Father stacking wood by the hearth. How can it be morning so soon? Samuel kissed me in a dream, and that rush of excitement lingers over me. But why was Abner Rollins there? And why Seth, and even Seth's old hunting dog, Molly?

I dress quickly, jamming my wild hair under my cap. Downstairs, Father is hunched over the fireplace coaxing a reluctant flame with the bellows. Please, please, I pray, let him be in a good mood.

"Were you up past midnight again?" Father asks, not looking up.

Here it comes, the lecture about wasting candles and paper and ink. I give him my best puzzled look and say no.

He nearly chuckles, and I breathe easier. Mother would have a fit if she knew how late I stay up. In fact, Mother doesn't even understand why I write in my diary. If nobody but you ever sees it, it's useless, she insists. I know she'd love to peek inside, though she'd be horrified if she saw what I've confided about Samuel. Lately I've taken to hiding Dear Diary in a crack behind the chimney, just in case she's curious.

"Mother still tending the Petersons?" I ask.

"Of course," he says with obvious bitterness. "I don't expect she'll be home any time soon, not with the pox raging."

"Polly still doing poorly?"

"I presume so. Unless Mother just prefers the company of severely ill children to that of her own family."

I don't know what to say. Then he laughs, as if it were a joke. Only, I know he meant it.

The fire finally roars to life, and I dish up oatmeal for him. Today I'll ask him. He looks almost happy, almost like the old days, as he rereads the essay he's written for the newspaper.

"Sarah, I took your suggestion and added something about how outnumbered the Americans are against the British," he says. "I believe I used your same words."

My heart leaps with pride, and I just about shout what I've wanted to ask, calmly and rationally, for weeks.

"Father, may I write something for the *Journal*?"

"Most certainly not."

He didn't give it even a moment's thought. "Why not?"

"The printing business is no place for a woman." He goes back to the essay.

His words gall me, but I hold my temper. "Father, I know as much about it as Samuel and you let him write."

He looks up. "Samuel is a young man, and he's my apprentice. Don't you know these are dangerous times?"

"I'm not afraid." I really mean it.

"Well, I'm afraid. I've already lost a son."

"But I—"

"No, not another word!"

———————

Still mad, I storm into town with Father's essay under my cloak.

A knot of anger and hurt sticks in my throat. Why does he treat me like a child? Haven't I read every newspaper that comes into the *Journal* office? And aren't I his sounding board as he composes his essays week after week? He even uses my words!

At the print shop I see Samuel tinkering under the press with an oily rag. When he stands up, I thrust the essay toward him and walk away without a word.

"What's wrong now?" he asks.

"Nothing!" I watch as he reads it.

"So he thinks there's still time for reconciliation with the Crown?"

I shrug. I know he's trying hard to make conversation.

Finally, he blows out a deep breath of exasperation. "Sarah, what in God's name is wrong? You're acting like a spoiled child."

I angrily spit out what Father told me. I expect Samuel to side with him, but he goes even further: He laughs—and it's a long, rollicking belly laugh.

"You? Write for the newspaper? What are you thinking? Can you imagine a girl judge? A girl pastor? It's insane!"

"If you want to help, just start pulling type," Samuel says.

Still furious, I begin to grab letters, knocking some onto the floor. I don't care that Samuel glares at me. I fight with every muscle to keep from dissolving into tears.

As I set the letters in place, I read Father's essay again. It's exactly what I would write, given the chance: "The hour is not past for the colonies and the Crown to again be one, as family. If the King sees fit to let the colonies tax themselves, no more blood need be shed in this senseless conflict."

When I arrive at the bottom of the essay where Father's name, BENJAMIN BARRETT, always runs, I hesitate for a second. How would my name look there instead? I've never seen my name in print. Something compels me to pluck the type and lay out SARAH BARRETT. A fabulous giddiness sweeps over me. Then, with a sigh, I reach for the B to start Father's name, but something holds me back. It's as if dismantling my name takes away my voice, my very existence. No! I leave it.

"Ready to print," I call out.

"We're running late," Samuel says glancing quickly at the type.

I nod silently, and take my place, ready to grab the damp pages as they come off the press. I feel triumphant, powerful, and exhilarated.

By late afternoon, I'm feeling awful. *What have I done?* To take my mind off it, I set off for Rev. Ichabod Evans's house. I like stopping by once a week to pick up his sermon for the upcoming *Journal*. He isn't at all like the last pastor, who frightened people half to death with his talk about divine retribution for everyday sins. In fact, Rev. Evans doesn't talk about the Bible or even God whenever I come to call. We might talk about stars or wolves or marmalade, anything at all.

Since Bunker Hill, however, everything is more serious. The pastor has just come from visiting Martha Bradley, whose husband, having survived the British, died of the pox. He was the third Bunker Hill veteran to fall ill.

"That's terrible news," I say. "People already have enough to worry about." I want to ask him how he can still believe in a God that dumps so much misery on everyone. But I can see he's in no mood for one of our philosophical discussions. Without the usual friendly chatter, he gathers a few loose papers from his desk and hands them to me.

"For next week's paper."

I scan the words and see trouble right away. "Are you sure you want to say this?" His eyes are intense. I can tell he won't back down.

"This order from the Continental Congress is the last straw," he says. "John Adams and the others have decreed a day of fasting and prayer next week. I'll not let anyone use a place of worship—*my* place of worship—to pray for victory over the British."

"You're going to defy the order?" I ask.

"It doesn't hold any legal weight. They can talk all they want about their new army and their General Washington, but the Crown's law is still the law of this land."

"Aren't you afraid of what they'll do?"

"I'd be more afraid if Matilda and the child were here with me."

His wife died in childbirth last year, and the baby didn't survive more than a day. Even Mother couldn't save them. "Someone besides your father must stand up to them. The town's losing good men. You heard about Tom Stone?"

"No." I know he's the town's barrel maker, and the *Journal* printed his letter urging men not to join the militia.

"People stopped buying his barrels. Then Abner Rollins threatened to burn down his shop. He got scared, packed up his family in the middle of the night, and left for Quebec."

"Quebec?" It might as well be the North Pole.

"It's safer up there. More loyalists. The Wyman family is talking about fleeing too. And William Scott says he's sailing back to England as soon as he can sell his farm."

It seems like half the town is running away. Are they that afraid of Abner Rollins and his band of outlaws?

"My father would never run. He wouldn't give them the satisfaction."

"We can't all be as stouthearted," Rev. Evans says.

As I hastily slip out, I wonder what the parson would think of me—putting my name on Father's essay. Now the awfulness of what I've done returns tenfold. Walking home fills me with dread.

During supper, I barely touch my food and avoid Father's eyes. I can't bring myself to tell him. By the time we finish, I'm in a full state of panic, and there's nothing I can do. The paper is printed and soon to be in the hands of readers.

I go upstairs early, hoping to write something in my diary to justify my blatant and vile plagiarism. The words don't come. Only: *I'm so ashamed.*

Sleep doesn't come either. I lie in bed, twisting and turning, certain that doom and disgrace await in the morning.

At least I've got that right, as it turns out. Rain pounds the roof as I feel each blast of Father's wrath.

"Stupid . . . stupid . . . stupid!"

I've never seen him so angry. His face is bright red and spittle flies from his mouth. He paces back and forth with a copy of the *Journal*.

"Have I raised a fool for a daughter? What possessed you to do such a thing?"

"I'm sorry, Father." My voice trembles.

"Do you even know what you've done? You've stolen my words, but worse than that—you've deceived the readers. If you were five years old, I'd take the branch to your backside. But you're 15, practically a grown woman, and you've displayed an . . . an . . . astonishing—no, a repulsive—lapse in judgment."

I wish I were dead. Every angry outburst feels like the sting of his hand across my cheek. If only I could go back a day and take my name from print, maybe forever.

"Don't you realize that people in town will think I put you up to this, that I didn't have the courage to use my own name? Even if I tell them the truth, you know they won't believe it. They'll just see a man they can't stand, who spouts opinions they can't stand, pinning the blame for them on his daughter."

I feel so small. If only I could disappear.

"Did Samuel put you up to this? I'll give him a good thrashing and fire his skinny hide."

"No!" My head aches from lack of sleep and worry. I've never heard my father talk this way and it scares me.

He brings his voice down a few notches, which is somehow even scarier than his full-on bellow.

"I thought I could trust you. You are a grave disappointment."

I ache for him to put his arm around my shoulder and forgive me. Instead, his eyes become more distant.

"The rebels will stop at nothing. For God's sake, Sarah, you were here when they killed your brother. You've put yourself and us in great danger, and if anything happens to you, I'll never forgive myself. I'll not have you at the newspaper putting all our lives at risk. From now on, you'll help your mother and stay clear away from the *Journal*. She needs you now more than ever—and God help you if you let her down."

CHAPTER 14

Aug. 19, 1775

Dear Diary,

I'm sure Samuel will never speak to me again. He must think me an idiot, or worse, a conniving plagiarist, a thief of words. I hate myself even more than before. I regret what I did, but I have to say that it wouldn't have happened if Father had merely given his blessing and let me write for the newspaper.

MY LIFE IS DISMAL. From sunup to sundown, I'm saddled with mountains of work—mending, cleaning, cooking, washing. If that weren't enough, Mother expects me to help tend her smallpox patients. I can't bear to look at another festering pustule. She's seldom home.

Tonight, as Father and I are eating yet another supper in silence, Mother arrives in a terrible state of distress.

"She's dead! Polly is dead!" Mother's face is twisted in anguish. She drops her satchel with a thud. "The poor child is gone."

I'm stunned. "I was there with you this morning and she seemed to be improving."

"She took a bad turn…," Mother says, too distraught to finish.

I wish Father would somehow comfort her, but he doesn't move.

She stands before us, her dark, hollow eyes rimmed with tears and her hands shaking. "It was excruciating. She was gasping for every breath. Her little face was so swollen she was unrecognizable. Her entire body was covered in pock marks."

I have to say something, do something to help. "Mother can I fix you a plate of bread and cheese? Tea?"

"How can I eat?" she wails. "I've come from the deathbed of an innocent child, and I could do nothing, absolutely nothing. Her parents are hysterical with grief."

Father clears his throat. "My dear, you've dealt with death before—"

"Not like this!" Mother shrieks. "I tried every comfort I know, and I'm the one who bragged to the rest of the town that I knew what I was doing." I've never seen her so upset. She finally sits down, but moments later she's pacing, clenching and unclenching her fists.

"Polly may not be the only one to die by my hand. Ezra Hill's fever still hasn't broken. He's worse today. I fear for him too."

I'm not accustomed to Mother blaming herself for even the smallest problem—she's always in control of her emotions, and everything else. Her sudden reversal is unsettling and makes me anxious.

"You did everything humanly possible, Mother."

"Sadly, I did not," she says, turning to Father. "Spare me your I-told-you-so. I knew there was a chance this could happen. I just didn't expect that I would….kill a child." Still, he doesn't move to comfort her.

"I feared this would happen," he says. "Everyone in town hates us, and now you've given them yet another reason: 'He's a dangerous traitor and she's a dangerous quack.'"

Mother stops her sniffling. "That's not fair!"

"I know," he says. "But in church tomorrow they'll be fired up plenty about poor Polly. They'll have a different idea of what's not fair."

"Maybe we'd best stay home from services," I suggest. I might be selfish but who wouldn't benefit from sleeping late, and then digging into a leisurely breakfast of pancakes and maple syrup?

"Perhaps she's right, Benjamin," Mother says.

But Father snuffs out that hope. "Mary, pull yourself together. The three of us will be in church tomorrow morning without fail.

I'll not have us hide from anybody."

———————————

The morning is miserably hot, and I keep my distance behind Mother and Father as we walk to the meetinghouse. I prefer it that way. Nothing I say to Mother seems to help, and I'm still smarting from Father's harsh words. I admitted I was wrong, and I apologized a thousand times. But I'm not ready to walk arm-in-arm and engage in pleasant conversation, and neither, I suspect, are they. Last night Mother wept for hours. Father drank all evening and scribbled his next tirade for the *Journal*.

Word of Polly's death has surely spread by now. I haven't wept a tear for the little girl with the sky-blue eyes. What is wrong with me? First Seth, now Polly. I remember sitting on her bed and telling her silly stories, one after another, to keep her from scratching the itchy rash that peppered her body.

The stories just sprang out of my brain—the one about the cat that could braid hair, or the boy who made naughty noises in church. Her favorite was about a girl who hated to go to bed. The memory of Polly's laughter makes me sad. I'll miss her joyous laugh.

No one on the road tips a hat to us as we plod onward. They look away. I daydream about whether Samuel will be there, and what I'll say to get back in his good graces. I put a little extra effort into dressing this morning. Even my hair is brushed and tidy under my cap, and I put on my best dress, the one with the white ruffles down the front.

As we approach town, a wagon rumbles up behind us.

"You've got a lot of nerve, showing your face in these streets," Matthew Stone yells down. He runs the sawmill and heads the local militia. His wife scowls at us.

Father yells back. "I've as much right as anybody—"

"I don't mean you, Benjamin," he interrupts. "Your wife, the midwife, or does she fancy herself a doctor now?"

Mother barely looks up.

"You can shield your face, but we know what you did to the

Peterson child," he says. "The whole town knows. You killed her and now Ezra Hill is damn close! Is this some redcoat scheme to drop us one by one?"

"It's just like you to make up some ignorant rot in the name of the rebels," Father says, sounding more like one of his editorials than like a man defending his wife.

"The town council doesn't think it's ignorant," Mr. Stone says. "They've called an emergency meeting about this inoculation business your wife has thrust upon us. She has to be stopped!"

Mother's clear voice rings through the waves of anger around her. "You don't know the first thing about—"

Father commands: "Hush, woman!"

"I'd watch my back, if I were you." Mr. Stone cracks his whip and the wagon creaks forward.

Mother is furious. Her tears are gone, and she'd shove Father off a cliff if one was nearby. "Benjamin, I am able to speak my own mind," she sputters. "Never, ever tell me to hush."

I want to cheer for all womanhood.

"Let the council meet about the pox," she says. "I have nothing to hide... unlike you, Benjamin."

"What are you talking about?" Father bristles.

"The letters. I know about the letters," she says.

Instantly, I'm alert. "What letters? Father?"

"I was going to tell you, Sarah. Letters sent to the newspaper. A number of townsfolk took strong issue with my—or our—words in the *Journal*."

"Took issue?" Mother says. "They threatened to hang you for real."

"They're just words on paper," Father says. "Takes a great leap for a man to put his words into acts."

"They've already put their words into acts, Benjamin. Have you forgotten about Seth so soon?"

"Of course not! We'll discuss this later."

Father never talks of Seth, and neither do I. I'm afraid he'll explode. And I worry I'll break down and upset him more. Besides, I still worry that he blames me. If only the hoe hadn't been so handy... I think about it every day.

Silently, the three of us pass the Essex Tavern just as Mr. Spooner hauls out an empty ale barrel.

"Morning to you," Father says, tipping his hat.

The tavern owner forgoes the customary greeting and gets right to business, planting himself in front of us and holding his hat in his hands.

"Benjamin, for God's sake," he says in a low voice. "I've always respected you. But you're simply wrong now, wrong not to take up the fight."

Father responds in kind, lowering his voice to nearly a whisper but relentlessly maintaining his message. "Silas, a man of your intellect should admit when you've gone too far. When all this is over you'll have the blood of boys and men on your hands, and you'll answer to the King. You'll lose everything—your tavern, your livelihood, God forbid, your family."

Mr. Spooner aims a shot of tobacco at Father's feet. "I see your daughter has now taken up her pen against us. Perhaps you're too afraid to affix your own name to your wrong-headed arguments."

Father somehow maintains his self-control. "'Tis the Sabbath. Have some common decency."

"Decency?" Mr. Spooner repeats, half-mocking Father. "We used to see it in our newspaper." His eyes fall on Mother. "For shame, Mary. Did the British put you up to it? Do they pay you per corpse?"

CHAPTER 15

WE HURRY UP THE granite steps to the meetinghouse along with the other church goers. The place is packed—could they all be here to see our humiliation? The next few hours promise to be torture as I take my seat between them—Father still fuming, and Mother ready to take on the town.

Samuel is nowhere in sight, and I regret all the effort I put in to making myself presentable. I hear a flurry of whispering and feel my face turn red. I'm sick of all their gossip, and I'm sick of having my face heat up like a red hot ember.

Craning my neck, I spot Emma's family in the back. I catch Emma's eye and smile until Mr. Jordan glares at me. I know every single person gathered here in their Sunday finest. Only a few share Father's loyalty to the Crown. As I count heads, many more are like Emma's family, solidly behind the rebels. But quite a few don't seem to be on either side. Father says they're too tired from eking out a living to care, or they're too afraid to take a side.

The meetinghouse is nearly filled now with a hundred or more people—the most I've seen at Sunday services. Then I remember Rev. Ichabod Evans's vow to defy the Continental Congress's order for a day of prayer and fasting. His sermons are stronger and louder each week, his voice thundering through the meetinghouse with such fervor that no one falls asleep. He gets so worked up that I think most people come just to see if he'll collapse in a heap.

He takes his place in the raised pulpit, towering over the wooden pews in which we so suffer. My back already hurts, and I dread the next three hours of captivity. At least I have something to pray about: Perhaps God will see fit to put Father—and Samuel—in a forgiving mood.

I'm not really convinced prayer works, though I can't tell a soul for fear of being branded a heathen. In fact, there are times when I doubt God exists at all. I prayed for Seth to live, and he died. And I prayed for Samuel to kiss me, and he's yet to produce one little peck on the check.

Mothers hush their children as Rev. Evans starts to speak. "Dearly beloved, we are gathered here to give thanks to the Lord for our blessings. Let us pray that he will guide us through this latest pox outbreak and give us the knowledge and tools to fight this menace."

"Mother," I whisper. "He means inoculation." She squeezes my hand.

"But that is not my main message today," he says. "There's an evil wind in the air." His deep voice resonates through the hall. "Maybe it's Satan, lurking so close that we can feel his breath. It is most certainly not God's will that we take up arms against one another."

At that moment the heavy wooden door creaks open. A late parishioner, I think. He'll get a scolding after services. Rev. Evans's eyes fix on whoever it is, and I turn to look. Abner Rollins and two other men stand silently at the back of the room. The blacksmith's beefy arms are crossed on his chest in a defiant pose. My heart thumps. Why are they here, and why don't they sit down?

"Gentlemen, this is the Lord's house, and you are most certainly welcome. Please take a seat."

By now everyone has turned to look, and I hear muffled whispers and gasps. One of the three grips a rifle at his side. Rev. Evans waits silently but the men don't move.

The blacksmith finally breaks the silence. "We're not here to worship, Reverend. We're here to make absolutely certain that you ask God for victory over the redcoats so more good men don't suffer the same fate as my son. Is it a fact that you refuse to lead our good people in a day of fasting and prayer?"

Rev. Evans's eyes grow huge with anger. "How dare you come into the Lord's house armed! How dare you speak with such disrespect before the altar!"

I can't take my eyes off the gun.

Father rises slowly from his seat, and I get an awful feeling in my stomach.

"Sit down, Benjamin!" the blacksmith yells. "You'd be wise to take heed, or you'll be next. My men are outside, and they're all armed. We've come for the preacher, unless he sees the error of his thinking."

"I will never pray for victory over my King on this day, or any other day," Rev. Evans bellows. "God save the King!"

He might as well have said "God bless Satan." I see only shocked faces. No one breathes; no one moves.

Abner Rollins stomps his feet, breaking the silence. "Come down from your perch, you pompous ass. Come willingly or we'll drag you out."

The pastor doesn't move. "I thought you would come for me eventually, but to put on such a spectacle in the Lord's house. For shame. Shame."

"Come down now, or you're a dead man," the blacksmith orders, grabbing the rifle from his henchman. Along with everyone else, I crouch in the pew, bracing for gunfire.

"I'll not have violence in the house of our Lord." The pastor steps down from the pulpit, his Bible in his hand, then raises his arms and faces skyward. "Let us bow our heads in silent prayer."

Others lower their heads but not me. I can't take my eyes off the pastor, his red cheeks blazing. He walks slowly down the aisle looking from parishioner to parishioner. As he approaches our pew, his eyes lock on mine as if he's found something.

"Pray for me child," he whispers, handing me the leather-covered Bible.

I'm startled but take the worn book as he moves on. "Where are they taking him?" I whisper to Father.

He doesn't answer.

As they reach the back rows, the pastor suddenly stops and turns around. His silence is crushing until he launches into a thundering prediction for those who dared humiliate him: "Vengeance is mine, saith the Lord."

When the men are out the door with the pastor in tow, the meetinghouse erupts in chaos, and a crowd streams onto the green where the blacksmith's wagon waits. I force my way to the front, and what I see horrifies me.

Mr. Rollins hauls a pail of steaming pine tar from the wagon and stirs it with a big stick. Two men hold Rev. Evans while another rips off his coat and shirt.

The pastor struggles in vain. "God will punish you," he shouts.

I clutch the Bible and look around for someone to step in and stop the madness. The crowd is getting bigger and louder. But no one steps forward. The pastor looks terrified, trying desperately to cover himself.

"Go back to England where you belong," a man shouts.

"You're lower than hog dung," another yells.

"Hang the bloody bastard," a woman screams.

I look around for Father. Surely he'll stop it.

The blacksmith picks up a mop and dips it into the hot tar. He smears it all over Rev. Evans's chest. The pastor shrieks from the pain and starts to sway but he's propped back up by the men.

"Father!" I scream. The pastor looks like a cowering dog cornered by wolves. Where is the sheriff?

Some people cover their eyes and mothers hustle away small children. I'm sure I'll vomit. I can taste oatmeal burbling up in my throat. But I can't take my eyes off the most grotesquely cruel thing I've ever seen.

The pastor moans and screams as yet more tar is smeared onto his smoldering flesh. "God help me!" he shrieks. Abner seems focused on his work, as if he were patching a roof before a storm.

I'm so close I can feel heat from the foul tar, and the smell clogs my nose. I pray silently for God's intervention. *If you're there, now is the time.*

"Bring me the sack, Hortense," the blacksmith shouts to his wife. A wisp of a woman with a dour face obeys his command. With his knife, he slits it open and with a grand flourish, he dumps a cascade of feathers on the moaning, writhing pastor. They stick to the tar, giving him the appearance of a strange, wailing bird with the trunk of a man.

The crowd roars with laughter. "Your precious King should see you now," someone yells.

Surely they're done with him. But alas, no.

"Men, bring the fence rail and we'll take the reverend for a ride," the blacksmith orders. "He'll wish a death by pox before we're done with him."

Helplessly, I watch them slide the coarse splintered board between Rev. Evans's legs. Then two men hoist it to their shoulders, and walk around the common, displaying their grimacing, groaning catch. Grasping the rail with his burned hands, he cries out in pain with every bump. Why will no one stop this? Where is Father?

By now some in the crowd are pelting him with eggs and rocks.

One man lobs a rotting hunk of pork. "Tell your precious King this is what we think of him."

I can't watch any more. I'm just as heartless as the others who stand by and do nothing. I open his tattered leather Bible, and a paper flutters to the ground.

CHAPTER 16

I'd KNOW REV. EVANS's neat, precise handwriting anywhere.

Dear Friend,

That you are now reading this means that I am in dire straits for my allegiance to the Crown. In my house in the bottom of the firewood box by the hearth you will find a paltry bit of money in a leather pouch. It's all I have, but it should be enough for my burial or, God willing, my passage to safety. God bless you.

He must have anticipated this terrifying turn of events, though he could have given his Bible to any other sympathetic soul. I tuck the note under my shawl. As the crowd breaks up, a handful of men, including Father, lift him into the back of a wagon. The pastor's tortured body, covered in hot tar and feathers, lies motionless. *He's dead—they've killed him!* Then a slight pained whimper proves otherwise, but who knows how much life is left?

Nobody notices me slip away from the common and run toward the reverend's place. But approaching the cottage, I hear raucous laughter, glass shattering, wood splintering. Am I too late?

Two front windows are smashed. Someone has taken an axe to the door. Crouching behind a boulder, I hear men's voices inside. Someone is bashing the pastor's furniture, making sure he leaves Essex with absolutely nothing.

Any sensible person would flee at this point. I can't—my feet feel rooted to the ground. I'm paralyzed. Two men stagger out of the house whooping and laughing. A third strolls out carrying a flaming torch.

"We'll show him hellfire!" he laughs. "Abner will be mighty pleased."

"Well, toss the bloody stick in there before we lose the flame," another says. "We have to get out of here."

As the men recede into the woods, wisps of smoke drift out the shattered windows. How long before the whole house bursts into flames?

The pouch! Before I have time to think it through, I race down the path and leap up the front steps. Inside, the smoke is so thick I can barely make out anything. The pastor's polished walnut desk lay dumped on its side, the 6-foot grandfather clock broken in two, the pine bookcase pulverized like kindling. Papers strewn everywhere.

My eyes sting from the smoke. Kneeling, I crawl toward the hearth, feeling my way as I go. The firewood box can't be much farther.

The fire is deafening. The heat burns my throat as I suck in air. I cover my nose and mouth with my shawl and crawl until I touch the rough edge of the wood box. Groping inside, I feel the sticky bark of pine logs, but no pouch. *Where is it, my mind screams?* Frantically, I heave each log aside until I come to the last one, which is lighter than the rest. The underside is hollowed out, and I feel the leather pouch tucked inside. How clever of the pastor.

I clutch it, elated. But as I crawl back toward the door, flames lick the ceiling. I fling off my cap as an ember burns through it. My cheeks feel on fire, and I can't see anything. Where is the door? A ceiling beam crashes to the floor, scattering embers onto my skirt. I open my mouth to scream but searing heat burns my throat. Frantically I brush off the embers, singeing my fingers. I don't know which way to turn.

Over the crackling roar, I hear the yowl, first soft then rising to a desperate screech. There it is again. It's the pastor's cat, Ezekiel. I follow the sound, and it takes me to the door. Ezekiel cowers in the doorway, black hair on end, meowing frantically. Saved by a cat!

I burst through and collapse on the ground coughing and wheezing. My skirts are scorched and torn, and my fingertips are starting to blister. But I have the pouch!

With the flames shooting through the roof, I have little time to get away before the fire draws the whole town. I scramble to my feet and run for the woods, scooping up Ezekiel on the way.

The cat yowls and digs his claws into my arm as I reach the road to my house. My heart is thumping wildly. I know it's a dangerous, foolhardy thing I've done. But I'm not dead, and I found the money. I only hope that Rev. Evans is alive to make use of it.

When I walk into the house, Ezekiel leaps down and dashes under the table.

"My God child, what's happened to you?" Father exclaims. He smells the stench of fire on me and surveys my clothing. "Are you all right?"

"Yes, I think so." In a rush of choking words, I tell him everything. "Is the pastor... alive?"

"Barely. Your mother is treating his wounds. She's made up a bed for him in the back hall."

I'm relieved, but still stunned by the horrible, shameful spectacle the whole town witnessed. "Why didn't the sheriff do something to stop it?"

Father runs his fingers through his straggly hair, something he does when things don't set right with him.

"The sheriff said there was nothing one man could do against an unruly mob. Seemed to me he was only too happy to let it be. I even went to Silas Spooner at the tavern. He said the Committee of Safety didn't authorize such cruelty, but that it was not unexpected when men are worked up to a frenzy over a noble cause."

Noble cause? What an astonishing thought. "What's so noble about torture?"

"A question these so-called patriots haven't the good sense to ponder," he says. "If he dies, it's outright murder."

"Will he die?"

"He's conscious, on and off, but in great pain. I'm sure your mother could use your help."

As I turn to go, Father puts his hand on my shoulder.

"What you did today was foolish and risky. But I can't say I'm not proud of you."

I'm elated, glad to be back in Father's good graces. But that fizzles when I see Rev. Evans's blackened body. "How could they do that to him—and then laugh about it!"

"Save your carrying on for later," Mother says.

The pastor moans softly as Mother pours a strong-smelling liquid from a jug onto a rag and gently scrubs his arms and chest.

"What is that, Mother?"

"Turpentine. Mr. Bascomb brought it over from the store. It loosens the tar but burns like the devil on raw skin." The smell makes my eyes water, and the stink of the tar and burned flesh is suffocating.

Mother seems unbothered by it as she works to free his body of the tar, inch by inch. Patches of skin, even hair, fall off with each tug, as the pastor grimaces silently.

Finally she wipes her hands on her apron. "I'll prepare some more camphor ointment to soothe the pain." As she gets up, she notices my clothing and swollen fingers. "What happened to you?" But Rev. Evans cries out, and she's distracted. "I'll deal with you later." She leaves in a swish of skirts.

I sit on the edge of the bed, and the pastor opens his eyes.

"Sarah, did you...?"

"I have the pouch, here it is." I set it on the bed. I don't tell him Father added a few coins to the pitiful amount.

"Bless you child. I knew when I handed you my Bible, you'd use your wits to—"

"I have more news," I say, looking down at the floor. I hate to tell him when he's suffering so, but he needs to know. "They burned down your house. Everything is gone. The furniture, your desk, your papers. I was lucky to get the pouch." I expect him to lash out at the injustice, even in his weakened state. By all rights, he should be furious.

He closes his eyes for a few seconds and when he opens them, his face seems at peace. "They are just things, my dear. Just things. How brave you were. God has spared us both."

I'm incredulous. "Don't you wish Abner Rollins a swift journey to hell?"

He shakes his head slowly and struggles to speak. "Did you know he goes to the cemetery near every day at dawn, and talks to his son's gravestone? I've seen him out there sobbing like a baby."

Abner Rollins, the devil himself, has a heart? I say nothing and the pastor, sapped, is done talking.

Mother returns with the ointment, and he winces as she dabs it on his burned skin. "I must leave tonight," he says hoarsely, with barely the energy to make the words and expel them from his throat. "Isn't safe for me here. Nor for you."

"Wait until morning," Mother says. "Until we're sure the fever hasn't set in."

"Where will you go?" I ask. "The British have blocked the port at Boston. The newspapers say people there are lacking food."

"It's all arranged," Mother tells him. "Mr. Bascomb will come for you before dawn and, if you're well enough, take you by wagon to Portsmouth. There you should find passage by sea to Canada or New York."

"Aye, safer there," he says.

I lean closer to him. "I retrieved Ezekiel as well. I'll take care of him for you."

"Ezekiel?" Mother asks.

The pastor is halfway delirious. "Ezekiel …land of milk and honey. Zeke knows…his mice."

Despite everything, Mother and I manage a bit of a smile, as Rev. Evans blinks back a tear.

"He's better off here with you."

"We'll see about that," Mother says, gently applying the soothing ointment. "I wish we could all be on that wagon in the morning."

CHAPTER 17

MY FINGERS STILL THROB as I carry a candle upstairs to my bedroom. Mother rubbed salve on them earlier, then subjected me to a sermon on the idiocy of what I'd done. I didn't fight back—she's right. But I'm still glad I did it.

I know sleep won't come soon—my heart is still racing. And I'm still angry. Sitting down at the little table that serves as my desk, I dip my quill pen into an ink bottle and feel swept along in a torrent of words. I work fast, while the horror is still fresh.

> *To the citizens of Essex,*
>
> *In the name of liberty, Rev. Ichabod Evans suffered unspeakable torture on Sunday. You who tarred and feathered him did not hear him shrieking as the hot, poisonous mess was removed from his raw flesh. Whether he'll heal is up to the Lord.*
>
> *You call yourselves patriots. You say you are fighting for rights and freedoms—the right to be free of the British, the freedom to say what you please and worship as you wish. Yet you won't allow those rights to others whose opinions differ from your own. Instead, you torture them and destroy their homes.*
>
> *How can you say your cause is pure and noble? Shame on you! Shame!*

My pen scratches furiously as my anger spills onto each sheet. I only stop to pat Ezekiel when he rubs against my leg. By midnight I'm done, and I sign my name at the bottom with a flourish. Then I fall into bed exhausted, but I lay awake another hour wondering what Father's reaction will be in the morning.

———————

At first light, I creep down the stairs and panic for a second. The pastor is gone! Did he die? But his pouch is gone, along with the pan of corn bread Mother baked. I never heard him leave in Mr. Bascomb's wagon. After throwing another log on the dying fire, I slice some rye bread and cheddar cheese for Father. Before long, he comes out of the bedroom, softly closing the door so as not to wake Mother.

Without a word I hand him the pages I wrote.

"What's this?"

"Please Father, just read it."

He puts on his spectacles and sits down at the table. He takes several minutes, then he reads it again. It seems like a lifetime. It must be awful.

He finally takes off his glasses and rubs his eyes. "My dear, this is a fine piece of writing."

I hold my breath as I wait for him to say more. He stuffs a piece of bread in his mouth and washes it down with cider.

"Is it good enough for the newspaper?" I finally ask. My hands are sweaty, my voice shaky.

"The *Journal*?"

"Yes, is it good enough?"

"Of course it's good enough," Father says. "I couldn't say it better. But it's far too dangerous to print with your name on it. You saw what happened to the pastor."

"I don't care. I'm not worried."

"I care. Do I have to remind you what happened to Seth?"

My hopes sink, and with heads down we eat in strained silence. All that work for what? Nothing!

"Maybe if you were a young man, tough enough to...."

"Obviously I'm not," I say peevishly, "and I *am* tough enough."

Father downs his cider. "What happened to the pastor sickens me. But I will not have you risk your life to bring logic to these fools."

"But it's *my* life," I protest.

"I won't have it."

"But—"

"No!" He slams his mug on the table.

I know it's useless to plead. The silence is heavy as I stoke the fire. Ezekiel whines and tries to jump on the table.

"Now git!" Father says, swatting at him. "I expect Rev. Evans won't be back for this witless creature. Or any of his belongings."

I look up at him. "There is nothing for him to come back for. Everything was destroyed, even his Bibles."

Silence again. Finally he clears his throat to speak.

"Perhaps there is a way," he says. "In Boston men are so worked up and the danger so high that some have resorted to publishing their commentary under different names."

"What?" I'm perplexed. "But I want to use my own name."

"Hear me out, daughter. One of them publishes under the name 'Candidus,' and the British press surmises he's really Samuel Adams."

"*The* Samuel Adams who stirred up all this fighting?"

"Yes. And he's not the only one. Pseudonyms have been around forever."

"What name would I use?" This is intriguing.

"Latin seems to be in favor these days."

"But I don't know any Latin."

"I do." Father scratches his chin and thinks for a moment, then he smiles. "I have it! You'll be *Destinatus*!"

"What does that mean?"

"Destined—and that's exactly what you are: Destined to raise trouble."

"Yes, I like that." The mystery of it sounds appealing, and I must admit, the danger excites me too.

But then an obvious, uncomfortable thought occurs to me. "Father, won't everyone in town know that Destinatus has to be you, me or Samuel? After all, we're the newspaper's entire staff."

"Of course not! We often publish items from the Portsmouth and Boston papers, even from London. Destinatus could be anyone."

"Even New Hampshire's own governor," I add, feeling better already.

"Yes, he's none too happy about this patriot uprising."

I'm, for once, speechless. I'm overjoyed about finally getting my writing into print but crushed at not seeing my name—that is, my real name.

Father holds out my essay. "Take this to Samuel and tell him to run it on the front page. With you there to help him, it's not too late for this week's edition."

"What's this?" Samuel asks. "Another rant?"

"Father says it's to go out front, right next to the announcement about the emergency smallpox meeting. He said it's a fine piece of writing."

"I'll be the judge of that."

As he reads it, he says nothing. I ache to know what he's thinking. Finally, he looks up at me.

"Who's Destinatus?"

I give him a vacant look and shrug my shoulders. "So what do you think?"

"Well, he makes a solid legal point."

"*He* does?"

"Yes. What's his name?"

I smile broadly. "*He* is me. It's the only way Father would allow it. So what do you think of the writing now?"

"Well, I wouldn't have written it quite like that, and this part here sounds too much like a woman." He points to a sentence. "And this here—"

"Do you like it or not?" My patience is withering.

"You wanted my opinion."

"And I'm still waiting."

Samuel stammers for a moment. "I guess it's good enough for

the paper. Yes, I like it. I like it fine."

I know that's the most I'll get and take his meager words as a compliment.

"Thank you." I give him the same satisfied look that I gave Seth that day he admitted I wasn't a bad shot with the bow and arrow.

"Aren't you afraid they'll find out it's you?" he says. "With all that happened to the pastor."

"Would you be afraid?"

"No, of course not," he says quickly.

"Then neither am I." That's not entirely true. I'm not so naïve I don't know the risk I'm taking. And I'll never forget the smell of the pastor's burning flesh.

"We'll have to hurry," Samuel says, adding, with a mock flourish, "Make room for the words of Destinatus, our mysterious new contributor." He winks at me, and I wink back.

CHAPTER 18

DAYS LATER THE MEETINGHOUSE is packed, thanks to the announcement in the *Journal*, a notice posted in Mr. Bascomb's store, and an ominous note nailed to a tree on the green.

Keep the pox out of Essex! Stop heathen inoculation!

Mother has no hesitation about attending. In fact, she can't wait to convince the town that she is its savior. Father would rather be chopping wood but he's sitting with us in this sea of hostile faces. I'm dying see if the town is also in an uproar over the mysterious new writer for the *Journal:* Destinatus.

Clearly on edge, Silas Spooner wipes his face with a handkerchief before he steps up on the podium.

"Ban inoculation!" Daniel Jordan shouts. Emma, sitting next to him, looks mortified.

Mr. Spooner bangs his gavel. "Quiet please! We have much business to conduct, and we'll do it in an orderly fashion."

I hear Father whisper, "Mary, we can leave if you wish."

She gives him a stern look and keeps her seat. I'm proud...and a little jealous.

The crowd quiets down as Mr. Spooner starts in. "Everyone will have a chance to air their concerns. As we all know, the pox has descended on Essex and is running rampant through our town. Six of our dear ones have already died, including little Polly Peterson—"

"God bless her soul!" Mrs. Rollins utters just loud enough to be heard.

"The question is this," Mr. Spooner says. "What must we do to protect ourselves from this vicious disease? Is inoculation the right path to take?"

Emma's father stands. "I'd like to speak, Silas."

"You have the floor, Daniel."

"We all know why this menace is spreading," Mr. Jordan says, aiming a finger at Mother as if he were shooting a deer. "That devil dressed as a woman is making money off the suffering—and sometimes even the death—of our loved ones."

Mother shakes her head. "Not true—"

"You'll have a chance to speak, Mrs. Barrett. Now continue, Daniel."

"Ever since she started giving the pox to all who want it, we've been besieged with sickness and death. Quarantine is a sham. I count six new names in the cemetery."

The crowd murmurs, and I cringe at the tally of newly dead.

"I say we ban inoculation," Mr. Jordan says. "We all have a better chance of avoiding the pox if we just take our chances with Mother Nature. Why invite disease into our community?"

"Hear, hear! He knows what's best," someone yells.

"Ban it, and jail the perpetrators," another yells.

"Settle down!" Mr. Spooner says, banging his gavel again. "Let's hear from Mrs. Barrett, unless her husband wishes to speak for her."

Mother is on her feet immediately. "Inoculation works," she says, her voice low and a little shaky. "Though it's inevitable that a few souls will die."

"Speak up!" someone yells.

"She's a Tory, just like her husband." It's Mrs. Rollins again, a thin, bug-eyed woman who reminds me of a poisonous frog. "It's a British plot to kill us, one by one."

Father shoots up out of his seat. "Let my wife speak!" he booms, startling even Mr. Spooner.

Mother resumes, her voice stronger and louder. "I said inoculation works—most of the medical profession agrees on that.

Done correctly, it produces a milder case and provides protection from ever getting the pox again."

"We know all that propaganda," Mr. Spooner interrupts. "Why are so many people dying, Mrs. Barrett?"

I fear Mother won't have an answer, and the doubters will step up their tirade. *Tar and feathers? Would they go that far?*

"I can answer that, Silas," Mr. Bascomb interjects. "We know our troops are bedeviled by the pox. With General Washington banning inoculation, his men are coming home sick and spreading the pox to others."

"Are you blaming this on General Washington?" Mr. Spooner asks incredulously.

"I'm just saying inoculation isn't the cause. It's the cure," Mr. Bascomb says.

"If I may continue," Mother says, drawing a nod from Mr. Spooner. "It's common knowledge that inoculation won't work unless patients are strictly quarantined for weeks. I've done my best to enforce that with my patients."

Mrs. Rollins jumps up.

"You're exercising Satan's will," she proclaims. "Disease and sickness are God's business, not yours." Murmurs of agreement follow.

"I would not presume to do the business of God," Mother says. "But if we are able to save lives, I would think the Lord would be mighty pleased."

I'm so proud of Mother I want to applaud. Even Father has a pleased look on his face.

The blacksmith rises to his full 6 feet, and I feel a flutter of nerves.

"Mrs. Barrett, or is it now Dr. Barrett," he starts off. "Polly Peterson didn't catch the pox from a soldier—she died by your hand. Isn't that right?"

Mother looks flustered. "Yes, I inoculated her, and I inoculated her parents."

"And are you a doctor?"

"No, but I've trained and studied—"

"No matter! You have no right to inflict the pox upon these people, no less gamble with their lives. I say we ban this cursed practice before we're all dead in our beds."

I can't stand to see Mother pummeled by these idiots. Father looks furious but he's not moving. I rise nervously.

"My mother is not a doctor, but she might as well be. She inoculated me, and I stand here as proof that it works."

Then Mrs. Bascomb stands. "I was inoculated as well and suffered only minor scarring."

Then five others follow suit.

"What about the dead? They can't pipe up so easily!" Mr. Jordan yells.

Mr. Spooner raises his hands. "Quiet please! It's plain to see that we're all of different minds."

"Perhaps I can provide some clarity." I turn to see an unfamiliar young man, smartly dressed, stand and face the crowd. "I am Dr. Josiah Potter, from Gilroy, and I have a proposition that may answer your concerns."

"You have our attention, Dr. Potter," Mr. Spooner says.

"I have opened a smallpox hospital in Gilroy, and I'd be pleased to do the same in Essex."

Mr. Jordan jumps up from his seat. "The pox-stricken will come in in droves! That's insanity!"

"Let the doctor speak his piece," Mr. Spooner says.

"I would provide inoculations to those who wish it and a comfortable place to quarantine until they've recovered and can't infect anyone else," Dr. Potter says. "Those who contract the pox naturally would be welcome as well."

"Young man, aren't you inviting an explosion of cases?" Mr. Spooner asks.

"Not if it's done correctly," the doctor says. "In Gilroy we've taken over an abandoned house on the edge of town and installed a 7-foot fence around it with a sturdy lock. We've stationed a guard to make sure no one enters or leaves without permission. We have a staff of nurses who board with us, and care for the sick for three to four weeks, however long it takes to fully recover. We even fumigate all clothing and bedding with sulfurous fumes."

Mother is on her feet. "That is all well and good, Dr. Potter, but surely you don't do this out of the goodness of your heart. Or do you?"

Dr. Potter looks a little uncomfortable. "I charge 8 pounds per person."

I gasp. That's more than Father paid for our milk cow. Judging by the buzz in the audience, others are stunned too.

"Only the wealthy can afford that, Dr. Potter." Mr. Spooner says. "With the fighting going on, many families are hard pressed to put food on the table."

"Nor can they take time off from their labors to be inoculated— certainly not weeks," Mr. Jordan says.

"If they don't quarantine, the pox will spread," Dr. Potter says. "Mrs. Barrett may do a fine job of inoculation, but she doesn't have the means to isolate the sick."

"What would you have us do? Build a fortress? With a moat?" Mr. Spooner asks. Hoots of laughter follow.

Mr. Rollins strides up to the podium and shoves Mr. Spooner aside.

"Let's end this foolishness now," he roars. "I'm calling for a ban on inoculation. And I say we send Dr. Potter back to Gilroy as fast as his feet will carry him and forget about his fancy hospital."

"Not so fast, Abner," Mr. Spooner says. "We'll not decide this now. The hour is late. The town council will take it up at the next meeting."

I can't wait to get out of the meetinghouse, away from the scornful crowd. We're finally down the front steps when Mr. Jordan confronts Father.

"Benjamin, you're a disgrace. First, your wife and this inoculation scheme, and now your newspaper prints this treasonous nonsense by some fool called Destinatus."

"It's my newspaper, and I'll print what I please," Father says.

Mr. Jordan moves in closer. They're practically nose to nose.

"Are you Destinatus? Are you the coward that penned that harebrained essay about 'poor' Rev. Evans?"

I want to shout to the treetops that it's me. *I'm Destinatus!*

"I won't divulge who it is," he says. "Just know that your torture of Rev. Evans has disgusted people of influence in Boston and beyond. Now, leave us be."

"We'll get to the bottom of this," Mr. Jordan says.

"Do what you must," Father says. "Come along, ladies."

"Don't think you'll get away with this, Barrett. We know you're working with the British, and your wife and daughter as well."

"Hogwash!" Father takes Mother's hand and leads us toward the road. "I was proud of you tonight, Mary."

Mother is thrilled. "So you'll do it? You'll get inoculated and write about its success?"

"Maybe," I hear him say. "When the time is right."

———

At home, Father lights his pipe and sets his ink bottle and paper on the kitchen table.

"I'm weary, but I must do this."

"Let me write it," I say. Since the meeting ended, my mind has been awhirl with ideas, and I can't wait to set them to paper.

Father gives me a long, hard look. "Give it a try but I'll decide whether it passes muster."

Upstairs, I ruin two precious sheets of paper, before the right words finally spill out of me. Two hours later, I'm done. Exhausted, I fall into bed fully clothed.

In the morning, Father reads it and gives what, for him, is a fabulous review.

"Well put, daughter."

I think I'll collapse.

"You've made a reasoned argument, backed up with the science Mother talks about so much. But I especially like this part: *A hospital, as Dr. Potter suggests, will ensure that quarantine works. However, it won't work if only the wealthy have the means to go there. Why not treat the poor at no cost? Essex will be a shining example to the rest of New Hampshire—indeed, the rest of the colonies—when we wipe out the pox*

103

and simultaneously show compassion for the needy."

Mother is listening and breaks into a broad smile. "Well said."

I must be dreaming. I've never done anything to her liking. Not that I've tried all that hard.

"I was hoping I could use my own name this time," I say.

"No." His answer is final. "Some people will heartily agree with you—rather, Destinatus—but more would want to shut you up forever. Are you prepared for that?"

I know he's right. "I'll be Destinatus, for now."

"Then take it to the *Journal* for the next issue," he says. "God help us!"

_ﾏﾟ_

CHAPTER 19

Two days later the issue is out. I nearly run to the print shop, my stomach in a torment. Samuel is in back unsaddling Lucky. It's chilly for mid-October, and steam rises from the chestnut mare as he hauls over a bucket of water and breaks open a bale of hay.

He's just finished distributing papers in Essex and as far away as the inn in Gilroy. Surely people in taverns, shops and meetinghouses have had time to pore over all four pages. Surely they're all dying to know about Destinatus.

I want to rush over and blurt out what kept me awake most of the night: What's the town's reaction?

Though it takes great effort, I hold it in. I don't want to seem consumed with myself. He wipes his face, brushing his damp blonde hair back from his forehead. Father's old leather coat hangs loose on his tall, thin frame. His cheeks are bright red from the cold. I can make out the wispy beginnings of a mustache.

Emma doesn't think him handsome in the least. "Too skinny," she says. But I see something—I don't know what it is, but something that excites me when I'm around him.

Finally, I burst out with it: "Samuel, what are they saying?"

He looks up, surprised to see me. "Saying about what?"

"The pox and inoculation!"

His face slowly eases into what he must think is a sly grin.

"Mr. Bascomb says there's been a run on feather pillows and pine tar at the store," he jokes.

"How can you possibly think that's funny? The pastor nearly died!"

The least he could do is tell me my essay is an adequate piece of writing. But no. Nothing! Emma thinks he's jealous, and I agree. That gives me some satisfaction.

"Just tell me what they're saying."

"I don't have time to chat with people," he says with mock irritation. "I'm tired and hungry. I'd be in a finer mood if you'd greet me with a mug of ale, some cornbread and a sweet 'Good day to you Samuel, how weary you must be.'"

"I'm not your handmaiden. Fetch it yourself."

I stride into the print shop. What is it about Samuel that makes me want to kiss him one moment and slap him the next? He treats me the way Seth did sometimes, teasing me as if I'm 12, not 15. Girls my age are already thinking about marriage—not that I want to soon, or maybe ever.

To take my mind off the most infuriating man in the world, I read the ads for the next issue. It's the usual fare, nothing scandalous. The widow Harris is looking for a boarder, or, as everyone surmises, a new husband. Mr. Bascomb needs an apprentice for his general store. He'll be hard pressed to find any takers, with so many of the men away fighting.

I'm still reading when Sheriff Willard hauls his portly frame into the shop. He takes off his hat, exposing his shiny bald head.

"Good day to you, Miss."

I nod suspiciously. He's never stopped by. Why now?

"Is Samuel, Samuel… Mason, about?" he asks.

"No, he's tending his horse," I say. "I expect he'll be in soon."

"I'll wait," he says without hesitation. "So Samuel's been apprenticing here the last six months. Is that right?"

"Approximately." I'm dying to know why the sheriff, or anyone, would need to see Samuel. "Anything I can help you with?"

"No. Well…yes, perhaps there is, as long as I'm here." He puts his beefy arms on the wooden counter and leans forward. "You could help with the bear."

"What bear?"

"The one that killed Daniel Singer's dog this morning. Busted up Daniel pretty bad too."

"What happened?"

"Daniel and his boy were out cutting brush in the lower pasture. They heard the dog yelp and howl like crazy. They looked up and saw he'd cornered a black bear. Big devil, at least 400 pounds. It had the dog by the neck and was dragging him away."

I know that dog. He minds the sheep at the Singer farm.

"The boy fired his rifle and missed. That's when this bear—maybe 7 feet tall on his hind legs—came after Daniel."

"That's terrible! What happened then?"

"Bear gouged him, but Daniel swung his hatchet and dug way into its front paw. It was enough to send it back into the woods."

"Is Mr. Singer all right?"

"We had to get him over to Gilroy so the doc could fix him up."

"Why? My mother could have stitched him up. She's right here in town."

The sheriff shifts his weight uncomfortably. "We thought it best."

I already know why. Some people would rather risk death than be treated by a loyalist, and a woman at that.

He looks around impatiently. "Where is that young man? You said he'd be back straight away."

"Any minute." I'm enthralled with the bear now. "Is the bear still out there, alive?" I'm already thinking ahead to my solitary walk home later.

"Yep. It probably ain't no more than a bee sting to him." He smiles pleasantly at me now. "I'd be obliged if you could put something in your paper to warn folks this cussed creature is in our midst. I'm certain he's the one that surprised Mrs. Spooner out by the privy last week."

"Of course," I say. My account will have all the bloody details, and Father couldn't possibly object to me writing it. "I'll gladly take care of that for you."

He cracks his knuckles impatiently. "Since we have time to pass, you can tell me who this Destinatus is that has everyone riled up. It's your father, isn't it?"

"I can't say."

"Surely you can—and will."

His chilling tone takes me aback.

"What are they upset about?"

"Upset about! This…Destinatus…suggests we turn Essex into the world capital of smallpox and pay for it ourselves with some outrageous tax. Isn't it enough that the British are already taxing us to death?"

"That's not—"

The back door opens and Samuel saunters in, stopping suddenly when he sees the sheriff.

"I've been waiting for you, boy."

"What can I help you with?" Samuel says as if he's handling an advertisement for the paper.

"You must know why I'm here."

"No." Samuel takes a step backward.

I'm afraid for him and haven't a clue what's going on.

"If this is about Destinatus," I say, "I can assure you it's not Father or Samuel. It's me."

The sheriff laughs. "Do you take me for a fool?"

"Sarah, it's no use trying to cover for me," Samuel says. "I'm Destinatus. I'm the one you want, sheriff."

"At least we have that nasty business settled," the sheriff says. "But I'm here on something even more treasonous."

Now I'm truly clueless.

"We know all about your father, Samuel, and we know you've been helping him."

"My father is a farmer and of course I help him with chores when I'm not needed here at the newspaper."

That's news to me. I thought he hated farming.

"That's not all your father does, is it?" The sheriff moves in closer to Samuel, his beefy face inches away.

"What are you talking about?"

"Your father breeds horses and sells them to the British. In fact, he's a fount of information for the redcoats, feeding them all manner of intelligence about our militias."

"You don't know the first thing about my father," Samuel says.

"And you're right there helping him," the sheriff continues, undeterred. "He's a damn spy—and so are you! We've seen you lurking around our meetings."

"I am *not* a spy," Samuel fires back. "But I'm proud to be British, and a subject of the greatest nation on God's green earth. I'll say it so even you can understand: Long live the King!"

"Samuel! Stop it!" I shout.

"Boy, you've done it now." The sheriff grabs a broom and slams Samuel against the wall, jamming the stout stick across Samuel's neck so hard he can barely breathe.

"What do you think of your bloody King now, boy?"

Samuel is choking, unable to utter a word.

I have to do something fast—and, as usual, I scream out the most ludicrous of possibilities.

"The bear! I see the bear!"

"What?" The sheriff whirls around to look, and Samuel grabs the broom with one hand and lands a blow to the sheriff's jaw with the other. He crashes to the floor and lies motionless.

"You've killed him, Samuel!"

"Hardly. He's just knocked out," he says with nonchalance, as if he renders sturdy lawmen unconscious every day of the week.

"You're in trouble now," I say. "Why did you have to yell, 'Long live the King?'"

"I'm not afraid of that ox." Samuel's face is still red and he's breathing fast.

"It's not just him—it's everyone else in town. You've got to leave, now!" My mind is going in a million directions.

"All right. I'll saddle Lucky," he says.

"I know a place."

Samuel grabs hold of my shoulders. "You're not coming with me. It's too dangerous."

"Yes, I am. It's the only way you'll find it."

"Wait!" Samuel strides into the back room and comes out with his knapsack and his old flintlock pistol.

"I'm ready now."

CHAPTER 20

Samuel kicks the horse into a gallop on the road out of town. I'm behind him in the saddle, clinging to his waist. With every bump I nearly fly off.

"I think it's just ahead to the right, after that pine," I say, relieved nobody is about. It's been years since I was in the cave that Seth and I discovered—our secret hiding place.

Finally, he reins in Lucky as we leave the road to follow an overgrown, barely visible path along the creek. The woods are dense and the horse falters, looking in vain for a way back to the road. He rears his head occasionally to protest the extra load on his back.

"I think the cave is to the left of those maples on the rise," I say, hoping I'm right. Everything looks so different from the way I remember it.

"Are you certain? I don't see anything."

"Not so loud!" He twists to look behind us, and my face brushes against his. For a second, our eyes lock.

"I'm sure it's nearby," I stammer. But, in truth, I'm not sure at all.

We follow the creek around another bend, weaving a path between the rocks that lay strewn along the banks. Poor Lucky! My eyes sweep the terrain, searching in vain until a faintly familiar notch catches my eye.

"There! Up on the hillside." I point to a pile of boulders nestled against the slope. It's unremarkable, but I recognize the lone pine tree that has grown tall, a sentry right in front of it.

I jump off, and Samuel slowly dismounts, tying Lucky out of sight behind a cluster of trees.

Pushing my way through bushes to the lone tree, I see a sliver of darkness just large enough for someone to slip through. Terrified I'll unleash a flurry of bats, I squeeze inside, and Samuel follows.

It's pitch black, and it takes a minute for my eyes to adjust. It's not as big as I remember, but just tall enough for Samuel to stand stooped over. Gradually my eyes make out the dirt floor with its ring of black from long-ago fires. I see the two stumps Seth and I hauled inside an eternity ago.

"This is where my brother and I would fancy ourselves Indians hiding from soldiers," I say. For a moment, I let that pleasant memory wash over me.

"This will do fine for tonight," Samuel says, easing his tall frame down. "Too risky to leave now. I'll wait until dawn."

The meaning of his words suddenly hits me. I hadn't thought beyond guiding him to safety. Now he's leaving, maybe for good. "Where will you go?"

"I don't know. I still have a little money my father gave me. He can't help me now—he's got troubles of his own. I can find work in New York, or up north in Nova Scotia. Perhaps I'll run into Rev. Evans and can return the pistol he lent me."

Samuel laughs, but I only feel sad and bitter that I'm losing someone again. All the months he so annoyed me: How time has slipped away—and now, so little is left. If only he hadn't struck Sheriff Willard. If only he'd kept his mouth shut.

"Why did you insist you were Destinatus?" I ask. "None of this would have happened if you'd let me take the credit."

"Or the blame. I was afraid for you. I thought—"

"They were my words. You had no right." The tenderness disappears from Samuel's eyes.

"Sarah, I saved you from Willard and whatever he had in mind, but all you can think about are your precious words. How about these words: 'Thank you, Samuel.'"

It's a slap in the face, but maybe I deserved it, acting like a spoiled child.

"I'm sorry. I *am* thankful to you."

"I believe those are the hardest words you've ever had to say, Sarah Barrett." He puts his arm around my shoulder, drawing me closer. The warmth of his body, the smell of his pipe tobacco: I suck it in like a bee on a nectar-filled blossom. My body relaxes against his, and I feel like I'm melting away.

He lowers his head and gives me a soft kiss on the forehead. Then I can't stop myself. I raise my lips up to meet his and we kiss for real—a long, tender embrace I hope will never end.

Finally, he pulls free. "I've wanted to do that for a long time, but I didn't think you'd welcome it."

I smile in surprise. "I'd welcome it again!" I raise my lips to his.

"Sarah, you are a conundrum. A lovely conundrum."

I think I will collapse.

Lucky whinnies outside, startling us. "Sarah, you must go. It's late and they'll miss you. Let's just say our goodbyes here and now, real quick."

"But you can't leave without food for the journey. And Lucky will need to eat hearty." Of course, it isn't Lucky I'm worried about; I want to see Samuel one more time, and maybe another after that...

"I'll return before dawn with some provisions," I say.

"I can't have you—"

"No trouble. Will you be warm enough here tonight?"

"Yes. I have a tarp I can spread on the ground. Now hurry."

A soft rain begins to fall as I walk through the woods back to the road. I want to think about what happened in the cave, re-create it in my mind, but I must stay alert.

As I approach the road, two horsemen sweep by at a gallop, headed toward my house. Panicked, I crouch in a tangle of bushes. They must be searching for Samuel, or who knows, maybe me. I wait what feels like an hour in the drizzle before I dare venture out to the road.

As I walk past Emma's house, I can make her out in the gathering dark lugging two pails toward the barn.

"Emma!" I hiss.

She stops. "You startled me. I was just going out to milk the cows. What are you doing, and why are you whispering?"

In a rush of words, I tell her what happened with Samuel, including every detail of the big kiss.

Uncharacteristically, she ignores it, talking instead about the riled-up militia looking for him after he socked the sheriff.

"He's in big trouble, and so are you. Be careful, Sarah."

Finally home, shivering and wet, I'm afraid of what I'll find.

"Sarah, where have you been?" Mother demands. "We were frightened to death. Abner Rollins and his brother were here looking for Samuel. They threatened to burn down the house if we were hiding him."

"Where is he?" Father asks.

"He's safe."

"Sarah, tell me this instant," he orders.

I have no choice. "He's hiding in the cave down by the pond where Seth and I used to play. He's leaving in the morning before light."

"I fear for him," Father says. "I heard all about the pummeling he gave Sheriff Willard."

"Soon they'll be back to pummel us," Mother adds, glowering at Father.

After they go to bed, I creep downstairs with a sack and gather a hunk of bread, some cheese, apples, potatoes, and venison jerky. I include the last piece of pumpkin pie, which will no doubt irk Father. If he knew my plan, he'd have a fit.

The rain ticks against the window. Strangely, I'm not scared by what I'm about to do. I know the danger, but I can't *not* help him escape. I relive that moment when his lips touched mine. The tingle returns, and with it, confusion. Is it supposed to feel like that?

I open the cedar chest in the hall, careful not to make a sound. Pulling out Seth's old gray wool scarf, I hold it close, hoping for my brother's scent, but all I can smell is the cedar. I fold it carefully and put it in the sack.

In bed I lie awake, hoping the rain will let up. As I drowse off, I hear the plinking of hail, but after a moment I realize it's pebbles hitting my window. I open it, letting in a blast of cold damp air.

"Sarah, get up!"

"Emma?"

"Hurry!"

I dress quickly and creep out with the sack. Emma is shivering, holding a lantern.

"What's happened?"

"Father came home from the tavern and said all the talk was about Samuel. They say he's a spy."

"That's rubbish! I'm sure of it."

"Father says someone saw you and Samuel leave the print shop and race away on Lucky.

Dread races through me. "Did you tell him about the cave?"

"Father was like a madman, threatening me with a whipping if I kept something from him." Emma is shaking. "I was so afraid. I've never seen him so angry."

"What did you say?"

"I-I-I told him Samuel was hiding in the barn at the pastor's old place. That he would head north at first light. Father left to go find him, and I came here to warn you."

Relief washes over me, but only for a second. Samuel will have to make his getaway sooner than later. "Thank you. I'll make it up to you. I promise."

"I'll make sure you do. Now hurry!"

I hug her, nearly knocking her over with the sack of food.

Then I head for the cave. Tree branches scrape my face as I feel my way in the moonlight.

"Samuel!" I whisper. "Samuel, come quick!"

He emerges slowly through the narrow passage with his pistol drawn.

"Sarah, what's wrong? It's not yet dawn."

"You must go now." I explain in a breathless rush of words, handing him the sack. "I packed some oats for Lucky."

He kisses my cheek. "Hurry home before they miss you. Stay

close to the creek and keep an eye out for that bear."

I watch him tighten Lucky's cinch and hop up. I crave just a few more minutes with him. "Where will you go?"

"If they reckon I'm going north, I'll head south, to Connecticut."

"Safe journey," I say, wishing I had more tender words at my command.

"Goodbye Sarah. I'll not forget you," he says, "and your beautiful words, and your wild red hair."

He disappears into the darkness, and I feel like a piece of me has been ripped away.

CHAPTER 21

I HAVE NO TIME to feel sorry for myself. At home, I wake up hours later to learn the pox has now claimed the young Boyle couple and their three-year-old son.

"They weren't inoculated and suffered terribly at the end," Mother tells me as I drag myself to the breakfast table.

"Mr. Boyle was blinded, and poor Mildred couldn't speak for the sores coating her mouth and throat. The boy went first with a raging fever that I just couldn't bring down."

"I'm sure you did everything possible." My thoughts are still in the cave with Samuel as Mother goes on.

"Mr. Spooner has called an emergency meeting of the town council today. If they have any sense, they'll set up the hospital fast and start inoculating before half the town dies."

"I hope so," I say rather absent-mindedly.

"I bet Destinatus hopes so too," Mother says, expertly drawing my attention back to the life-or-death matter at hand.

Suddenly, I'm back in the moment. I can't deny my excitement, the power of my words. God help me for being so selfish at a time like this.

Hours later, only a few people are at the meeting, including Dr. Potter from Gilroy. The council members are all huddled around Mr. Spooner near the podium, murmuring things I can't make out. Something isn't right.

Mr. Spooner bangs a gavel and calls the meeting to order. "We're here about the pox," he announces as if it weren't obvious, "and what, if anything, we can do."

Mother's hand shoots up. "I'd like to make clear that the latest victims, the Boyle family, were not inoculated. They might still be here—"

"Enough, Mrs. Barrett," Mr. Spooner says. "The council has made its decision. We want no part of Dr. Potter's pest house, and we are banning this dangerous practice of inoculation you so favor."

"Sir, I beg you to reconsider," Dr. Potter shouts. "You are going against current medical wisdom, and families are dying as a result."

Mr. Spooner bangs his gavel some more and demands that everyone quiet down.

"We've heard all the arguments," he declares somberly, "and we are tired of the rhetoric. The council has made its decision: A ban on inoculation starts immediately. Offenders will face a fine of 5 pounds, and that applies to the one doing it and the one getting it. For subsequent offenses, the fine will double, and we may have to consider the possibility of imprisonment." He looks straight at Mother but forgoes further comment.

"This meeting is done," he says quietly, with another flourish of the gavel.

Mother and I catch up with Dr. Potter outside. "A terrible night," she says.

"Indeed. I hope that you'll tell your patients they're welcome in Gilroy."

"That's a fair distance to go, and a big burden to take on when they're ill," Mother says. "But thank you for the offer."

As we walk home, I grow angrier, spouting off to Mother. "They can't do that! They didn't even let us speak."

"There's nothing we can do, Sarah," she says as we arrive home to find Father stirring a kettle of yesterday's stew.

I'm too worked up to eat. "How can they just make their own law?"

"So now you're challenging their authority to make laws?" Father asks, slurping his stew.

"No, just bad laws that are cruel, ignorant, and unfair."

"Says who?" he asks as if we were playing some childish guessing game. He seems to be having a jolly time of it.

Now I'm fuming and can barely get my words out. "They're telling us what we can and cannot do with our own bodies!"

"So you would make it law that *everyone* be inoculated?"

"Why not? It's for the good of everyone."

"Those who don't want pus stuffed into their bodies could say the same thing: It's *my* body. And remember, there are people like the Whistlers down the road that had their whole families inoculated only to see two of their children die anyway."

"Whose side are you on, Father?"

"I'm on the side of finding the truth. Anyway, if you want to challenge the law, you'll need proper grounds. You'll need to petition the town council and do it in proper legal language. Maybe even file a lawsuit."

"*I* can do that?" Suddenly, I'm alive.

"Anyone can do it," he says. "That was the whole point of the Magna Carta and all the laws that followed it hundreds of years ago."

"Benjamin, don't feed her harebrained ideas," Mother says.

"It's not harebrained. She's hardly the first person to think about getting a bad law reversed."

After dinner, Father and I draft a letter to the town council:

> The council has made a terrible mistake that will needlessly cost Essex some precious lives. They approved a ban on pox inoculation, and that alone is bad enough, but they did it without hearing from all sides. That is why this newspaper is demanding the council reconsider its decision at a proper meeting. That is also why every citizen—even those who agree with the ban—should insist that proper, democratic procedures be followed.

I argue for threatening a lawsuit, but Father talks me into some calmer—that is, duller—language about "the prospect of litigation."

"I'll deliver the letter to Spooner in the morning, and then we'll run it in the *Journal*," he says.

For hours I lie awake going over every word in my head, wondering what Samuel would think, wherever he is.

I hear Father chopping wood in the dark, though we have a hearty supply. I wonder what he's thinking. *Have we gone too far?* For the first time, it occurs to me that I might be dead-wrong—about inoculation, about the patriots, about everything.

———

Predictably, Essex goes into a full-blown uproar. Emma says her father is so mad he's pushing everyone to stop buying the newspaper and shun Mother's services. One minute I'm thrilled *my* words have done that, and the next I'm terrified. It doesn't help when I'm alone cleaning the press, and a rock, complete with a note tied to it, smashes the front window.

Drop your threats to the council or be destroyed.

I race home and find Father in the barn trying to fix the eternally broken plow. When I tell him about the rock, he barely reacts.

"What should we do?" I ask.

"We should do our job," he says quietly.

That doesn't comfort me in the least. "Father, maybe we should tell the sheriff."

"A lot of good that will do. He's already cast his lot with the rebels." At that point the plow handle splinters again and Father heaves it across the barn.

"I'll heat up the stew," I say, glad to make a quick exit.

Inside, I stoke the fire and add some potatoes to the watery gruel. If Mother were here, she'd make it edible, even tasty. But she's off tending a smallpox sufferer and might not be home for days. I don't know one herb from another and care even less.

Finally, I ladle the glop into a couple of bowls, slice some stale bread, and call Father to the table.

"Smells good, Sarah," he says.

I think he's just trying to make up for his foul mood but that's fine with me. It gives me a chance to ask the question that has been weighing me down.

"Father, could you ever see yourself supporting the rebels?"

"What are you talking about?"

"Well, they say it's all about lowering the King's taxes and demanding representation. Don't you believe in those things too?" I know I'm asking for a lecture, but the rock has set me to thinking: All this trauma could go away if Father had a change of heart—and I know he can be open-minded at times.

He's about to answer when a loud knock cuts him short. He grabs the bread knife as he goes to the door.

"Who's there!"

"It's Silas—Silas Spooner," a voice outside yells. "Please let me in, Benjamin."

"What do you want?"

"I'm alone and I want to talk with you."

Still clutching the knife, Father slowly opens the door.

"Put that thing down. I mean no harm."

Ever the gentleman, Mr. Spooner graciously acknowledges me, which is more trouble than most men take.

In his fine blue coat with gold buttons, he looks so elegant next to Father in his shabby work shirt.

Father eyes him cautiously.

"What brings you here, Silas?"

"I come as a friend, as a neighbor, as a man who respects all you've done. After all, we've known each other a long time, Benjamin. Your Mary helped birth my young ones."

"What's this about, Silas? You haven't paid me a social call in near a year."

His smile fades. "The town is at the breaking point. This challenge to the inoculation ban is the last straw. We might as well string up a banner announcing to the world: *Come and get your pox here*."

"Silas, you're being an ass. Doing nothing is the worst thing we can do."

"You might be right...in a perfect world," Mr. Spooner says. "A world where everyone could afford to take a month off to quarantine. A world where crops don't need tending and chores don't need doing. But we've got children to feed, farms to run, and a war to fight. We've got our own imperfect lives to lead, and no one has a penny to spare."

"I see your point," Father says. "But I'm not backing down, and neither are the doctors who say inoculation is the only thing that can save most of the folks in towns like ours."

Spooner is undaunted. "I'm not a one-man band, Benjamin. Nearly the whole council feels as I do."

"That doesn't make it right."

"You can't ignore our pastors, pastors all over New England, who say this inoculation scheme is tinkering with a divine plan beyond our understanding. Do you want the wrath of the church on your hands?"

Father just smiles. "My wife is a God-fearing woman," he says, "and her conscience is not troubled."

"You stubborn fool! The town is rallying at noon to demand that you cease printing. If you don't, I fear for your safety, my friend." He looks at me. "And your family's."

I sit next to Father and look about the packed hall. There are only two other women, and they sit as far from us as possible. It's as if we're lepers.

As Silas Spooner walks to the front of the room, he lays his hand on Father's shoulder and whispers: "I hope you've come to your senses."

Everyone is staring at us, and I feel my face turning red. My stomach is roiling, and I know it's more than old stew.

Emma's father, Daniel Jordan, strides in with his usual bluster. Behind him, her brother Thomas hobbles in on a crutch. He nearly lost his leg at Bunker Hill. Blood is leaking through the bandage, and he winces with every step.

Billy Slater, younger than me by a year, sits with his father and brothers. A rag is wrapped around his head.

"What happened to him?" I ask Father.

"Musket ball grazed his head, tore off his ear."

At the front of the meetinghouse, Silas Spooner faces the crowd and clears his throat. "Abner Rollins and some others asked for this meeting. They have grave concerns about Benjamin Barrett and his *Essex Journal*."

The blacksmith stands up and leans on the pew in front.

"This inoculation nonsense is the last straw. He's a damn redcoat! He doesn't wear a uniform, but he might as well. And why not? His appointment as the King's printer pays him from the royal coffers. And to top it off, he harbors a spy and passes him off as an apprentice."

"No! That's—"

Father hushes me. and I swallow the rest of my outrage.

Jack Nims, a farmer with a perpetually sour face, gets up. "You ask me, there's only one reason he's pushing this inoculation deal— and that's because his wife makes a few shillings every time she stuffs a load of pus into her next victim's arm!"

Mr. Spooner jumps up. "Mary Barrett is one of the finest midwives and most caring neighbors in this entire colony," he declares. "On inoculation, she's wrong as can be, but let's not go down the bloody path of character assassination, Mr. Nims!"

Many in the crowd seem to be murmuring their assent with Mr. Spooner's impassioned words but Emma's father shouts them down.

"I say we let the Committee of Safety do its job," he yells. "They're the ones supposed to ferret out the redcoats among us."

The hall erupts in a roar of approval. Suddenly, I'm very afraid. I look around for the sheriff, but he's cheering just like the others.

Mr. Spooner yells for quiet. "Let Benjamin Barrett speak his mind."

Father, wearing his best waistcoat and breeches, rises slowly to speak, and the room grows silent.

"All I'm saying is that it's not too late to work out our differences with the Crown. If you silence me, you silence all who have ideas different than your own. You talk about freedom of speech—but if you fight only for the speech that you agree with, then you're fighting an empty battle."

I applaud, but I'm the only one.

"I'll not shut down the press," he says. "Come Thursday, the *Journal* will publish as usual."

"We'll see about that," Abner Rollins snorts.

Mr. Spooner tries to keep order. "You'll not reconsider, Benjamin?"

"No. I will not."

I swell with pride. *He didn't back down.* If he's afraid, he doesn't show it. As we leave the meetinghouse, a woman spits at him, leaving a slimy glob clinging to his coat.

"Shame on you!" I hiss.

"Shame on you," she fires back. "You haven't lost a child to the pox, have you?"

Outside, a crowd gathers, and I stay close to Father. Then someone yells, "You'd best git to your print shop. Hurry!"

Running across the green, we hear a crash, then another, and then the sound of wood splintering. We dash inside just as Abner Rollins raises an ax above his massive bulk and swings it down again on the battered wood frame of the printing press. It collapses like a pile of kindling and cheers ripple through the crowd.

I watch in disbelief. It feels like it's *my* press they're destroying. My life, my family, my future. Father surveys the damage with a look of despair I've not seen since Seth died.

"God will deal with you, Abner," he says slowly, enunciating each word.

"As he will with a traitor," the blacksmith says.

His henchmen carry out tray after tray of metal type.

I step in the way, but Father pulls me back. "What good is the type to you?" he asks the smirking smithy. "You can't sell it. There's not another printer for 50 miles."

"We'll melt it down and make bullets. The patriots have more need for ammunition than fancy words."

The men finally leave, taking with them every scrap of metal.

"I hope he burns in hell!" I say, choking out the words.

"Damn fools!" Father sputters. "They don't know I have something far more valuable than the press and the type."

"What?" I'm thoroughly confused, but I follow him to the back of the ruined shop, where, on an ordinary day, he'd be mixing his ink.

"Ink? What good is ink now?" I fear he's been driven insane.

"It's not the ink—it's the formulas," he explains as if he were telling a three-year-old the difference between bread and bread pudding. He cradles the leather-bound volume where he records his concoctions.

"Sarah, fetch me the sack Samuel used to deliver the papers."

He loads it with the aging book, along with boxes and bottles containing powders and potions. I wonder if he's lost his mind.

"We'll find a safe place at home for these," he says, scaring me more than Abner Rollins ever had. "They'll be our salvation."

CHAPTER 22

Dec. 5, 1775

Dear Diary,

Still no word from Samuel. One minute I fear he's dead or never cared about me. The next minute, I can smell his pipe tobacco. I poked around his old quarters at the print shop and found a novel under the bedding: The History of Tom Jones, a Foundling. *No wonder Samuel hid it!*

MORNING COMES WELL BEFORE it should, and my head aches from lack of sleep. Last night, I penned a long letter to Samuel—though I have no idea where to send it. Emma doubts I'll ever see him again.

The house is frigid. Snow blankets the ground nearly two feet deep. Getting out of bed is out of the question. I burrow deep under the covers to stay warm.

"Sarah?" Mother calls out from downstairs.

"I'm almost dressed." I nestle deep in the warmth for a few more minutes. Mother will have a list of chores for me before I've eaten breakfast. The privy needs a good scrubbing, she reminded me last night. And there are the soiled linens from the twins' birth at the Webster farm. She has only a few calls for catching newborns these days—only those mothers who don't care that she's a loyalist.

Thank God the pox epidemic is nearly over. It's been a hellish couple of months, especially for Mother, who can never turn down a plea for help. Of course, she obeyed the inoculation ban, despite my urging to do otherwise. Dozens died, needlessly, although we'll never be able to prove it.

The cases are dwindling, since everyone is stuck inside like trapped squirrels. With the newspaper gone, Father has quietly dropped his threatened legal action against the town. No one took it seriously anyway.

"Sarah!"

There's no escaping it. I inch out of bed, shivering, and dress quickly. Downstairs, Mother is by the hearth stirring the oatmeal. How big the bulge in her clothing has grown! In a few months I'll have a brother or sister. I feel nothing. I'd give anything to hear Seth outside shoveling snow. Instead, it's Father I hear, his shovel scraping the granite steps.

"Sarah," she says, "I'm told Emma's brother needs looking after, with that leg still festering. Mr. Jordan won't like it, but he's got to realize that no one else can help."

Father steps inside, letting a burst of cold into the house.

"Firewood is getting low, Benjamin," Mother says. "Could you find the time to chop some more?"

I hear the usual prickly edge in her voice.

"Can't. Axe needs sharpening," Father says.

"I thought you took it to be ground yesterday. You were gone most of the day." Mother gives him the same scowl she gives me when her patience is raw.

"I did."

"Well?"

Father glares at her. "Ebenezer Crawford won't grind it. Said he won't do business with a damn Tory. We argued but he didn't come around. It was the same at Woodard's. I expect I'll have to get my own grindstone."

Mother's sigh fills the room, and I dread the tension that will follow the rest of the day.

Without another word, he heads to the oak desk where he keeps his ink bottles, chemicals, paper and quills.

"I suppose you're going to tinker with your precious ink now," Mother says to his back. "Waste more time."

He turns around slowly. "You make it sound like I'm going off to play cards. I assure you, I'm not."

"Why do you bother with ink now that the *Journal* is gone?" she asks.

I wonder the same but keep it to myself.

"Ink is more than just ink," he says angrily, apparently presuming that everyone with a half-working brain would know what he's talking about.

"Ink happens to be the last thing I care about right now," Mother shoots back. "Our provisions are low, and in case you haven't noticed, we have a baby coming soon."

"I've always provided, and I'll continue to do so," Father says. "Now pull yourself together."

Mother goes back to the oatmeal pot, clanking her spoon against the sides just to let him know she's still angry.

I don't understand him. He spends his days poring over formulas, smelling up the house with his experiments. Staying up past midnight, he burns candle after candle. Two nights ago, he accidentally set a napkin on fire. I thought Mother would strangle him.

At his desk, he lights a candle, despite the daylight streaming in. He scratches out what I assume is another rant on the rebels' cause—a futile effort without a place to publish it.

I daydream about running away from the bickering, the boredom, the rebels, this stupid town, the whole sorry mess. I imagine Samuel in Philadelphia or New York, and I spend hours plotting my escape, and how I'll take up with him, and write my novel, and become famous.

Father, hunched over his desk, waves his scrawled-upon paper over the candle flame, singeing it. Is he deliberately provoking Mother?

I'm desperate to get out and see Emma for some sympathy. "Mother, I'll go to the Jordans. I can treat Tom's wound."

"No. I'll do it myself. Seems I have to do everything around here."

"Mary, for the love of God!" Father shouts. "Do you enjoy being the martyr? Is that it? Let Sarah help you. You've been after her to do just that."

"She doesn't know how to lay on the poultice," Mother shouts back.

"Yes, I do! I've seen you do it a hundred times." That's a partial lie, but how difficult can it be to slap a bag of ointment on a cut?

Mother doesn't need much convincing. "I've mixed him my slippery elm poultice to draw out the infection, and I think some elder blossom tea would do him some good. I'll go fetch it."

Praise God! In a few minutes I'll be free.

———————————

Bundled against the cold, I step outside and feel like I'm in a magical land where everything is white, blinding white. The tree branches are heavy with snow, and for as far as I can see, the ground is pristine.

I strap on my snowshoes and stagger slowly out to the main road. Fortunately, someone's sleigh has laid a track so I'm not sinking up to my hips as I trudge along.

When I knock at the Jordans', Emma cracks the door. "Come in quickly. Father will be back from hunting soon."

"What's wrong?"

"He still thinks your whole family are working for the British."

"That's just twaddle."

"I know. Besides, it's important that Tom's leg is tended. He's in terrible pain. It was healing nice and proper but then it took a bad turn. Now it looks so horrid and stinks so bad I can't bear to change the bandage."

"I'll take care of it." I try my best to sound convincing, but I dread the whole prospect.

"Mind you, Tom is still not himself," Emma says. "He's thin as a fence post and barely talks."

I follow her into Tom's tiny room behind the kitchen and stop abruptly when I see the slight figure in bed. He's not the husky boy I remember. His eyes are hollow and his face gray.

"I told you, no visitors," he says before looking away.

"Sarah brought a poultice her mother made up for your leg."

"And some tea Mother says will perk you up," I offer.

Thomas keeps his gaze on the bare wall.

"I'll go fix the tea," Emma says.

He remains stony, finally insisting that only Mother can treat him and no one else.

I quickly come up with a lie—something I find myself increasingly skilled at. "Mother is ill and mustn't go out. Why don't you let me have a look?"

"No!"

"The poultice shouldn't hurt." I just want to set the warm, moist, cloth-wrapped lump by his bed and leave. But I'm puzzled by his behavior, and curious about the wound. I have a huge distaste for the bloody mess of newborns, but this is different somehow.

I summon up my nerve. "Just let me—"

"I said no!"

"Why?"

Thomas finally glares at me. "I don't want a Tory to lay a finger on me. You've already done enough. I'm as good as dead."

I take a step back. His words sting but also make me furious. "You're not dead and I'm no spy. Now let me have a look at your revolting leg before I change my mind."

Immediately, I know I've gone too far.

"I'm sorry, Thomas."

Neither of us speaks for what seems forever. Then, for some reason, I feel an urge to spill my own torment. "I've never told anyone this, not even Emma," I say softly. "Sometimes I imagine it was me, not Seth, shot and bleeding to death on the step. I wonder if things would be any different now."

Tears pool in his brown eyes. "I wish that soldier's aim had been better, and he'd shot me dead."

"No, Tom!"

"I'll show you what the Brits have done." He throws the quilt aside and I see the swollen, discolored leg. He grabs a corner of a yellow-stained bandage and tears it off, pulling the festering scab off with it.

"There, have a good look."

I nearly gag from the smell as well as the sight but do my best to stay calm.

"How did it happen?" I ask.

"It was last June, after we got orders to fortify Bunker Hill against a British attack." He seems calmer now. I move my hand closer to his leg and slowly pick up the poultice with the other hand.

"We built a wall taller than the tallest man among us. The British attacked again and again, and we kept pushing 'em back, until we ran low on gunpowder. They kept coming and finally broke our fort."

"What happened then?" I firmly plant the poultice on the wound.

Thomas doesn't notice. "Are you sure you want to know? You won't be so fond of your redcoats."

"Yes, I want to know." I hold tight to the wet mass and keep my eyes on Thomas, his face white with terror as he relives the moment.

"We were fighting hand to hand, trying to thrash them with our muskets. But it was no use. Their bayonets cut us up real good. I can still hear the screams."

"What did you do?"

"Retreat. We had no choice. We ran down the hill. Musket balls dropped all around me like hail. Men were falling everywhere."

"What happened to you?" I'm swept up in his story.

"I was running like the devil when an explosion threw me to the ground. My leg was tore up pretty bad."

"You were running *away* and they still fired?"

Thomas's eyes narrow. "That's not the worst of it. A boy no more than 13 stopped to give me aid. But one of your noble redcoats came along and jabbed a bayonet into his back. That boy wasn't even armed!"

I feel nauseous.

"I couldn't move to help him, and he died right there. Everything went black. Next thing I knew, the doctors were telling me to bite down on a stick."

"Your leg?"

Thomas nods. "They give the officers rum before they operate, but the enlisted men get a stick. Two men held me by the arms and the doctor suddenly cut down to the bone with a knife just like he was butchering a deer. I blacked out again before he dug out the musket ball."

I swallow the bitter taste of bile. Somehow, I hold the poultice firmly against the wound.

Thomas's lips turn up in a strange smile. "The good docs can saw off a limb in less than a minute. I saw it while I was there."

"Dear God," I whisper. "What happened after that?"

"I don't recall much. Spent weeks in one place or another. Infection set in, and no one thought I'd live. But I got better. Father came to Boston and fetched me before the first snow."

I feel a strong urge to cradle him like a kitten. Instead, I gently wrap his leg in a clean linen bandage. "There. I'm done. Would you like me to come back and change it in a few days?"

Thomas doesn't respond. His eyes seem to look right through me.

I struggle with what to say next, so I just do a bad imitation of Mother. "'Tis a very hard time you've come through. God will reward your bravery."

Thomas gives me a weary look. "My reward will be to blow the head off an Englishman."

I start to say, "You don't mean that," but I'm sure he does. And who can blame him?

Emma walks in with a cup of steaming tea.

"You'd best go, Sarah," she says. "Father will be here soon."

I stand up slowly, my mind still reeling. I don't know whose side I'm on anymore. Both are savage.

"I hate what's happening," I cry out to Emma as we leave Thomas's room. "The town despises me and my family, and I even have to sneak about just to see you!"

"If only your father weren't a loyalist," Emma sighs.

"He only wants the fighting to stop. What's so horrible about that?"

"It's more than that," Emma says, eying me warily. "He's against the patriots. Did Thomas nearly lose his leg for nothing? Don't you feel even a little bit proud of our men and what they're doing?"

"Thomas was brave for sure. But why must anyone risk death in a fight over taxes? Is it worth that much?"

"Of course it is! How can you even question it? What's wrong with you?"

"Nothing! What's wrong with you? What's wrong with everyone?"

CHAPTER 23

March 25, 1776

Dear Diary,

Still no word from Samuel. I'm beginning to think Emma is right: He's gone for good. Even my memory of how he looked that last night is fading—but not the kiss, thank God. If it weren't for Emma, I'd go insane from boredom. Her brother has become comfortable—maybe more than comfortable— with my visits, and his leg is healing nicely. It irks me that I still must see them only when their Tory-hating parents aren't around.

"Meet me after services," Emma whispers as we enter the meetinghouse. "You know where."

Wedged between Mother and Father, I fidget through the service while the pastor yatters on about sin and salvation. My back aches. My feet are freezing. My stomach growls. What is it Emma needs to tell me? Probably something trivial, like whatever she supposedly did with Will Patton, her latest obsession. Or maybe Tom asked about me again, now that his leg is healing.

The new pastor's shrill voice is like a mosquito buzzing in my ear. Rev. Isaac Stanford is a slight man with squinty eyes that seem to land all too often on me and my parents.

"May the patriots' courage free us from the chains of tyranny King George has thrust upon us," he drones on.

Emma's father beams. He leads the Essex Committee of Safety and has already sent the tax collector, Hiram Stone, to jail for trying to levy the King's latest tax. *Will this fight ever end?*

Just when I think I can't sit another minute, Rev. Stanford runs out of words, and I slip out, telling Mother I'll see them at home.

Our secret meeting place is the old barn next to Rev. Evans's burned-out house. I slip inside, imagining for a moment that Samuel is there waiting for me. In the dim light, I wrap my arms around my shoulders pretending it's his body I'm hugging to keep the chill away.

"Sarah? What are you doing?" It's Emma, peering inside.

"Nothing! Just waiting for you."

"I couldn't break free of Father," she says. "I don't have much time."

"What's your big news?"

"It's about your father. Well, not just him, all the loyalists."

"What? Speak plain, Emma."

"Do you know about the oath?"

"What oath?"

"The Committee of Safety says all the men must sign an oath of support to the patriots and not the King."

"What happens if they don't?"

"At the very least, they must give up their guns. That's what my father says."

"The least?" Now I'm sweating, anxious for Father.

"I'll just say it." Emma is clearly uncomfortable. "They're going to throw your father in jail if he doesn't sign. They still think he's working for the British."

"They won't really go through with it, will they?"

"They will! I overheard Father say they're going to your house this afternoon. You can convince him to sign, can't you? He'll listen to you."

I know Father won't sign. Nothing I'd do or say could change that. We walk silently out into the sunshine.

"Thank you, Emma. I know you risked a lot to warn me."

I hurry home, hounded by thoughts of Father fending off rats in a filthy jail. I find him sitting by the fire reading month-old newspapers from New York. Mother is churning butter with ferocious intensity.

"Father, they're coming for you today." In a rush of words, I relate what Emma said.

"Benjamin, you told me we were safe for now," Mother says. "Why should I trust anything you say?"

"Be still, Mary. Let me think." He removes his spectacles and rubs his eyes. "I heard talk of this at our meeting."

"What meeting?" I ask.

"A few of us met at Bascomb's to talk about our… predicament."

He grabs the rum from the shelf and takes a long swig.

"Jud Bascomb brought news that Washington and his men have driven the British from Boston. Now the rebels are so cocky they're talking about full independence from the Crown."

"What does that mean?" I ask.

"All-out war, no longer a squabble over taxes."

"I'll tell her what it really means," Mother says as she slams a glob of butter into the beans cooking on the hearth. "It's even more foolhardy to stay here. Tell her about Hiram Stone and his family. If you had any sense, we'd do the same."

Father takes another swig. "They're fleeing to New York, where it's safer for loyalists. Leaving in a day or two, before the roads are full of rebel checkpoints and patrols. They're counting on a few sympathizers along the way to give them shelter."

"As for the damn oath, I'm not concerned," he says. "Legally, it won't hold water. It's just bluster from the so-called patriots."

"Why not just sign it, Father? At least we could stay here without being harassed all the time."

"Sign something I don't believe in? Is that what you're asking? For shame!"

Slapped down for asking a perfectly logical question. I retreat to my bedroom and my diary, asking: *"Why does he have to be so high and mighty? Is he insane?*

I'm still pouring out my hurt, when I hear heavy pounding on the front door: "Benjamin Barrett, we've come to speak to you."

It's Silas Spooner, and I slip down the stairs.

"So you've come with your oath, I suspect," Father tells him, Abner Rollins, and Emma's father as they stride inside.

"Don't be a fool," Mr. Spooner says. "Renounce the King. It's not too late to back your countrymen." He holds out a sheet of parchment. "At least take a look."

Father studies it, and like so many times before, strikes a defiant pose with his arms folded across his chest and says nothing.

"I told you he wouldn't sign," the blacksmith says. "Let's get on with it."

"Give the man time." Mr. Spooner says. "Most all the men in Essex have already signed the Association Test—143 of them willing to take up arms against the King. The Continental Congress has ordered it in all the colonies. They want the names of those who won't sign."

Father *can't* be the only one.

"How many in Essex have refused?" I ask.

"Four, so far, but they'll come around."

"And what happens if they don't?"

Mr. Spooner looks at me as if I were a bothersome toddler.

"Benjamin, if you don't sign, we have the authority to take your guns, block your travel, take your property, and even arrest you. And that's just the beginning."

"You have no legal grounds," Father says. "You're all damned outlaws."

"Just sign it, Benjamin. Please, just sign it!" Mother commands. "Don't be a martyr at our expense."

"For God's sake, Mary. This is not your concern."

"It *is* my concern, and Sarah's," she lashes back, turning from her cauldron of simmering beans. "We'll have a baby soon. Think about us. Forget your lofty principles for once."

"Listen to your good woman," Mr. Jordan says. "It's what your boy would have wanted too."

"He's right, Benjamin," Mr. Spooner adds. "Think of Seth."

At the mention of Seth, Father's jaw stiffens, and his eyes narrow.

"I *am* thinking of the boy. I'm thinking that my family has already lost one life to this insanity."

Mother is near tears. "Please, Benjamin. I don't want any more trouble."

"Father, will you sign it?" I whisper.

He downs the rest of his rum in one big gulp. "I will not! Hell no! I'd sooner take up arms against all you damn rebels than go against my King."

As if in a stage play for which he'd been rehearsing all his life, Father sticks out his chest and slowly, loudly enunciates: "Long...live ...the...King!"

"You leave us no choice, Benjamin," Mr. Spooner says somberly. "We're locking you up where you can't spread any more of your bile."

The blacksmith pushes Mr. Spooner aside. "I say we hang him!"

"Stop!" Mother unleashes her commanding, woman-in-charge voice and everyone goes silent. Using muscles I didn't know she had, she lifts her steaming pot of beans off the fire, inserts herself between Father and Mr. Spooner, and issues a deadly serious warning: "Come any closer to my husband and I'll scald you good."

No one moves. It doesn't feel real. There's Mother with her big belly, armed with the bubbling beans. And on the other side, there are the town fathers, men who have never before been threatened by a woman, no less a woman bearing beans. It's crazy.

Finally, Mr. Jordan speaks. "There'll be no hanging, Mrs. Barrett. Not as long as I'm leading the Committee of Safety."

Father takes the cauldron from Mother's shaking hands and puts it back on the hearth. Then he tells the men to just do whatever it is they came to do.

I can't believe they're taking him away. My mind races, searching for a way to make it stop.

Father seems resigned to it. "First I must fetch my Bible."

The blacksmith starts to object, but Mr. Spooner raises his hand. "We can't deny a man his Bible. Make haste."

"I'll get it, Father." I'm desperate to help him in some small way.

"No, my dear, you get my overcoat."

He goes to his desk and pulls out the Bible—a book I have never actually seen him open—from behind his pens and ink bottles.

As I help him on with his coat, he slips something into his pocket. His eyes lock on mine in a stare that tells me to keep my mouth shut. "Take care of your mother," he says softly as he walks out with his captors.

CHAPTER 24

MOTHER AND I WATCH helplessly as the men mount their waiting horses, with Father, his hands bound, in a sheriff's wagon behind.

"Mary, I may be gone a long spell," Father yells out. "My brother Hiram will help you and Sarah. Seek him out as soon as you can."

She clings to the doorway until they're out of sight.

"Mother?"

She doesn't answer. She doesn't move.

"Mother!"

Finally, she looks at me.

"Father doesn't have a brother Hiram, does he?"

"No, not even a cousin."

My mind races for an explanation.

"Hiram Stone is the only—"

Suddenly I know what he meant.

Mother is ecstatic. "He wants us to flee south with the Stones. He figures we'll be safer in New York, and he can find us there when he's able."

I know she's right, but my heart sinks. I can't leave Essex. I *won't* leave. Emma is here, and Thomas. And Samuel: How will he ever find me? Besides, Father is here—in jail, but still here. We can't leave him when he needs us most.

"We haven't much time." Mother's eyes dart about the house. "We'll take only the bare necessities. And you'll need to go to the

Stones to let them know we'd very much like to join them."

"I'm not going with you, Mother." I wait for the world to end.

"Of course you are!" She looks at me with disbelief. "This is not the time—"

"No, I'm staying! I'm nearly 16, old enough to take care of myself."

She's shaking with anger. "I'm still your mother, and with a baby due soon, I happen to need you a great deal!"

"All you care about is yourself!"

In a flash, she slaps me so hard it nearly knocks me down.

"What do you know? You're still a child," she screams.

That infuriates me even more. Although some weak inner voice is telling me to hold back, it goes silent as I explode.

"You don't care what *I* want, and you never have!" I've crossed a line and couldn't care less. "You're a terrible mother!"

"How can you say such hateful things?" Exasperated, she lets out a dreadful cry. "Stop all this nonsense and go to the Stones!"

Without a word, I grab my cloak and slam the door. I'll head for the Stones all right—anything to get away from her.

Stomping angrily down the road, I still feel the welt from her wedding ring raking my face. I pass Emma's house, wishing I could stop in and find a sympathetic ear. No chance of that!

Finally, I reach the green. The jail is just a stone's throw away, a squat log hovel, in front of a not-much-bigger house where the jailer, Ezra Rollins, lives with his family.

Maybe it's the idea of Father being so near, or just doing something that would shock Mother, but whatever the reason, I sneak over to the jail's tiny, barred window. I'm about to call out to him when I see Abner Rollins and his brother, Ezra, emerge from the house with a coil of stout rope. The loop at the end can be taken for nothing other than a noose.

They're going to hang him right here! How convenient—a mighty elm just steps away.

Then I remember what Samuel told me once. I run across the green to the meetinghouse and climb the stairs to the bell tower. In the musky blackness I hear the flutter of bats swirling around me, and I swat them from my face.

At the top, I pull the rope with all my might, and the huge bronze bell booms. Samuel said the rebels' secret code is two clangs and a pause, followed by two more to alert the town that the British are approaching. After the second set of clangs, my ears are throbbing. I scramble down the stairs and run outside.

Crouched behind a tree, gasping for breath, I see men with their muskets running to the green, some still dressed in their Sunday clothes.

"Step smartly, men," one yells. "Take your positions!"

In another minute or two, several dozen armed men swarm the green, swiftly falling into formation.

"Where are the bloody redcoats?" a young man yells.

But it's Abner Rollins, still clutching his rope, who asks the more pertinent question. "Who rang the warning?"

While my diversion worked, I knew it wouldn't last long. Back at the jail, I find the door wide open and the jailer sprawled on the floor, moaning. His face is a bloody mess.

No sign of Father.

Men are still milling about the green in noisy confusion. Soon they'll figure out it was a false alarm and hunt down the culprit.

Where is Father? Whether he's escaped or been taken somewhere, he's certainly not headed home. Then I have a hunch: *The cave*. Soon I'm tearing through the woods, branches scratching my legs and snagging my skirts. I don't care. I trip on a tree root and fall, bashing my forehead on a rock. Shakily I stand up and press on.

At the cave, I squeeze inside.

"Father?"

Silence. Nothing, no one. Exhausted, I collapse on one of the stumps. I have no idea where he is. That animal Rollins could be slipping the noose around his neck as I sit here, unable to do anything.

Suddenly all the awfulness of the past year wells up inside me. Why is it some people are stricken with such misfortune? I cry until I'm good and ready to leave and go face Mother with the horrible prospect of Father's fate.

I've taken maybe 10 steps from the cave when I hear something crashing through the brush. I stop and stand perfectly still. Then I hear it again, closer. The bear? A wolf? Wolves have been attacking the sheep nearby.

Then something grabs my arm. I start to scream, but a hand clamps over my mouth.

"Sarah! Be still!"

I see Father's face, and I'm flooded with relief. He puts his arm around my shoulder, and I burrow into his chest sobbing.

"Was it you who rang the bell?"

I nod.

"Ah, my quick-witted daughter." He hugs me tighter. "They were going to hang me, for sure. They dropped everything when they heard the bell."

"What about the jailer?"

"The fool was so drunk he unbolted the door when I asked for water. I smacked him in the face, probably broke his nose, and ran out. I would have been here sooner, but I wanted to make sure no one followed me."

Suddenly he gives me a quizzical look. "Why aren't you packing to leave with the Stones? Didn't you understand—"

"I understood." I look away.

"Well?"

"I can't leave. Emma's here and—"

"You can't stay here, my dear. These bloody fools will find a reason to go after you and Mother."

With his handkerchief, he gently wipes the blood and tears from my face. "I must flee before they find me."

"Where will you go?"

"New York. I have people there."

"It's so far. How will you get there? You don't even have a crust of bread. I could—"

"No, you've risked enough. And I know I'll find you and Mother once you're in New York too."

We sit silently on the stumps in the cave. I inhale the damp air and pick up the scent of Samuel's pipe tobacco. But then it's Father who takes my hand. "Sarah, hurry home before they come after me with their dogs. I'm counting on you to help your mother. Promise me you'll not abandon her."

I have no choice. "I promise."

CHAPTER 25

WHEN I FINALLY BURST through the door, Mother is packing a quilt into the big oak chest she brought from England.

"Sarah, where—?" Then she gasps. "Your forehead! Come here and let me have a look."

"No, no time. They could be here any minute."

I yank off my bloody, torn clothes and explain what happened. Mother takes it all in without a word. The anguish in her eyes says it all. As I wipe the crusted blood from my face, I hear the clop of horses.

Then heavy pounding on the door.

"Open up by order of the Continental Army!"

The pounding resumes, so hard I fear the wood may splinter. I open the door slowly. Outside are a dozen men, some holding torches and others with muskets at the ready.

"We've come for Benjamin Barrett," Silas Spooner says. "You'd best not conceal him if you value your lives."

Abner Rollins barges in ahead of the tavern owner. "And if we find out you or anyone else aided his escape from jail, may God have mercy."

"Father escaped?" I say in my most incredulous voice. "How can that be? Did you hear that, Mother?"

"Yes. He's not here. Now please go."

"Not so hasty," Mr. Spooner says. "We'll have a look around. We've already searched the town. He can't get far on foot."

"Look all you want." I swing the door wide open. "Search the privy, if you want."

"Men, scour every room and the barn," the blacksmith says. "Be careful, he's a desperate man."

"My father wouldn't hurt a fly. He's not some desperado," I say.

Mr. Spooner eyes me suspiciously. "How did you get that bruise on your forehead?"

"I, I—" I stammer, unable to think fast enough.

"The child is clumsy," Mother says without hesitation. "She was carrying an armload of wood and tripped, banging her head on the doorway. I was about to prepare a salve and send her to bed when you and your men barged in. Child is probably feverish."

I can't believe what I've just heard come out of Mother's mouth. And with such ease and confidence.

"You men have no right to be here," she goes on. "We've done nothing. If he escaped, my husband is likely miles from here. He has more sense than to come back here and await a mob of outlaws."

"Hold your tongue," Mr. Spooner says.

They open cupboards and rattle dishes. What they hope to find, I can't fathom. Suddenly I remember Mother's tea hidden in the flour sack, just as one of the plunderers pulls out the jug of rum next to the sack.

"I can sorely use a trifle of this," he says, tipping the jug back for a swig.

"Don't be a hog. Give it here," the other says, grabbing it.

"Pass it here," a third says.

The jug goes around again, then one of them slams it on the shelf, sending a tub of molasses crashing onto the floor.

"Look what you've done now," I yell, as the sticky black goo oozes through the kitchen.

But the imbecile just laughs. "Toss me that flour sack, and we'll pretty it up some more," he yells at the others.

"No!" I scream, as one of them snatches it. "Give it to me." But he cuts the sack open with a knife, sending up a cloud of flour.

"What do we have here," he says, pulling the bag out of the flour by its drawstring. "Perhaps some money?"

"Nothing you'd be interested in." I try to grab it. He snatches it back.

"It must be something. Let's have a look."

He takes out a handful of loose tea and sniffs it. "Silas, I reckon you'll want to come see this."

"Tea?" he smirks at us. "You do know you can't drink British tea? You do recognize that it's contraband and individuals are forbidden from possessing it? You do acknowledge that you're committing a serious violation just by having it here, no less by drinking it, right?"

"On whose authority?" Mother says. "Certainly not our King's."

With his calm, polished demeanor fraying at the edges, Mr. Spooner gives her a look that could stop a snake.

"Damn redcoats," the blacksmith mutters.

Still holding the tea, old Spooner glances at Mother's swollen belly then looks away. "I'll deal with you later."

He turns back to his men. "Start with that desk. Look for hidden drawers. Go through every document you find."

The men pull out drawer after drawer, dumping everything on the floor. Mr. Spooner pores over old letters, discarded essays, ledgers for the farm. He grunts now and then, apparently unable to find anything incriminating.

I fight to hold back my anger.

"Silas, what about all these ink bottles? There must be dozens."

"Empty them all. We don't need any more of Barrett's claptrap."

Good thing Father isn't here to see the wreckage as the men fling the bottles against the hearth, shattering them. Ink smears the brick like an angry child's painting. Then they tear through the rest of the house, tipping over the table and breaking off a leg. Ezekiel howls from all the confusion and one of them heaves a bucket at the cat, narrowly missing him.

I scoop him up and try to comfort him, but he's too frightened and leaps off my lap. Mother and I huddle on the front step, fearing the men will set fire to the house after they finish ransacking it.

Mr. Spooner and a few henchmen search the barn. He orders one of them to check the woods around the pond. A couple trot toward the trees with their hunting dogs, and I choke down my rising panic.

But after several minutes, he calls his men together. "He's not here.

Could be halfway to Quebec by now. Nothing more we can do here."

The worst is over, I think.

Then Abner Rollins snorts in disgust. "I say we talk to the girl. I would bet my sow she knows where he is."

My heart races as I mop up the mess on the floor.

"Leave her be, you idiot," Mr. Spooner sputters. "If you hadn't tried to hang the man we wouldn't be in this fix. Let's get out of here."

"Wouldn't take much to pry that secret out of her," the blacksmith says.

Mother lets out a cry. "She doesn't know and neither do I. Now, please leave!"

Ezekiel rubs against my leg, meowing inconsolably. I pick him up to quiet him, and to still the shaking in my hands.

The blacksmith eyes the cat and gives me a sickish grin. "You wouldn't want anything to happen to your kitty, would you?"

I clutch Ezekiel tighter, and that sets him to wailing worse than ever.

"You'd sure hate to see him drown in that pond." He reaches for Ezekiel but a shriek from Mother startles everyone.

Her huge belly heaves as she sprawls on a chair panting.

"Mother! What is it?"

Another shriek stills the room again, and I know.

"The baby! The baby is here," I yell.

"Please, we haven't much time," Mother says. She groans and screams with such pain that it rattles the men. They turn away in embarrassment.

"Get the horses!" Mr. Spooner shouts.

Mother lets out one more ear-crackling scream as they leave.

It seems the baby will arrive any second. Usually, it takes hours. Something must be horribly wrong.

As the sound of horses grows dim, Mother pulls herself up from the chair and walks to the window. "They're gone."

"Mother, let me help you—"

"No, no, I'm fine."

"But the baby?"

"It's not here yet."

"But the pains?"

"What pains?" Mother says, smiling slightly.

"You were *pretending*? But the screams were so real." I'd never seen such a performance. Is this really *my* mother?

CHAPTER 26

March 26, 1776

Dear Diary,

I hate them—I hate them all. What they did made me want to scrub everything they put their filthy hands on. I've never felt so violated and I'm only a little grateful that I didn't have a gun at my side when it happened.

I PUT DOWN MY pen at the sound of heavy scraping across the floor downstairs. It's after midnight—what's she cleaning now? We've already swept and mopped the floors and put the house back in order as best we could. I scalded my fingers washing the dishes in near boiling water. The ink stains on the walls and floor didn't come out, permanent reminders of both Father and of the men who would hang him.

I go down to find Mother trying to push the table against the door, despite her big belly.

"In case they come back," she says. Her eyes have a look of wild determination, and I know better than to question her.

Together we jam it in place and do the same at the back door with a chair shoved under the door latch.

"Nothing will budge," she says. "We're safe."

Neither of us believes it, but it's comforting to hear. My staying behind seemed like a grand adventure just a few hours ago. But now, it's clear even to me that we should pack up and go.

"Mother, it's not too late for us to leave with Hiram Stone."

"I thought you were dead set against leaving."

"I was. But not now."

"You *do* have a choice," Mother says. "I was wrong. You aren't a little girl anymore. You proved that tonight."

I don't expect this—Mother never admits she's wrong. It feels good to know she's finally seeing me as I am, but my promise to Father weighs heavy. Even more than seeing Samuel again.

"I'll go with you. I *want* to go with you." I hope I sound convincing. "And I'm sorry I called you a horrible mother. I didn't mean it."

What she does next stuns me. She kisses my cheek, just a little peck. I feel a rush of tenderness toward her.

"God knows when I'll see Benjamin again," she says. "I wish our last moments together hadn't been so fraught with sharp words."

Mother has never confided in me such intimate feelings, and I don't know what to say.

"He doesn't have food, or heavy wool stockings or his warm scarf…" she drifts off. "And his spectacles—he'll need those. We could—"

"No, Mother. It's not safe for Father or us if we venture out."

She looks totally defeated and exhausted. "Then we should try to get some sleep."

As I climb the stairs, I turn around and see her carry his rifle to their bedroom.

For hours I try to sleep, but every time I ease into drowsiness my eyes pop open at the slightest sound. At dawn, pounding on the front door jars me awake.

Has the ragtag band of haters returned—this time for Mother and me? I slip down the stairs, thankful I slept in my clothes. Wrapped in a quilt, Mother is at the door with Father's gun.

"Who's there?"

"Mary, it's Jud Bascomb. I mean no harm."

"How do we know for certain?"

"I'm here alone, and I have word from Benjamin."

She unbolts the door, and he slips inside. As I light a candle, he surveys the wreckage from the raid just hours ago and shakes his head in disgust.

"Abner and his hoodlums?"

I nod. "You saw Father? How—"

"He came to my house two hours ago, desperate for a horse. I gave him my mare, Lady. Said he'd make it right once the British win."

And if they don't? I keep that thought to myself.

Mr. Bascomb takes a wrinkled paper from under his shirt. "He wanted you both to have this letter. It pained him terribly that he had to flee without seeing you."

Mother reads it aloud:

My Dear Ones,

My heart aches that I could not say goodbye. Know that I am safe for now and heavy with purpose that I cannot disclose. With God's help, we will be reunited soon. Be strong. Let these words give you comfort and the vision to read between the lines and see things as they truly are.

PS: Find solace and understanding in the words of Mark 4:21-22

I grab it from Mother, utterly confused. "What does this mean?" I ask. *"The vision to see things as they truly are…* Does he think we can read his mind?" Truth be told, Father saw the whole notion of Scripture as meaningless twaddle. If he ever quoted it, it was as a line in one of his silly songs.

I recognize the gold edging of the paper. It's a blank page torn from the back of his Bible. It could be the first time he's used it for more than a paperweight.

I'm worried about his sanity, but Mother sounds irritated. "I fear he's involved himself in something that's far beyond his control and put himself in great danger and us as well."

Ordinarily, I would come to his defense, but I'm hurt that he fled so abruptly, leaving such confusion and mystery.

"Was he in his right mind?" I ask.

"He said little to me," Mr. Bascomb says. "Only that his efforts would pay off. He was frantic, as any man on the run would be."

Mother and I spend hours trying to understand. One minute we're fearing for Father's safety and the next we're railing against him for leaving.

Over a solemn breakfast of ham, cheese and bread, I can't help but wonder about Samuel and whether I'll ever see him again. Why is it the men in my life keep disappearing?

"Best you forget that boy," Mother says, sipping her tea. I know she means well, and I keep from reminding her that he's not a boy, but a young man.

Soft tapping on the back door startles both of us.

"Father?" I run to open it.

Instead, it's Emma, breathing hard. "Have you heard?"

"Heard what?"

"Abner Rollins is dead! Murdered!"

"What are you talking about?"

"They found him last night near Rev. Evans's old place," she says, still breathless. "Somebody slit his throat. They say it was your father."

"What?" That anyone would suspect *my father* is more incredible to me than the fact that the brutish blacksmith is dead. "Father would never—"

"Never mind that! You're not safe here. They'll be coming any time now."

"Mother, we have no choice but to leave with the Stones," I say.

"Hiram Stone? How do you know he'll take you?" Emma says.

Hiram Stone, the pompous little rat of a tax collector, is the most hated man in Essex. Even Father, who is quick to defend fellow loyalists, dislikes him. He says Stone delights in squeezing as much as he can from the residents to gain favor with the British—not to mention keeping a healthy slice for himself. Father's editorials took him to task more than once.

"He'll take us," Mother says. "It's time I collect on an old debt."

CHAPTER 27

"I'D SOONER CUT OFF my arm than take you with me," Mr. Stone tells us when we appear on his doorstep. "How dare you come here, you and your stinking pox." When he tries to shut the door, Mother blocks it with her foot.

"I well remember the night your son Luke was born," she says.

He eyes her suspiciously. "What of it?"

"The poor babe was blue, not a sign of life in his little body. Do you remember what you said?"

His chubby, round face grows red. "That was three years ago."

"I remember it clearly. You begged me to save him. 'I'll do anything for my son to live,' you said."

His eyes dart about like cockroaches in a cupboard.

"I breathed life into that child." She draws out each word for emphasis. "I put my lips to his and filled his tiny lungs with air. I brought the color back to his cheeks. I brought that loud, shrieking cry to his lips."

I have mounting respect for Mother.

"Too risky to take you with us," he sputters. "I'll not endanger my wife and child. Besides, we're ready to go right now."

I fear it's over, our great escape, snuffed out before we even leave town.

Martha Stone, a wisp of a woman, has been silent since she stepped forward to see the commotion. Now, she looks straight at him, her eyes filled with disgust. "You *will* allow them to accompany us."

Mr. Stone has effectively been wrestled to the ground. He turns to us. "We'll be by your place within the hour. Bring only the clothes on your back—we won't have room for more. If you're not on time, we'll leave without you, so help me God."

———————

The fat little rat is true to his word, and before long Mother and I are wedged under a hot, itchy wool blanket in the back of the couple's farm wagon.

"I feel like a criminal," I whisper. "We've done nothing wrong, and there's no way Father would have killed Abner Rollins."

"Hiram doesn't want to take any chances," Mother says. "And I don't want to upset him."

Of course, any loyalist would have good reason to be cautious. The muddy roads are filled with rebel soldiers streaming to New York where the British are massing now that they've been thrown out of Boston. Anyone on the road is viewed with suspicion.

We can barely breathe as the wagon bumps and slides out of Essex. Hiram Stone and Martha sit up high on the only seat with little Luke. Their belongings poke us in the ribs—two straight-back chairs, table, battered chest, grandfather clock that sticks out the back end, pots, barrel of flour, jugs of molasses, smoked pork.

The filthy old blanket is swarming with fleas. I can't stop scratching in places no flea has any business going. Miserable doesn't begin to describe it. But I don't complain to Mother. She winces with every bump as she clutches her belly and her old satchel, jammed with all the tinctures, herbs and salves she could gather at the last minute.

I lift the blanket to let in some fresh air and peek outside, but Mother yanks it down.

"Careful! Silas Spooner and his men must be hunting everywhere for Father and now the two of us."

I know she's right. I hunker down into my dismal hole, wondering what would drive someone to murder the blacksmith. For the first time, I grapple with the possibility that Father may have done it.

I've wished the brute dead more than once, and maybe Father, in a fit of rage, slashed his throat. I shake off that notion. Impossible!

I wish I could have said goodbye to Emma and Tom. I imagine her jolly laugh when I tell her about Mother dressing down old Hiram at the front door. She risked everything to help us escape and will pay dearly if her father finds out. Just the thought of it makes me feel dreadful. I *have* to return to Essex. It's the only connection I have to Samuel. But I know he's likely long gone as he makes his way to New York or Philadelphia. Will he even remember me? The skinny girl with the unruly red hair he poked fun at for using words like "anarchy" and "ambiguous" and "feline." Feline? Oh no!

"Mother! We forgot Ezekiel!"

In the suddenness of my realization, I jostle the grandfather clock and the chimes clang, making such a racket Mr. Stone reins the horses to a stop.

"Shut up!" he hisses.

The wagon lurches forward again and I roll my eyes.

"Don't fret about Ezekiel," Mother whispers. "He'll survive on his wits."

I wonder if I will. We are crammed in a wagon heading God knows where with the most disagreeable man in the world. I know from Father's editorials that the old goat bought his own protection from tar and feathering by lowering the taxes for Abner Rollins and some of his friends. But only days ago, rowdy rebels beat him for daring to drink ale at the Essex Tavern.

That was the last straw for Mrs. Stone, who wanted so desperately to flee to England, but at the last minute her husband told her New York would have to do. They're still arguing about it as the child fusses on her lap.

"We haven't the money to sail back. How many times must I tell you?" he growls. "We've barely enough to get to New York."

"We'll be no safer there," she says.

"Yes, we will. We'll be among folks who respect the Crown. Not these savages. I can find work there."

"You're a fool, Hiram."

"Quiet! Before I toss you out and leave you by the side of the road."

She snorts in disgust.

"Maybe you'll think twice next time you decide we should transport a murderer's wife and daughter," he says, cracking the whip to speed up.

"Benjamin Barrett didn't kill anyone," she says.

"The whole town thinks he did," he snaps. "Who else would have done it?"

"You don't think it was despicable that Abner tried to hang him? And for what? Refusing to sign their loyalty oath?"

"Well, then, it makes perfect sense that Barrett would want the loudmouth dead."

No! I want to scream. *You're wrong about my father, you ignorant fool!*

Mother must sense I'm about to erupt. She puts her hand on my arm and touches her finger to her lips.

As I settle into grim silence, I start putting together Father's defense. If anyone deserved hanging, it was that miserable ox, but Father, would argue *no one* deserves to hang without a fair trial. No, he's no cold-blooded killer. He even aroused a mob by daring to stand up for peace. He went to jail for refusing to bear arms.

As we bump along, I try to concentrate on the bright side of my situation—I hate it when Mother says things like that. I allow myself to imagine life in New York with its fine shops and bookstores. I dream about the novel I would pen about my heroine, strong-willed, opinionated Samantha, who loves a sea captain, a handsome rascal who dabbles in piracy.

New York must be full of publishers. Would they look kindly on a woman author? If need be, I could use a man's name or just go with the tried-and-true Destinatus. Still, it galls me that I'd have to resort to subterfuge when I have a perfectly good name of my own.

Mother has been silent for several minutes. "Are you all right?" I whisper.

She takes a deep breath. "I wanted to leave Essex, but not like this, not like a criminal. I wanted to return to London, but now we—"

"Quiet! Don't move!" Mr. Stone orders. The wagon rumbles to a stop amid the sound of men's voices and the clop of other horses.

"Good morn," he greets them in an unusually cheery tone. "Where are you headed?"

I recognize the gruff voice as Emma's father, Daniel Jordan, and fear the worst.

"New York. Moving my family there," he answers.

"Must be Tories," another voice yells.

"Where's your permit? Tories can't travel without papers." Emma's father again. He says "Tories" as if we were lice.

I hear Mr. Stone fumble for a moment. "Here it is."

I hold my breath and will myself to be still—not easy with Mother squeezing my arm so tightly that it throbs. It seems like minutes drag by.

"We're searching for Benjamin Barrett," Mr. Jordan finally says. "You wouldn't be hiding a killer in that wagon, would you?"

"No sir!" Mr. Stone answers. "We're God-fearing Christians."

"We'll have a look anyway."

As the men dismount, I squeeze my eyes shut and try to still my shaking.

"Poke under that blanket."

I feel a sharp jab to the back of my head.

"Ow!" It just pops out of my mouth.

Someone flings the blanket off. "Well, look here."

The daylight blinds me as I rub my head.

"I'll be damned. It's Benjamin Barrett's wife and daughter," Mr. Jordan says. "Tell us where he is, and we'll spare you harm."

"We don't know," Mother says firmly. "My husband is no murderer. You should know that."

"What I know is you can't be trusted either. You would have us all dead of the pox if you had your way, pretending to be a doctor."

Before Mother can answer, he turns to me. "And you, I see you've inherited your father's poisonous pen, spreading nonsense in that Tory newspaper."

For once I say nothing.

"Just tell us where he is."

"I told you, we do not know," Mother says speaking clearly and slowly as if Daniel Jordan were a child. "Neither do the Stones."

"They're aiding the enemy—we'll deal severely with them," he says. "But right now you two leave me no choice," he says. "You're both under arrest until you decide to cooperate."

"You can't do that," I burst out. "We've done nothing wrong."

"We have reason to believe you're aiding a traitor. That's treason."

The man behind him is restless. "I say parade them through town. See how they like garbage flung at them. Before long they'll cooperate."

"We'll do no such thing!" Emma's father says. "Mrs. Barrett is heavy with child.

"Well?" He looks hard at me and Mother and waits for us to "cooperate." I stare back. So does Mother. Silence fills the air.

Then he turns to the others. "Perhaps they'll feel more like talking after they sit a spell in jail."

CHAPTER 28

THE JAIL FOR WOMEN is little more than a shack attached to the jailer's house—not quite the miserable hole that held Father that awful night. But it's a grim prospect when we're finally shoved inside. The stink is awful.

"Our last guests were a couple of dirty whores, so it may not be up to your high standards," says the jailer, Ezra Rollins. His smirk makes me furious. He's big, just like his recently departed older brother Abner, with coal black hair and eyes. But he's more fat than muscle, and his hatred for us is obvious.

"Smell ain't so bad after a few days."

"Is there no privy?" Mother asks.

He gestures to a filthy bucket.

"My child is due very soon. This is not a fit place to bring a soul into the world."

The jailer spits. "What about my brother's soul? If you know anything, you'd be wise to spit it out." He pulls the heavy oak door shut behind him and turns the key in the lock.

"Toad!" I want to kick something. Could our circumstances be bleaker? We'd be better off in the cave. The one small, barred window, no bigger than a dinner napkin, is too high up for me to look out. Loose boards cover the dirt floor. There are two wooden stools, one with a splintered leg. The tattered straw mats in the corner are for sleeping, if anyone could sleep in such filth.

"At least there are no drunkards or thieves to bother us," Mother says, seeing the bright side, as usual. "And they allowed us our quilts." Fortunately, for what's left of my sanity, she doesn't break into a prayer of thanks.

A soft rain starts to fall, both outside and through the roof. It's damp and chilly and it will be worse come night.

I drag the stool over to the window. Standing on my toes, I can just barely peer outside. The tents of patriot soldiers have begun to pop up on the village green, a troop likely heading for New York to bolster Washington's forces. Men laugh as if they were boys playing at war. *Damn their good cheer!*

"They can't keep us here forever," Mother says softly.

"It already feels like forever."

She stands slowly, her hand resting on her bulging belly. "Someone will…." Her voice trails off and her face wrinkles with pain.

"What is it?"

"The child, I fear."

"Didn't you say it was weeks away?"

A puddle of pale, yellow water appears at her feet, a clear signal the baby has begun its descent.

"The pains started this morning. Perhaps with all the excitement…"

For a second, I think Mother is playing another joke. But it's no joke, and I'm frightened. "What should we do?"

"Call the jailer. If he's got a shred of decency, he'll get us to a decent shelter."

"Mr. Rollins! Mr. Rollins! Come quickly." I pound on the door until my fist hurts. No one comes. I bang on the window bars with a tin cup I found on the floor. People walk by on their way to the shops, but nobody seems to hear.

I even yell out the window to the men on the green, but they're cheering on two soldiers in a brawl. Minutes tick by.

Frustrated, I take a long, deep breath and scream so loud that Mother jumps.

A few seconds later the jailer opens the door.

"What the devil do you want?" he says, slurring his words. He stinks of rum and looks like he's just been slapped awake.

"It's my mother. Her time is close. We can't stay here."

He eyes Mother suspiciously as she sits sprawled on the stool fanning herself. "Is this a trick? I heard all about your act the other night. It might have worked on Silas, but I'm not that stupid."

"It's not an act," I plead. "Can't you see she's suffering?"

"My brother told me what a lying little hussy you are. I'll not be made a fool of."

Mother sits silently awaiting another wave of pain. Her face contorts and a low moan emerges from her lips. If she's acting, it's quite a performance.

The sight unnerves the jailer. He slams his jug of rum on the stool. "Here, this will help. Now give me some peace."

I ease Mother onto the straw mattress. Despite her big belly, she looks so small and frightened—not a sight I'm accustomed to, and it unsettles me.

"This one isn't like my others," she says.

I fight to hold in my own panic. But a terrifying reality overtakes me and soon Mother confirms it.

"Sarah, you must attend this baby, just as if you were me at any of the births you've helped with."

"No! No, I can't."

"You've witnessed it a dozen times. We have no choice."

I want to scream that I can't possibly do such a thing. "I'm afraid. What if something happens and the baby dies, or you—"

"That's natural. I still fear it at every birth. Remember: It's in God's hands."

Now isn't the time to launch into my doubts about God's powers, so I just confess the awful truth. "Those times you told me to watch …I didn't. I couldn't. All the blood and wailing, it makes me dizzy and sick. What if I faint and—"

"You won't."

"What if I forget what to do?"

"I'll guide you. Besides, there's little that you need do. Let nature take its course." The weak little smile fades fast as another pain grips her.

Unnerved, I climb onto the stool again to look out the barred window. The rain has slowed to a drizzle, and soldiers march in formation around the green, their muskets to their shoulders. I watch for a while, tapping my foot to the drummer's beat, anything to avoid facing the task ahead.

The rain casts a gloom on everything, and it will only get worse tonight. At least there's a candlestick holder with a long stout candle. Will the jailer sober up enough to light it? Will he bring us food? We haven't eaten since morning, not that Mother is the least bit hungry. She struggles to get comfortable, and I put aside any notion of complaining.

The hours tick by slowly. There are so many questions I want to ask. What is the pain like? How does it feel to have a living thing kicking your innards? Is she afraid the baby will get stuck on the way out, just as it happened with Emma's mother? Of course, Mother always knows exactly what I'm thinking, a maddening feat.

"God will see me through this," she says after another scream causes the jailer to pound on the wall. "Though God appears to be occupied when I most need him."

I laugh out loud, and it feels good. Soon Mother is grinning. It's the first time I've sensed a crack in her faith, and it makes me feel better about my own doubts. It puzzles me why God would put any woman through such pain. And then do it over and over, year after year.

"When you have your own children, you'll—"

"I don't want any babies."

Mother doesn't lash out as she has in the past when I've expressed myself on the subject of children. She's thoughtful for a moment. "But it's what God wants. It's our purpose, to bear children. It's in the Bible, in—"

"It's not what I want. I want something else, something more."

"Nonsense! You'll find that having children and making a home are quite enough."

"No, I meant—"

Mother stifles a shout of anguish as long as she's able but finally gives in. She relaxes when it passes. "Is it the pain you fear, child?"

"No," I lie. That's only part of it. It's fearing death too. But mostly, it's that a child will keep me from what I want to do more than changing diapers or dishing out oatmeal: I want to make a difference in the world, not just to my family. I want to write.

"I suppose you'll not take a husband then."

"Probably not." When Samuel kissed me in the cave, I felt a strange, wonderful stirring—something I suppose Mother would call lust. I crave it again, but I'll likely never see him again.

Thankfully, Mother doesn't pry further. She shakily reads her Bible between pains. It's the one she carries in her medical bag and often reads aloud while waiting for a balky birth. She likes reading from the Book of Job—she says it comforts the mothers, but I have my doubts.

By evening the pains are closer together, and Mother is in even greater agony. My own stomach rumbles constantly, making it hard to think of anything else. The soldiers on the green are eating supper and the smell of roasted meat nearly drives me mad.

The single candle will be our only light tonight. But we can't count on the jailer returning to light it. The idiot must be sleeping off his drunkenness.

"Mother, do you have some flint in your bag?"

"Yes, have a look."

I pore through herbs and ointments, knives, scissors, needles and thread, even a small mirror she sometimes puts under a newborn's nose to see if it's breathing. I find her little tinderbox, with its flint and a scrap of charred linen to use as tinder.

I've lit many a fire, but never under such dire circumstances. I scour the dirty floor for bits of kindling to shape like a bird's nest, just as Seth showed me years ago. Is there enough tinder to spark a flame? I feel Father's letter in the pocket under my skirts but discard any notion of using it.

I strike the knife against the flint, causing sparks to fly. *Please God, if you're listening, give me a flame.* Minutes pass by with each frustrating try. But finally a spark catches. I gently blow on it and the tiny red spark grows.

The soft glow of the candle fills our dismal cell, and I see a faint smile on Mother's face.

"I'm so fortunate to have you here," she says, and my spirits lift.

In between the pains, she hoists herself off the mattress and paces the room. Huddling under the quilt, I'm wracked with uselessness as night settles in.

The noise on the green finally dims as the soldiers bed down. The pains are minutes apart. "The time is close," Mother groans, triggering a surge of panic in my gut.

She sits on the footstool with her back against the wall and takes a long swig of rum. The pain must be awful. Mother never drinks— she hates the taste.

"Take off your petticoat," she commands.

"What? Again?" Last time, it was for Seth's gaping wound.

"To wrap the child."

I unhitch the woolen petticoat and it slips to the floor.

The next pain brings Mother to tears, and great sobs shake her body as she slumps on the stool. She guzzles the rum as if it's cider.

"What's happening Mother?"

"The pain…I don't think I can bear it." She looks at me with pleading eyes, and I feel even more helpless. I'm not accustomed to her not being fully in command.

I grip her hand. I don't know what else to do.

Minutes later another pain. Mother shrieks. Then more pains. "I can't do it."

"Yes, you can," I say in a take-charge voice that surprises even me. "You did it with the twins. You did it with me and Seth."

"It's so hard this time."

"Be strong, just a little longer." I have no idea how long it will take, but it's already been more than any human should have to withstand.

After another hour, the pains are even closer. Thank God! I don't think Mother can survive much more. I kneel in front of her and push back the skirts.

"I see him! The very top of his head."

Mother is panting and crying. The news doesn't seem to please her. "Dear God, where are you?" Even though the room is cold, sweat streams down her face.

"It's almost over," I say, not really sure it's true. "You can do it. I know you can." I sound more and more like her.

Mother grimaces, shuts her eyes and pushes hard. Then again, and again.

I grab the petticoat, folding it into a little nest, and brace myself to catch the baby. Finally, Mother pushes again, screaming as if it's her last breath and the baby's head pokes out. I cushion it, and seconds later the rest of the slippery bundle slides out so fast I nearly drop it.

"A boy! I knew it." He's smaller than most and covered in white muck. I wipe his face and realize he's no beauty—he looks like he's been bested in a fight.

He starts to wail, and I'm flooded with relief.

"Let me have a look," Mother says, still breathless.

With some hesitation, I gently hand him over.

"My beautiful boy!"

How she sees beauty in that little face is beyond me, but I know better than to ruin the touching moment. Besides, I'm so happy the whole ordeal is over I'm practically dancing.

Then Mother closes her eyes and repeats the incantation she uses at all her births. "Our God in heaven, thank you for giving us another soul on this day, March 27, 1776."

It feels like Mother did all the work, not God. But I keep that to myself.

"What name shall you give him?" I ask.

"Benjamin."

That makes me smile, and I jump in to finish the second half of her usual welcome. "May you bless my brother Benjamin with good health and a strong spirit." Silently, I hope God can do something about his sorry-looking mug.

"Sarah, fetch the scissors. You have the honor of cutting the cord."

When it's all done, Mother and baby fall asleep exhausted on the prickly straw mattress. I lie there too, but I can't sleep. I'm too excited. I survived it, and so did they.

Finally, sleep overtakes me, until something interrupts a perfectly good dream. A noise? A rat? I lift my head, still half asleep. Then I hear it again.

"Sarah!" A vaguely familiar voice. "Over by the window."

"Samuel?"

CHAPTER 29

I LEAP TO MY feet and scramble atop the wobbly stool by the window, craning my neck at an impossible angle to see what I can.

"Samuel?"

"Shhh, keep your voice down."

In the moonlight I barely recognize him. His blond hair is longer, stringy, and hangs in his face. A scraggly beard makes him look older.

"I joined a regiment—I'm fighting for the Crown."

For a moment, I think I'm still dreaming. He looks like neither rebel nor redcoat. His tattered shirt and muddy breeches aren't the Samuel I know. For all anyone could see, he's just another homeless pauper.

"My orders are to keep a close eye on the rebels and their stock of munitions," he whispers. "Those I meet on the road assume I'm a beggar or a drunkard. I even splash rum on my face so I stink of drink."

I can picture Seth playing the drunk with great relish. But Samuel? Samuel, who loves his pipe and law books, and wouldn't go out for a stroll if his pocket handkerchief wasn't folded just so?

"Aren't you afraid you'll be recognized?" I ask. "Abner Rollins would surely…" I forgot for a moment the blacksmith is dead.

"I know about Abner. And your father's escape."

"You don't think my father—"

"No, no, of course not." He looks back toward the soldiers on the green.

A whimper, then a hearty cry from little Benjamin startles us. "I have a new brother. Benjamin. I delivered him a few hours ago." Loud voices on the green stop me from bragging.

"I must go," Samuel whispers. "Your father is with the British too."

"A soldier? Fighting?" The idea strains belief.

"No, he's engaged in some kind of mission. Nobody knows much about it, and he wouldn't tell even me."

We hear footsteps and freeze.

"Goodbye for now, Destinatus."

"How can I find you?"

"The cave." He's gone in a flash. My heart is pounding so, I nearly trip stepping down from the stool. Samuel risked everything to see me, if only for a minute!

Questions flood my head. How did he know we were here? Where was he all those months? But more puzzling is Father's "mission." At least he's safe somewhere, but will I see either of them again?

I can't go back to sleep. The candle has burned down to a nub, and I warm my hands over the dying flame. I take out Father's letter and reread it for the hundredth time.

Let these words give you comfort and the vision to read between the lines and see things as they truly are.

They give me neither comfort nor vision. Nothing about any secret mission. It sounds like Father is delusional, and I still need a way out of this stink hole. Expecting nothing helpful, I turn yet again to the Book of Mark, as he urged in his note.

And he said unto them, Is a candle brought to be put under a bushel, or under a bed? And not to be set on a candlestick? For there is nothing hid, which shall not be manifested; neither was any thing kept secret, but that it should come abroad.

It makes no sense. It's not even a passage about hope and strength and keeping faith. Is Father playing games with us while we wither in this hell?

Disappointed, I blow out the candle and crawl onto the mattress next to Mother and my new brother. Despite the prickly straw that pokes my skin, their warmth feels good, and I feel my body giving way to sleep.

———————

I wake at dawn to Benjamin's wailing. Mother puts him to her breast and the screaming stops instantly. He sucks with such fury you'd think he's possessed. In the daylight I see the exhaustion on Mother's face and the bloody mess from the night before.

My stomach rumbles with hunger, and it's hours before Ezra Rollins finally unlocks the door and brings in two bowls of cold oatmeal and a hunk of hard rye bread.

"Quite a racket in here last night," he grumbles. "Upset my sleep."

He turns to leave without a word about the baby. I want to shove the oatmeal in his face.

"You can't keep us here now," I say. "Not with this newborn."

He shows no emotion, not even any mild curiosity over this tiny human being that drew his first breath hours ago. "Ain't up to me."

"But—"

He's out the door. Pig! I loathe him even more than his swinish, lately deceased brother.

The oatmeal is half water. I pick specks of mold out of the bread before offering it to Mother.

"No, I'm not hungry." Her voice is weak. She's shivering, though her wool cloak is pulled tight around her.

I press my hand to her forehead. "You're burning up with fever. We can't stay here." I'm desperate for a way out before Mother takes a turn for the worse.

Mercifully, she and the baby drift off. Childbirth is exhausting for both. This much I've learned at Mother's side.

I climb up to the window and watch the rebel troops build their fires and prepare breakfast. The smell of salt pork wafts through the bars and I think I will go mad.

The town comes alive with daily business. Across the green Mr. Bascomb opens his store. A woman lugging two pairs of shoes strides toward the cobbler's shop. Wagons arrive at the green with more supplies for the soldiers—piles of blankets, sacks of flour, and boxes of ammunition.

From my treacherous perch, I glimpse a familiar red cloak and recognize Emma approaching. "Emma!" I whoop with joy to see her.

"I came as soon as I heard you were here," Emma says, craning her neck up toward me. "I told Father I was delivering the shirts I sewed for the soldiers."

The baby whimpers and I announce, "I have a brother, Benjamin, born last night. But mother is doing poorly. I need your help. We can't stay here."

"I don't know what I can do—Father watches me like a hawk."

"Emma, please think of something."

"I'll try, but I can't promise anything. I must go."

Emma slips away and I allow myself a pinch of hope.

The baby wails and I pick him up so Mother can sleep. I hold him close to my chest and he nuzzles in. I've helped Mother before with other babies, but they all seemed like squirmy, beady-eyed fish, ready to slip out of my grasp at the first opportunity. Benjamin seems so at home in my arms. Something comes over me, and I kiss the top of his head.

By late afternoon the jailer finally returns in his predictably foul mood, followed by Emma's parents and Silas Spooner. I clutch little Benjamin while Mother lies half-conscious on the reeking mattress.

Mrs. Jordan squints in the dim light and surveys the squalid room. "Oh, dear God in heaven." She glares at the men. "How could you allow this? This isn't fit for my hogs."

She kneels by Mother and takes her hand. "Take comfort Mary, I've come to help."

I want to hug her till she breaks in pieces. God bless Emma!

But her husband bristles. "Mind what you say. They're criminals. They're aiding the enemy, and that's treason."

"Can't you see the poor woman is no danger to anyone right now?" Mrs. Jordan's beefy face is red. "She could easily succumb to the fever. And the child, a tiny thing, he's done nothing to deserve this hellish place."

I want to applaud.

Old Spooner looks ill at ease. Men always stay clear of birthing matters. He shifts from one foot to the other, surveying the bloody mess from childbirth and the swarm of flies.

"Perhaps Mrs. Jordan is right," he finally says.

"Perhaps Mrs. Jordan should tend to her own business and leave serious matters to those who know better," Mr. Jordan snaps.

"The welfare of my friend and her children is most definitely my business, as you put it, and I know it better than—"

"I'm warning you, woman! We can't just let them go free. What does that say to all the other Tories who would do us harm?"

Mr. Spooner rubs his face and inhales deeply. "He makes a good point. I say we put them under house arrest. We can keep a close watch in case Benjamin Barrett tries to contact them."

"They could bring him right to us," Emma's father says with a rare smile.

The baby fusses and I jiggle him. Mother is shivering violently.

"I will consent, provided they stay at my house," Mr. Jordan says. "I'll keep a close watch, by God. Mrs. Jordan can tend them both."

"Both? Surely you mean for Sarah to come as well," she says.

"She's not ailing. She can stay here."

"She's still a child! She can't stay here. She belongs with her mother."

I've never seen Mrs. Jordan so angry. Normally, I would take issue with her describing me as a child, but not now.

Mother winces with pain and slowly raises her head off the mattress. "I will not leave this place without my daughter."

Before the men can respond, Mrs. Jordan speaks, her voice calm and reasoned. "Sarah can help sew overcoats for our soldiers. We're behind on the new batch. And we've still to do the men's stockings. I hear she's a fine seamstress."

I can't believe what I've just heard. What lies has Emma told her mother about my sewing skills? Pity the soldier who would wear something I make. My stitches are crooked as bottom teeth. I once sewed two sleeves together. But if it means freedom from this misery, I'll sew circles around everyone in town.

Mr. Jordan knows he's been bested. He turns to the jailer. "I will take custody of the traitors and the infant."

CHAPTER 30

May 20, 1776

Dear Diary,

I can't stop thinking about Father and his secret mission. What could he possibly have to offer? True, he knows Latin and can write as eloquently as Shakespeare. Do the British need such a man to write their orders and messages with pomp and flair? In Latin?

EMMA'S HOUSE IS TWICE the size of ours, with five bedrooms off the long upstairs hall. We're assigned the tiny storage room off the kitchen where Thomas was laid up with his mangled leg. There's no window but the bed we three share is clean and warm.

Mother finally seems on the mend, after weeks of loving attention from Mrs. Jordan, despite her husband's frequent grumping about Mother's alleged treason. But she's still weak, and Benjamin's care falls to me, though I feared I'd bungle it at first. I fretted over his breathing. Did it sound raspy? Too shallow? Was he breathing at all? What if I drop him?

The house is busy with people from morning until late at night. In the roomy front parlor Mrs. Jordan directs a regiment of women from town who sew shirts and jackets for the militia at a frantic pace. Those who aren't sewing are knitting stockings, their needles clacking like chickens.

Putting it off as long as I can, I finally join the dreaded sewing circle, certain they will uncover my incompetence in short order. In the corner, one neighbor hunches over a loom weaving linen while two other women turn out yarn on their spinning wheels. They take breaks only to drink bitter "Liberty Tea" made from raspberry leaves. They'd sooner die of thirst than sip the detestable British tea, or so they say.

I'm certain these ladies will not take kindly to a loyalist in their presence, nor do I want to be here anymore than they want me here. Emma, true to form, warned me to keep my opinions to myself, though everyone knows exactly who I am. Keeping my mouth shut may be tougher than sewing a straight stitch.

Finally, I force a smile and take the linen shirt pieces from Mrs. Jordan and clumsily thread a needle. I glance up to see if anyone noticed. So far, so good.

Emma only adds to my discomfort. She sits beside me knitting a sock, stifling laughter as I struggle to sew two pieces together.

Martha, Emma's terribly proper older sister, gives us a look. "What are you two going on about?" she demands.

"I was just telling Sarah about the big dance that's coming up soon."

"What's the point. Surely you realize that prisoners aren't permitted to go dancing."

"I know, but everyone is talking about it," Emma says.

"Everyone being you," Martha says. "You have nothing better to do than flaunt your wares on the dance floor. It's unseemly."

"Oh Martha, my dear, lighten your heart," Mrs. Jordan says. "I think the dance is a good idea. These are difficult times, and it will bring us some cheer."

"Is it true that Pierre Chevalier himself will be here?" one of the ladies asks.

"Yes!" Emma gushes. "He teaches in Boston and travels all over. He'll show us all the latest steps."

Martha rolls her eyes. I can picture Emma spending hours gussying herself up for Monsieur Chevalier. Even if I wanted to go, which I don't, I'm sure that I'll be locked up here.

As I struggle with the sewing, the women yatter on about the new unmarried pastor, the poor quality of this year's maple syrup, and the shortage of pork and molasses now that the soldiers are encamped in town.

"I hear another of them is stricken with the smallpox," Mrs. Jordan says. "That makes four this week."

"The first one died horribly," Patience Sanders says. "Poor man was out of his mind and covered with hideous sores."

I'm all ears now.

"There's new talk of turning the schoolhouse into a hospital now that so many are afflicted," Mrs. Jordan says. "At least it's a way to keep them away from the rest of us, the poor souls."

I know I should keep quiet. Emma gives me another warning glance, but I can't hold back.

"How can they open a hospital without doctors and nurses?" I'm beginning to see a way out of our predicament.

"I don't figure they can," Mrs. Jordan says.

"Once you're inoculated and suffer through a mild case, you're immune for life," I say. "That's what the doctors say."

Now I have their full attention.

"My mother and I have been through it. We can help. And Mrs. Bascomb, and others."

I feel like I've just handed them a tidy solution to their troubles, and our troubles as well.

Dead silence follows my little lecture.

Finally, Tess Hudson, a thin woman with a constant frown, speaks up. "We know what your mother did, what she did to Polly Peterson. We'd have to be crazy to let you loose on our sick ones. You're all working for the British and would sooner see us dead."

"Amen!" Martha says, giving me a haughty look that makes me furious.

"Don't be foolish," Mrs. Jordan snaps, signaling the issue is closed.

I feel defeated, trounced really, and wish a pox on all of them.

As I rethread my needle and knot the end, I feel something brush against my leg.

"Ezekiel!"

"I found him hiding under the wood pile," Emma said. "I've been feeding him, though he earns his keep as a mouser."

The cat climbs into my lap, and I stroke his stomach, setting off a strong purr heard across the room. When I dangle a snippet of yarn, he swats it, prancing around on his hind legs. I laugh so hard my sewing falls to the floor.

"Is that all the stitching you've done?" Martha grumbles.

I want to tell her there's more to life than perfect little stitches. But it's my supposedly brilliant sewing that saved me from jail. So I work faster, not caring whether the stitches are even and close together. What does it matter anyway? It'll be worn by someone I'll never see—a rebel at that. Finally, the sleeve is sewn in place, and I examine it. One swift jerk of the shoulder and it will burst. It will just have to do.

We work until 2 o'clock, when the ladies go home to prepare dinner. Soon, Mr. Jordan and his sons trudge in from the fields. His farm is the largest in Essex, a fact he praises God for every time the family gathers for grace around the long dining room table.

I hear his booming voice as Mother and I sip bowls of turnip soup in our tiny quarters. Prisoners that we are, we're not permitted a seat at the table. Emma risked life and limb yesterday to slip us slices of custard pie.

Mother sits up and eats heartily, the first sign of an appetite in a while. "How long do you think they'll keep us here?" she asks.

"I don't know. Perhaps until they find Father."

"I'd be dead now, were it not for Mrs. Jordan's kindness," she says, pulling the baby to her breast and lying back against the pillow.

Mother seems so at peace, but my mind is racing. I hate being a prisoner. They're watching our every move. I'd enlist Emma's help, but I've already put her in too much danger.

When I leave the room with our dirty dishes on a tray, I bump into Emma's brother, nearly knocking him to the floor.

"Thomas! I didn't see you. I'm so sorry."

"No harm done. How are you, Sarah?"

"I'm fine, for a prisoner."

"Yes, I know all about it."

"You're looking quite well, Thomas." I feel awkward. I haven't seen much of him since my confinement. "And you're back on your feet."

His gait is slow and stiff, but the color has returned to his face and the heft to his body. He's pleasing to look at, and there's something playful in his smile. He seems older now, not the angry, bedridden boy of months ago.

"I never did thank you proper for tending my leg," he says. "So, thank you."

"No need. Where are you off to?"

"I'm still a member of the militia. I can't go back to the battlefield yet, so I guard the armory. Anyone tries to steal those munitions, I'll blow their head off—and probably take half the town with it."

"Hope you leave the better half, Thomas." We share a laugh and for a split second I feel like I'm back with my brother.

"You can help the patriots' cause," he says, lowering his voice. "Tell them where your father is. It's not too late for you and your mother."

"Not too late for what?"

"To be on the right side. Don't you know they'll put you back in jail once your mother is well? Who's to say what will become of the baby?"

His words cut me like a knife. "I don't know where Father is, Thomas. I wish I did, I'm so worried about him."

I can tell he doesn't believe me. "At least think about it," he says, as he buttons his coat and limps out the door.

I'm left standing there with Thomas' words ringing in my head. What *is* the right thing? Father always knew, and I mostly trusted him. Now I have no idea.

CHAPTER 31

I'M SEWING THE COLLAR on a linen shirt for the tenth time when Emma returns from delivering another load of shirts, breeches, and socks to the soldiers on the green. She gives me a sly smile and flicks her eyebrows, and I know instantly that she's got a tasty piece of news.

It's all I can do to keep working. When I can stand it no longer, I break into a fit of wheezing, gasping, and coughing.

"I need ...a...drink, please," I choke out in mock desperation.

"I'll see to it, Mother," Emma says on cue. "Come with me, Sarah." She thumps me on the back as if to dislodge an elephant. "That should help."

In the kitchen she pours me a mug of cider as I continue my little act.

"So what is it?" I whisper between coughs. "I know you know something."

"Guess who I saw on the road?"

"Who, Emma? For God's sake!"

"Samuel! I didn't recognize him at first when he staggered out from behind the stone wall reeking of liquor."

"I know about the liquor. What did he say?"

"Said he has to see you, that he has something important to tell you."

"What is it?"

"His undying love for you? How should I know."

"Emma! What did you tell him?"

"Told him the only time you're not under constant watch is when my whole family goes to church on Sunday. I forgot to tell him Martha stays behind to make sure you don't escape."

"Does Martha really think I'd flee without Mother and Benjamin? Without a horse or wagon?"

Mrs. Jordan suddenly appears. "I'm glad your coughing spell is over, Sarah. Come back to the parlor girls, we have much work yet to do."

———————

For days, all I can think about is Samuel and why he wants to see me. Maybe he loves me and wants me to know it—a thought that excites me, though I'd never let on to Emma. She'd make merciless fun of me. Besides, I think it's far more serious than that, and the more likely answer is that he has some news about Father.

"I hope it's so," Mother says as we bed down after a grueling day of stitching breeches. "I would give my life to know that he's safe and well."

"I know you would." I consider mentioning my love for Samuel, but Mother and I have been getting on so well, I don't want to complicate things with excessive honesty.

As she nestles Benjamin between us, she voices doubt about Samuel showing up. "If he comes even close to the house on Sunday, he'll never get past Martha."

"The guard dog," I grumble. "If only we could distract her."

I'm almost asleep when Mother nudges me. "There may be a way. I have some valerian root in my satchel that we could slip into that raspberry tea Martha so loves."

"Valerian?"

"It makes you drowsy and, if you take enough, you nod off. I recommend it to my ladies for insomnia."

Suddenly I'm wide awake and loving this conspiratorial side of Mother. "You would help me?"

"Yes. Anything for your father."

Yes, anything for Samuel.

Sunday morning, the house is busy as Emma's family trot out their best clothing for church. Chaos erupts when Mr. Jordan discovers he's missing a button on his waistcoat, and everyone drops to the floor to search for it. Minutes tick by. Fortunately, I find it on the stairs.

"Good eye, Sarah," Mrs. Jordan says. "Martha, would you sew this button back on?"

"I'll do it, Martha," I pipe up. "I'd be happy to help out." I smile sweetly at Martha, and the nasty buzzard even smiles back."

"Thank you, Sarah. How kind."

I manage to sew the button on at lightning speed, a feat that surprises everyone, especially Martha.

As the family heads out, Emma whispers, "Be careful."

Back in the parlor, Martha stretches out on the blue velvet sofa, the first of its kind in Essex and now the talk of the town. She opens her Bible, and after she's settled in for a few minutes, I initiate my brilliant plan.

"Martha, would you like some raspberry tea?" I flash her a dazzling smile.

"How nice of you, Sarah. Thank you."

In the kitchen I put some loose raspberry leaves in the tea pot, along with a pinch of Mother's dried, chopped valerian root. As an afterthought, I dump in another bunch of the sleep-inducing herb for extra assurance. But when I add the boiling water, the concoction smells repulsive, so I drip in a teaspoon of honey.

She barely notices me when I set it before her. "I hope you like it," I say. "I used a little honey, knowing your fondness for sweets."

Martha looks at me with the slightest hint of suspicion. "You're very agreeable this morning. I find it pleasing." Then she gives me a tiny smile, as if it would pain her to show some teeth.

"There's more tea, should you need it," I say, returning the pinched smile.

I sit by the window watching for Samuel and counting Martha's sips. The minutes drag by, and I wonder if he'll even show up.

The first sign of hope from Martha is a huge yawn. Then her eyelids droop. Still no Samuel. A few more minutes pass. Finally, her eyes close and I start to rise out of my chair when they spring open again. I plop down and wait. Eventually, they close, and a soft rumble emerges from her lips, followed by a snort, and then the blessed sound of snoring.

It all seems for naught as I wait and wait. Finally, a soft scratching at the back door. I tiptoe out of the parlor and open the door a crack.

"Sarah!"

"Shhh!" I slip out the door into the sunshine and behold the bedraggled creature that is Samuel.

"I can't believe it's actually you," I say.

"Let me kiss you and I'll prove it."

He gives me a passionate kiss on the lips, but I'm too focused on his scraggly beard to enjoy it.

"Emma said you had something important to tell me," I say. "What is it? Something about my father?" I wait what seems like an eternity for his answer.

He pulls back from our embrace. "You must keep this secret."

"Of course."

"The rebels are stockpiling munitions—cannon, gunpowder, muskets, everything they can get their hands on for the fighting in New York. It's hidden in Rev. Evans's old barn under piles of straw."

"Why are you telling me this?" I ask, disappointed it's not about me.

He squeezes my hands. "The redcoats are going to raid the barn and seize the munitions. The rebels sure will be surprised, and whatever happens, their defense will be pitiful. But the whole scene will be chaotic—a perfect time for you and your mother to escape."

"It might work." My mind is scrambling to put it all together.

"I'll get word to you when it's about to happen, probably in a few days. But now I must go, before I put you at risk."

"Wait! Where's my father?"

"I can't tell you," he says with a bit of an edge.

"Why? He's my father, Samuel."

"He's safe with the British. Let it go at that."

"If you care at all about me, you'll tell me more."

"Sarah, you put me in a terrible bind. All I know is that it's highly secret. Only the very top commanders know." He pauses. "There is something more."

"Tell me."

"It's strange, unsettling. And, anyway, I don't believe it."

"Please, I have to know."

Samuel is silent for several excruciating seconds. "I heard rumors that he's invented some kind of chemical that can help the British win the war.

"What are you talking about?"

"Forget I said anything. Now I must—"

"Surely, you can tell me if he killed Abner Rollins?"

"He did not."

Relief floods me for a second. "Then who did?"

Silence, then a deep breath. "Abner found out about our plan to seize the munitions. It was at the Essex Tavern. I was there playing the drunk, trying to scare up information about the rebels. Two of our men were also there, disguised as rum traders. One of them let it slip about the munitions and Abner overheard. He confronted us outside and—"

"Did *you* kill him?" I have to know.

"He pulled a knife on me. Must have recognized me. We wrestled in the dark like a couple of madmen. He's a bear of a man, and he had me pinned down, my face in the dirt."

I can barely breathe.

"I thought he was going to stab me in the back. He would have, if my men hadn't gotten to him first."

I feel lightheaded and start to sway. Samuel grabs me.

"I'm not saying I did it, Sarah, but it had to be done. One yelp from Abner and we would have all been dead."

"But murder?"

"It wasn't murder," he says. "This is war, and people die. It was him or me. Surely you see that."

"What I see is another death."

"I'm not sorry, Sarah," he says as if reading my mind. "I hated

178

what the rebels did to your family, your father, your brother, now you and your mother. And poor Rev. Evans. Then all that business telling us what we could and couldn't print. I had to do what I could."

"But you—"

"Enough about all that," he says, pulling me close.

He tilts my face upward and kisses me tenderly on the forehead. Then his lips find mine.

I'm deliriously happy. Until I hear Benjamin cry, and I remember Martha.

"I have to get back inside."

"I'll return," he says, letting go of me.

I slip in, hoping my face doesn't show the scarlet signs of torrid love—if, in fact, such things exist outside novels. In the parlor, Martha begins to stir.

"I must have dozed off," she says, sitting up. "I'm so sleepy." She has a sloppy smile on her face and drool running down her chin. She's never looked happier.

———————

That night Mother and I prepare for bed in the dim candlelight. She's happy too, even giddy, knowing that Father is alive. I hold back the news about the redcoats' planned raid. No point in getting her worked up.

"I knew he would be involved in some grand, mysterious adventure," she says. "That's so like him." She's totally forgotten how furious she was with him over the last six months.

"Do you really think he's some kind of crazed chemist?" I ask her.

"It wouldn't surprise me," she says. "You know how he constantly fiddled with his precious ink and paper."

"And nearly burned down the house when he set the napkin on fire."

Suddenly I have what the Bible calls an epiphany. It's an unexplainable flash of knowledge when everything comes together, and you can't move or talk fast enough. "The candle, the flame, the paper! That strange Bible passage."

"You're not making any sense."

"Don't you see! He directed us to a passage about holding something over a candle."

I take out Father's letter and reach for the candle.

"What are you doing? Don't burn it up!" Mother tries to grab it from me.

"No!" I yank it away. "I know what I'm doing."

I hold it over the flame until scorch marks begin to appear on the paper. Then I pull it away and study it in the dim light.

I can just barely make it out: *"You have discovered my mission. I will write again soon."*

"That's what it says!" I thrust the paper in her face, unable to contain my excitement. "It's written between the old lines."

"But how?"

"I don't know, but it has to do with Father's ink concoctions. It makes sense now."

"Not to me."

"Don't you see? He's invented an invisible ink that only shows up with the heat from a candle. That's what he was working on all those months, so the British could send secret messages and the rebels would never catch on!"

"And I thought he was just wasting his time," Mother says, breaking into an absolutely lovely grin.

CHAPTER 32

May 25, 1776

Dear Diary,

Why do men thrive in the awfulness of war? Samuel isn't bothered by Abner's death—one less bully in the world, one less threat to the monarchy. Are men tougher about such things than women? No doubt Samuel and his men are doing what they feel they must and are heroes to their commander. I'm troubled by it, but I have to admit, a little thrilled.

I SELDOM KEEP SECRETS from Emma, and this one is like a fireball in the pit of my stomach.

I've thought of little else, and I'm jumpy at the slightest sound. I dropped a tray of teacups and drew a scolding from Mrs. Jordan. Mother can always sense when I'm holding something back, but mercifully, she hasn't said a word.

My life as a prisoner is one dreadful chore after another. When I'm not sewing those uniforms, I'm in the kitchen scrubbing the floor or plucking feathers from the hapless chicken that will be the day's dinner. Not that Mother and I will eat any of it—our meals are skimpy at best. This morning my hands are raw from churning the butter for an eternity.

Of course, Emma knows I'm hiding something, but she's consumed by plans for the dance, what she'll wear, and whose eye she'll catch.

While I sweep up chicken feathers, she tries to jolly me with her imitation of the great Pierre Chevalier giving a dance lesson.

The racket draws Thomas into the kitchen, and he smiles at me for the first time in days.

"I have something for you," he says, handing over a polished wooden box.

I'm immediately wary, surmising he's being nice as a ploy to find out where Father is.

"Go on, take it," he urges. "It's just something I thought you could use while you're here. Emma told me you keep a diary."

"I did, until the patriots ransacked the house, and it was lost in the mess. Lately, I just use scraps of paper."

"Open it," he says, ignoring my chilly tone.

Inside is an ink bottle, a quill pen, and a few sheets of paper. I'm stunned.

His initials are carved on the outside. "I got this after I was wounded. Doctor's wife thought it would improve my spirits, but I'm not the sort to write letters." He looks away. "You were so kind to tend my leg. I wanted to thank you for getting me back on my feet."

I hold the pen up and examine the quill tip. "Thank you, Thomas. That's very kind of you." I want to say more but he hurries away.

"He likes you," Emma says, grinning like a fool. "If you weren't a prisoner, I bet he'd work his charms on you at the dance."

"Don't be ridiculous."

Mrs. Jordan's sewing group is becoming halfway tolerable. My stitches no longer look like the work of a toddler. To tell you the truth, sewing gives me time to think while the women drone on about someone's new bonnet or the best way to make piecrust or the big dance which, more's the pity, will not be graced by my presence.

I thread my needle and begin sewing the pieces of another linen shirt. It's my third since arriving at the Jordan home. The first two were sloppy, and frankly, I just didn't care.

Something changed with this one. My stitches are more even and closer together. I don't really know why it suddenly matters, but it does. I keep imagining the young man who will ultimately slip it on. Someone like Thomas. Will he be tired of war or eager for more of it? Will he be frightened, or will he be cocky? Has he killed any British soldiers?

I even imagine meeting him one day. Will he hate me for being a loyalist? Could he hate me just for favoring the King? There is so much more to know about me than that. Could he hate Mother, nodding off in the rocking chair with the baby nestled on her chest?

I stitch the shoulder seams twice so they'll hold better. On a whim, I use tiny stitches to create my initials "SB" on the inside of the collar. If he never meets me, at least he can wonder who I am. Maybe he'll put it all together when he sees my first novel.

A new worry has cropped up in my trove of worries. Thomas could be guarding the munitions the night of the redcoats' raid. Barely able to run, he'd be easy prey for the British. I can't let that happen. He's Emma's brother, and I care about him.

———————

While the Jordans' home isn't exactly jail, Mother and I are still very much prisoners. She's still weak from childbirth but I spend my non-sewing time mopping the floors, boiling rancid bacon for soap, and scrubbing the linens. We're not allowed to take meals with the family—you'd think we're contaminated with the pox—so we eat bowls of mush and stale bread in our cramped little room. Now and then, Emma sneaks us a couple of apples.

When she whispers, "I have something for you" on this gray evening, I expect another aging fruit, but she adds: "It's from Samuel," and slides a slip of paper into my raw, red hand.

In the privy I finally have a chance to read it.

Destinatus: It's Sunday night. I promise we'll meet again.

It's signed simply *"S."* Visions of him smothering me in kisses any time soon are gone. I wonder if I'll ever see him again.

In the meantime, the Jordans gather for supper—my cue to retire with Mother to our little jail-away-from-home. But I can tell that tonight something is different. Usually mealtime is full of chatter, but Mr. Jordan is somber. As I head down the hallway to our room, I stop to eavesdrop as Thomas quizzes his father.

"Father, isn't it a good sign the British troops abandoned Boston?" he says. "The tide is turning, don't you think?"

Mr. Jordan says nothing and neither does anyone else. The silence is broken only by the tick-tock of the tall grandfather clock in the corner until, finally, he speaks.

"'Tis only good news until they decide to harass us where we least expect it," he says in low, conspiratorial tones.

As I enter our room, I shush Mother before she can open her mouth. Without closing the door, I can hear just enough of the talk in the dining room.

"Our women finished four more shirts and two woolen coats today," Mrs. Jordan chirps as if to ease the tension. "Sarah has turned into a passable seamstress."

"She'd be a lot more valuable to us if she told us the whereabouts of her father. Instead, she's treated like a princess—eating our food, sleeping on our bed, warming herself by our fires."

He's on a rant now.

"She's got the run of the house as if she were an honored guest, not the prisoner that she is. It's time she and her pox-loving mother went back to jail where they belong."

Mrs. Jordan starts to say something, but he shuts her up with one word: "Enough!"

I hear footsteps and a knock at the front door. Mr. Jordan opens it to Silas Spooner, who wastes no words on pleasantries. "It's true. It's what we feared."

"Come into the parlor where we can talk. Tom, join us."

Suddenly my brain comes to full attention. Something has happened, and I have to know—but there's no way I can penetrate the closed parlor doors.

All I can do is offer myself up for extra service in the kitchen.

And I do want to keep myself in Mrs. Jordan's good graces, as she might be the only person on earth who can keep me, Mother and little Benjamin out of more dire circumstances.

"I'm here to help clean up," I say to Mrs. Jordan as they all leave the table.

"Thank you, my dear."

"I thought I heard someone at the door," I say. "Did something happen?"

"It's not your concern," Mrs. Jordan says abruptly. "Now make haste with the dishes."

While Emma builds up the fire and heats water, I clean up the supper dishes very quietly, straining to hear any little scrap of conversation from the men in the closed-off parlor. But all I hear are muffled sounds, glasses clinking as if in a toast, and occasional bursts of laughter. After an hour or so, I give up and go to our room, where Mother is already sleeping with Benjamin.

Finally, Mr. Spooner leaves. As Mr. Jordan trudges up the stairs, he bids Thomas goodnight. "Yes, the tide may very well be turning."

After a few minutes I hear Tom rattling things in the kitchen. Curiosity is making me crazy, and I tiptoe back there.

"Oh, Tom—you startled me. I came out for a sip of cider."

"So the prisoner would like a sip of cider to ease her poor parched throat." He's slurring his words and has a sloppy grin.

"You're drunk!"

"That I am," he says, pouring himself a glass of whiskey. "And why not?"

"You'll find out in the morning when your head feels like a pincushion."

"Why don't you join me?" he says pulling out a chair that nearly topples over. He staggers to the cupboard to get another glass. "Let me pour you a bedtime nip."

"I'll join you but save the whiskey. I prefer cider."

"Ever the cautious one. Don't worry. Father is snoring by now."

I'm beginning to see an opportunity, and I want to keep my wits about me. I pour myself a little cider and sit down. Tom moves his chair even closer.

"What was the big meeting about tonight?" I ask as casually, as if I simply wanted the time of day.

"Wouldn't you like to know!"

"Yes, I would," I say, pouring him more whiskey. "It's not as if I can do anything about it, being trapped here awaiting execution."

He laughs a hearty drunken laugh. "You have it pretty easy for a prisoner."

"It must have been important, given your father's earlier sour mood."

"It was." He puts his hand on mine. I leave it there. "But he was in a much better mood after old Silas left."

"He must have heard some good news," I say, wondering how to extract my hand.

"Yes, you're very clever," he says, squeezing my hand. "The patriots could use someone with your cleverness." He stumbles over the word "cleverness."

"Could they?"

"Certainly, they could."

"What would a person have to do to make that happen?" I say, realizing immediately that I may have gone too far. But what is too far? I'm suddenly aware of what a kiss, or more, could get me. Am I willing to make that trade?

He's squeezing my hand even harder. "You don't have to do anything, except tell me where your father is."

"Honestly Tom, I don't know." I hold back the rest—that I'd never tell even if I knew.

"For some reason I believe you."

My hand is still trapped, and I make no move to free it. I gaze into his eyes with what I imagine is a come-hither look and get right to the point.

"So why was your father so distressed at dinner? You might as well tell me. Being a prisoner, I can't do anything with the information—not that I would want to hurt the patriots."

"Since your loyalty to the King is waning, I'll tell you," he says. "The British are planning to attack the armory and seize our weapons."

I try to act nonchalant, as if this is something I might hear in my sewing circle. "And you know this how…?

"Captured a redcoat sniffing around the ammunition. Beat him nearly senseless till he talked." His words are barely understandable.

"What are the patriots going to do?"

"This is the best part. We'll ambush the damn Brits as they march in, *before* they know what hit 'em."

"That's…wonderful!"

"I'm loving this new Sarah, the rebel," he says, leaning over to kiss me.

I pull back. "That'll be a big Sunday surprise for the redcoats," I say.

Suddenly he looks wary.

"Sunday? I never said Sunday. What made you say Sunday? Where did you get that idea?"

I realized my mistake as soon as I said it. My mind scrambles for any half-baked explanation.

"Sunday? I didn't say Sunday. I said 'someday.' Of course, *someday* the redcoats will be plenty surprised."

The dreamy look in his eye is gone. Have I destroyed whatever goodwill I thought I'd conjured up by flirting? He yanks his hand off mine and slides his chair back.

"I must be off to bed," he snarls. "And you, get back to your room now!"

Did I ruin everything—maybe even jeopardize lives—by putting my foot in my mouth? I don't know. As I tiptoe back to Mother and Benjamin, one thing is sickeningly certain: Come Sunday, Samuel will have no idea he and his men are walking into a trap.

CHAPTER 33

IN THE PARLOR'S MORNING sunlight, I pretend to focus on my sewing, but all I can think about is Samuel. He'll meet a bloody end, killed by the loose lips of a redcoat who couldn't stand up to a rebel beating. Both sides are despicable, but never mind that for the moment: Somehow, I must warn him.

I prick my finger, and a drop of blood soaks into the linen shirt in my lap. The red spot startles me out of deep thought.

"The men don't know whether they'll join the fighting up north or go south to New York." It's Emma's mother. "Could be on their way in a week. We'd best hurry if we're going to finish these."

Only I know that the choice between north and south is irrelevant. They may never make it if the war erupts right here in Essex. I wish I could share my secret with someone. Too dangerous to tell Emma; she can't keep her mouth shut even if *my* life depends on it.

The talk turns to how the men will fare in battle.

"I pray they'll take comfort in their Bibles," Martha says as her knitting needles clack away.

"Isn't their Bibles they'll take comfort in," one of the younger women says.

I glance at Emma, who's already feigning shock for my benefit.

"'Tis the drink and the cards and the gambling," another says.

I know it's none of those that cause the most worry. It's the camp followers, the women who travel with the troops to cook, nurse the injured, and more often, to peddle services that no one here in the lovely parlor talks about. I've heard about camp followers from Emma and try to picture Samuel wounded, with one of them hovering over him. Would he find her pleasing to the eye, more pleasing than me? Or, more to the point, would he—

"I hear the hanging is in all the newspapers in New York," Mrs. Jordan says, and suddenly I'm alert.

"What hanging?" I blurt out.

"Thomas Hickey, one of George Washington's aides," she says. "Seems he was part of a huge plot to assassinate the general. Even the mayor and the governor and half of New York high society were in on it."

"But they didn't actually do it, did they?" I'm incredulous.

"No. Someone spilled the beans," she says.

Martha pipes up. "But the plan was to not only kill the general and his staff but blow up a huge store of rebel guns and ammunition. Thank the Lord for the rat who talked."

"Yes, thank the Lord," I echo, imagining the tortures that must have awaited "the rat."

"Sounds like something your father would have a hand in," Martha says. "The way he always spouted off about the patriots' cause, calling us a pack of rabid dogs and the like. He certainly prided himself on bringing light to us, his ignorant readers."

I'm livid. "My father is principled. He would never be involved—"

Now it's the dour knitter, Tess Hudson, standing right in front of me, her hands on her hips like a stern school mistress, her eyes boring into my soul.

"Don't be so sure. He killed Abner Rollins, or he wouldn't have gone on the run."

"No!" A knock on the door interrupts my response.

Martha returns in a moment. "It seems the prisoners have a visitor," she announces with disdain.

My heart thumps for a second, until I see Mrs. Bascomb, the store owner's wife.

"I've brought something for the new baby," she says, handing me a small blue and white quilt, carefully folded.

"How kind of you. Mother will be pleased." I take the quilt and start to unfold it to show the other women.

"Oh no my dear," Mrs. Bascomb says, grabbing it back. "Tisn't fit to show such fine seamstresses."

Mrs. Bascomb is twitchy and nervous. Something is amiss.

"May we show Mother?" I ask Mrs. Jordan sweetly. "She's with the baby in our room."

"I shouldn't allow…Mr. Jordan…oh, just for a minute. But Mrs. Bascomb, let's don't make a habit of visiting our 'guests.'"

Mother is surprised to see her old friend. "Bless you for coming."

As I shake the quilt open, a folded paper drops onto the bed.

"What's this?" Mother sits up.

"Hush!" Mrs. Bascomb warns. "The others mustn't hear."

I snap up the paper and hold it so Mother can read it as well.

To my dearest wife and daughter,

It pains me to write this because my heart aches to see you both. My dears, I have bad news. I'm quite sick with the pox and may not have long to live.

As I lie here, I think constantly of dear Seth. Were it not for me, the boy would be alive.

If we don't meet again, know that my love for you both has sustained me and that I'm going to my grave an honorable man.

Your loving husband and father.

Mother covers her mouth to stifle a cry. Her body shakes with silent sobs.

"He's not dead, I'm sure of it," I tell her. "People survive the pox. You know that." Father has never been sick. I can't even imagine him frail and bedridden. "We'll find him, and you can make him well." I don't add how relieved I am that he's not in jail for plotting to kill Washington.

Gradually, Mother calms down.

"How did you come by his letter?" she asks

"My husband." She looks warily toward the door. "He was in New York at a print shop buying stationery and such for the store when he saw Benjamin. He was quite sick and half-mad, but he was set on helping the Crown."

"Do you have more news?" I ask.

There's a sharp rap on the door, and Mrs. Jordan bursts in. "You must keep this door open. Come along Mrs. Bascomb. Your time is over."

I jam the letter in my sleeve just in time and force a smile. "We didn't want to disturb you."

That night I wait for Mr. Jordan's snoring then tiptoe out to the kitchen to light a candle. Every time the house creaks, I fear someone will awaken and find me outside my room. Emma's sister Martha would love to see me in big trouble.

Ezekiel is lazing by the glowing hearth. He pads over, erupting in frantic meows before settling into a soft purr.

I unfold Father's letter and hold it up to the flickering light. My hands shake as I lower it over the flame. Surely Father would use the invisible ink to say his dying is all a ruse, a trick to keep the rebels off his track. Surely, he isn't sick.

The flame slowly singes the paper, and I can make out new words emerging between the lines. My hands are sweaty, and my throat is dry.

"Money under rock behind privy. Flee to New York. Jonah Livingston at Loyal Gazette will help. Godspeed!"

I sink into the rocking chair. My gut tells me he really is dying from the pox. Ezekiel jumps into my lap, licking my hand as if he's scrubbing his own paw. I scratch his head as I try to sort through all that I've learned.

One thing is certain. We need an escape plan, even with Mother still recovering. But there's something even more urgent: The rebels will be lying in wait when the British launch their raid on the pastor's barn. I picture Samuel with a gaping gunshot wound bleeding to death in the dirt—just like Seth. And if Thomas were to die, Emma would be devastated. Again. All the people I care about most are dead, dying, or about to die. How can either side in this war claim honor?

I rock, stroking the cat and mulling how little I can do. Then, the plan comes to me, bit by bit. At first, I shrug it off as preposterous, too dangerous, and too likely to yield unthinkable consequences. But if I succeed...

With the first hint of dawn, I get up from the rocking chair, sending Ezekiel to the floor in drowsy bewilderment. I tiptoe upstairs to Emma's room.

"Wake up!"

Emma sits up with a start. "What is it? What's wrong?"

"Nothing, nothing at all."

"Then why—"

"I need your help. It's important."

Emma slumps back on the mattress. "What can be so important—"

I shake her awake. "I need you to fetch Seth's bow and arrows from our barn and bring them to me."

CHAPTER 34

"What do you mean you have a plan?" Emma is fully awake now.

"Shhh, you'll wake everyone," I whisper. "No one can know about this. Promise me you'll keep it secret."

"How can I promise when I don't even know what it is?"

I move closer. My voice is raspy with fatigue and excitement. I have to convince her, and it means trusting her with my life.

"Listen carefully."

Emma rolls her eyes. "You sound like Mother."

I hold onto my patience. "This is important. It's not some silly game. Lots of people could die."

"Die? I'm listening, go on."

"British soldiers are planning a raid on Rev. Evans's barn to grab all the patriots' guns and ammunition."

"When?" Emma's eyes focus intently on me, as if she's trying to gauge how much of this madness to believe.

"Sunday, when they think everyone will be in church."

"Not Thomas! He'll be guarding the munitions. We have to warn him."

She starts to get up and I stop her. "Wait, there's more."

"Sarah, how do you know all this?" She eyes me suspiciously.

"Samuel. I saw him. He's here with a British regiment."

"He's fighting for the redcoats? How—"

I slap my hand over Emma's mouth. "Quiet! He's got his reasons."

She yanks my hand away and angrily tells me she's sick of my schemes. "Besides," she says, "it's my responsibility to tell Father!"

"No!" My voice is louder than I intend, and I fall back into a whisper. "He and Thomas already know. That's what they were talking to Spooner about in the parlor. They and their patriot friends won't be in church because they'll be lying in wait to ambush the redcoats. The British will march right into their trap."

"And Samuel?"

"He doesn't know. I'm so afraid he'll die."

"What about Thomas?" Emma's voice quavers. "Even if he knows, something could happen to him...."

"I know. This could turn into a bloodbath. It could be awful."

Her eyes reflect her confusion. "What's your plan?"

I choose my words carefully. "I'm going to blow up the munitions before the raid, before the ambush, before any of it happens."

"What?" Emma breaks into a big smile. "You can't be serious. You're joking, right? Just like Seth."

"No. I'm not."

"You're serious. You really mean to do it, don't you?"

I nod.

"How? Tom says there's dozens of barrels of gunpower, muskets, even five cannons. They've hidden explosives from five towns here."

"My plan is to set the building on fire with Seth's bow and arrow."

"Now you're talking crazy, and you're scaring me."

"I know it sounds preposterous, but I'll use a flaming arrow. I can do it, Emma. You know I'm a great shot. If Seth were here, he'd tell you so."

"If Seth were here, he'd tell you what a fool you are."

I had a feeling she'd react this way. "I need your help, Emma, not your sarcasm."

"I am helping you. I'm telling you that this is foolhardy. You could set yourself on fire. You could set the whole town on fire! If they catch you, they'll hang you."

"I won't get caught. Don't worry so much." Truthfully, I hadn't thought about the consequences beyond stopping the ambush. And now Emma is throwing doubts into my beautiful plan. And she could be right. I know it's risky, but it'll be worth it. Why can't she see that?

Emma is fuming. "Don't tell me not to worry. How selfish can you get, Sarah? What about my brother? Are you going to blow up Tom as well?"

"Of course not. That's where I need your help, to divert his attention so he'll be safely out of the way."

Emma is flabbergasted. "Now you want to drag me into this? No!"

It will be dawn soon, and we don't have much time before the whole family is up. I take a deep breath and press on as if I never heard her say no.

"If I do nothing, men on both sides will die. Maybe Samuel. Maybe Thomas. Your father. Men we see in church. Boys we grew up with. It could be a bloody disaster. It could be as bad as Bunker Hill."

"Haven't you forgotten one little detail? You're still a prisoner. You can barely go to the privy without someone trailing you."

"That's the least of my worries," I say as convincingly as I can. I'm not ready to tell her that part of my plan. I strike a confident pose and jut out my jaw as if I were Joan of Arc, sitting for a portrait.

Emma smirks. "If escaping here were the least of your worries, why haven't you just walked away?"

"And abandon Mother and Benjamin?"

Emma is still hesitant.

"My father and the others will be furious over losing all those munitions," she says. "They've been guarding that barn and hoarding weapons for months. No, I can't do it."

"Emma, think about the lives we'll save!" I summon a softer voice. "Doing nothing is far worse. This way no one gets hurt."

"Only if your idiotic plan works."

"It will only work if you help me."

"You must love Samuel something awful. Otherwise, you wouldn't take such a chance."

"I do. I think I do." It's not the time to get into the meaning of love. "I don't want to lose him."

"Nor can I lose Thomas."

Emma's resistance is wearing thin. "Then you'll help?"

Her face is filled with uncertainty, but she doesn't say no.

"Good!" I squeeze her hand.

"But I didn't say—"

"I'll need you to gather a few things besides Seth's bow and arrows. Some turpentine, a small pail and… oh, would you stop by Mr. Bascomb's store and tell him I need his help again? That it's urgent."

"What do you mean?"

I hear footsteps downstairs. "I can't explain now, but we have to act fast."

CHAPTER 35

My hand shakes so badly I can't thread my needle. The other women are all hunched over their sewing except for Martha, who's watching me intently. Does she know something?

Even Emma doesn't know everything, and that's partly why I'm a quivering mess. I was lucky she didn't press me on why I so urgently needed Mr. Bascomb's help. Without him and his wagon, I can't carry out the final part of my plan—the part I can't bear to tell Emma about.

I'm hoping Mr. Bascomb will help Mother and me escape in the chaos sure to erupt after the explosion—that is, if my aim is true, if the flame catches, and if we don't get caught. So many ifs...

I should tell Emma about the escape. But if all goes as planned, we might not see each other, at least for a long while. I'm already torn up about that more than keeping a secret from my best friend. Soft-hearted Emma would be an angry, weepy mess, and I don't think I could bear it. Worse yet, she might let something slip. No, better to keep it secret.

I know she's already started the mission I assigned her. She announced early this morning that the coffee supply was nearly gone, and that life simply wouldn't go on if she didn't rush over to Mr. Bascomb's to fetch more. It was just a ploy, and I knew it. She returned an hour later with the coffee, and her smug look told me she'd taken him aside to seek his help.

Now I would just have to wait. Would he even want to help me, the prisoner under close guard? He'll likely think it's too risky to waste his time on such a wild venture.

I feel the folded paper inside my sleeve—the note I intend to slip to Mr. Bascomb, if he shows up. The best chance for my insane plan is tonight, with nearly everyone at the dance.

The sewing ladies are all buzzing about what they're grandly calling a ball. My attention drifts in and out. Mr. Spooner, it seems, has offered up the Essex Tavern for the big event. A renowned fiddler and a piano player will provide the music while the glory-covered Monsieur Chevalier will once again lead the ladies and gentlemen in the elegant dance steps he learned in his native France.

To hear Emma talk, you would think the King himself is planning to attend what is sure to be the most thrilling event that has ever graced our boring burg. That's why I dread telling her she won't be attending, because that's precisely when we'll be blowing up the barn.

For the rest of the day, I force my mind back to my sewing without jabbing myself. When it's done, the shirt I so frantically stitched is still puckered in the wrong places. I should tear it out and start over but there isn't time, given Mrs. Jordan's demand that we work faster. The sleeve will hold just fine, though it won't win any prizes.

"Were you asleep when you stitched that?" Martha's voice startles me. "Pity the poor soldier who'll be wearing that sorry scrap."

The other women snicker, and I'm fuming when Mr. Bascomb walks up the steps.

"Come to see my husband, I expect," Mrs. Jordan says.

I smile to myself. Emma has done it again! Mrs. Jordan opens the door to let him in.

"Good afternoon to you, ladies," he says, stooping to enter. His head nearly reaches the ceiling.

I try to catch his eye, but, with appropriate caution, he doesn't even look at me. A clever move on his part.

"Is your husband about?" he asks Mrs. Jordan.

"He's in his study. I'll fetch him. Feels like we might get more rain tonight, doesn't it?"

"Hate to see rain during the festivities," he says.

Soon Mr. Jordan lumbers in.

"I've brought you some tobacco from Bailey's spread over in Gilroy." Mr. Bascomb hands him a pouch from his haversack. "Good crop this year."

Mr. Jordan pulls out a handful and inhales. The aroma fills the room.

"A sweeter smell than the flowers of May."

I've never seen Mr. Jordan in such a pleasant mood, and with a loyalist no less. Of course, Mr. Bascomb doesn't wear his loyalty on his sleeve. He's discreet. Few people in Essex know that he's the one who spirited away Rev. Evans after his tar-and-feathering. As they say, he keeps his own counsel—unlike Father.

"Thank you," Mr. Jordan said. "'Tis even better than the rum you brought last month. Now come into my study so we can have a word."

The friendly chatter makes me anxious. Why has Mr. Bascomb brought him rum and tobacco? He's not a rich man, or at least he doesn't dress like one. His breeches are clean but patched, and his once-white shirt is frayed and worn.

Mr. Jordan then turns to me. "Fetch us some whisky, and don't tarry."

I return with the bottle, and the two men disappear. They talk for an hour, and occasionally I hear them laughing.

Now I'm frantic. What if Mr. Bascomb is telling him about my plea for help, and the two of them are having a good laugh at what an ignorant girl I am? For a moment I wish I'd never sought his aid. But there's no one else I can trust—if I can trust him.

Finally the door to the study opens. "I'll leave you to your business," Mr. Bascomb says to Mr. Jordan. "I'll just get my coat."

"I'll get it for you," Martha says before I can blink.

"No bother, Martha," Mr. Bascomb says quickly. Sarah is closer. She'll fetch it."

I leap up and practically race to the coat rack. With my back to the women, I slip the paper from my sleeve into his coat pocket.

"Here you are, Mr. Bascomb. And your bag."

"Thank you." He looks intently at me. Is he trying to tell me something?

It seems like all eyes in the parlor are on us as I futilely grasp for something to say. Finally, it comes to me:

"Looks like we're in for another thunderstorm. Darker than a pocket out there." I put a barely discernible emphasis on the word pocket.

Our eyes lock for a moment as I try hard to convey my desperation.

Mr. Bascomb nods ever so slightly. "Just a shower. Won't ruin the ball. Good day, Sarah."

When he's out the door, I exhale. Something in that nod tells me he understands, but I'm not sure. I'll just have to trust that he finds the note and will risk everything he holds dear in Essex to help us.

And now Mother, the last hurdle. When I open the bedroom door, she's tending Benjamin. Still weak, she seems stronger every day. She's already talking about catching babies again if we ever leave this prison.

"Mother, we must talk."

"What is it? Are you ill, child?"

"No." I've given up on reminding her I'm not a child. "I have a way for us to escape, a way to get to New York. But we must act fast." I hope she'll be pleased, even excited.

"What? What are you talking about?"

"Not so loud! Mr. Bascomb will be here with his wagon at 10 tonight. He'll take us part way. He has friends who will help us, just as they did Rev. Evans."

"Sarah, how did you—"

"I slipped him a note. He'll be here, I know he will." I don't *know* anything of the kind. Maybe he didn't catch my pocket reference. Maybe he'll turn us in, and we'll be in an even deeper mess.

"But everyone will come after us."

"Don't worry. Emma and I have it all figured out. We'll create a distraction." That's at least half true.

Mother shakes her head fiercely. "No, too risky. And you have no right to put Emma in such peril."

I know she's right. But I plow ahead anyway.

"This is our only chance to see Father," I tell her. "I'm certain he's alive."

"Don't get your hopes up. He'll likely not survive the pox. If only he'd let me inoculate him."

Mother closes her eyes and goes silent. The baby fusses, and I pick him up to comfort him.

After an agonizing minute, she finally speaks. "There is nothing more I would ask of God than to let me see my dear, sweet husband. My heart aches every day for his touch, his voice."

Is this *my* mother talking? I've never heard such tender talk from her. She and Father were barely speaking when he left. "So you'll do it?"

Mother nods.

I suppress my urge to let out a full-throated cheer. "Then we must prepare quickly. We'll need a sack of food for the journey."

"I'll take care of that tonight when I help with supper." Mother's face shows a resolve I haven't seen in months. Now it's all up to me, and what I have in mind is nearly impossible.

On my way to the privy I pass Emma. "Tonight's the night," I whisper.

"But the ball—you know I'm going."

"Perfect time to do it."

Emma shoots me a look of pure hate.

Later, when I deliver fresh linens to her room, she lets me know exactly how she feels.

"It's the only thing I've had to look forward to in this dismal place, and you've ruined it for me."

"There will be other balls."

"You *would* say something simpleminded like that."

"What about me? Don't you think I'd like to get all dressed up, leave this prison and dance away the night?"

"You know you can't do that. Father would—"

"Of course I know," I snap. "Doesn't mean I can't dream about it."

Emma rolls her eyes. I brush it off, relieved to see she's recovered Seth's cedar bow from the barn. Nearly four feet high, it's strung with the leathery sinew from a cow's backbone. I grip the smooth wood, and feel my brother's presence, his smell, his laughter. My heart aches to see his sly smile and put up with his teasing just one more time.

"Are you sure you know what you're doing?" Emma says.

I glare as if it's a question that doesn't deserve an answer. Pulling back the bow string ever so slowly, just the way Seth taught me, I feel the muscles in my shoulder tighten. It's been so long since I've done this.

I couldn't bear to look at the bow after Seth died. Panic seeps into my chest. Will my aim be true? Suddenly I'm not so sure. I'll have to be more accurate than I've ever been in my life. Emma found only three arrows. I pull back the bowstring several times until I feel strong and steady. Then I let go and the sharp ping startles her.

"Don't do that!" she says. Then, with her fingertips, she touches the bow's smooth wood. "Where did Seth get it?"

"He made it. The old Indian working at Mr. Dodd's stable showed him how. The arrows, too, with wild turkey feathers at the end."

"I had no idea," she says. So much she doesn't know about Seth.

"Have you thought of a way to distract Thomas?" I ask.

"How could I? I thought I was going to the ball tonight in my new gown with the lacy bodice."

"Well, I have an idea."

"What?" Emma eyes me with suspicion.

"Offer to bring him his supper just after dark when he's on guard duty at the barn."

"And then what?"

"Stop in the woods about a hundred yards away and scream as loud as you can. Scream as if someone is holding a knife to your neck."

"What? I can't do that!"

"Let me finish!"

"But what am I screaming about?"

"You just saw a bear. Probably the one that tore into Ezra Collins and nearly killed him. Remember how the men went looking and never found it?"

"Yes…" Emma's still hesitant.

"Well, you found him, the biggest one you've ever seen, and if you scream 'BEAR!' loud enough, Thomas will race over."

"And when he sees there's no bear?"

"He'll be so relieved to see you—and you'll have scratches to show you put up a fight."

"I will?"

"Yes. On the way, I'll find a branch or something to scrape up your arms and face. I'll make sure you're bloodied up good."

"No, you won't. You're crazy, and I don't want anything to do with your idiotic plan." She starts to leave the room.

"Wait! I need you. I can't do this without you." My only hope of stopping the ambush is slipping away. "If you won't do it for me, do it for Seth."

"This has nothing to do with Seth!" she practically shouts. "Don't use him to justify this madness."

"I'm not. I only thought—"

"This is what you always do, wear me down with your words, until I agree to something that goes against everything I believe."

"I don't do that."

"Yes, you do. You get an idea in your head and you're like a dog with a bone until you win. You're the one who talked me into walking across the pond last winter before the ice was solid, and I fell in. I could have drowned."

"But you didn't."

"And you don't think things completely through before you go off half-cocked." Emma is on a rant, and I can't argue with the truth of it. "Have you even thought about what would happen if we're caught?"

"*You* won't be caught," I say. "All you did was see a bear and scream. I, on the other hand, have nothing but my life to lose."

"What about Tom? Won't he come under suspicion for leaving his post?"

"No! He was just rushing to the aid of his dear sister. Who could blame him?"

"All right Miss Know-it-all," Emma says. "What about this: Won't my entire family think it strange if I say I'm not going to the dance when it's all I've blabbed about for days?"

"Maybe you're feeling sick. It's the course, your time of the month, and you're bleeding buckets."

"No!" Emma is so exasperated she pounds her forehead. "Well, here's the biggest flaw in your harebrained scheme: No one with any sense would believe that I came away from a brawl with a bear and have only a few scratches to show for it."

"You might be right about that."

"It's much more believable that I'd see what I think is a bear and scream," Emma says. "Then I'd flee in terror, tripping and falling, and scratching myself up good."

She's right. "Yes! That's much better!"

"I didn't say I'd do it," Emma angrily retorts. "Have you forgotten? I'm the one who wants to go to the ball and dance till I collapse. Bloodying myself for you and your daredevil mission isn't what I had in mind."

I hang onto the thinnest shred of hope. "I would do this for you," I say, not quite certain that I would.

"Well, I would never ask. I think you're being selfish. You just want to be the big heroine."

"Not so!" Though I can't deny the whole idea excites me. "My plan would save lives—Samuel's, Tom's, your father's, others—and all you have to do is get a few cuts and a lot of sympathy. If we do nothing, it could be one big slaughter of men and boys. Do you want that on your conscience?"

"No," Emma says slowly.

"Neither do I. Then you'll do it?"

Emma, once again, looks beaten down, and I halfway hate myself for manipulating my friend. "Yes, but you're not scratching my face. My arms, maybe. But not my face."

CHAPTER 36

THE JORDAN HOUSE IS a blur of activity as everyone prepares for the ball. Hair must be curled, braided, wrapped, and pinned. Cheeks rouged, but not too much. The sweet scent of rosewater is everywhere as gowns are freshened and perfume dabbed in critical places. I ache to be part of it, and I know Emma does too.

At first, I thought they were all going, leaving Mother and me unguarded for the evening. But that hope fizzles when Mr. Jordan announces he has better things to do with his time than prance around on the dance floor under the tutelage of Monsieur Chevalier.

"Everyone will be there," Mrs. Jordan says, trying to coax him into sociability. "It will be quite a spectacle."

He stands firm. "Someone must stay here to guard the prisoners," he proclaims. "I am quite content to do that."

But later I overhear Mrs. Jordan complain to Martha, "Father would rather drink himself to sleep than join the festivities."

It's true. Every night he enjoys a glass or two of rum at supper then retires to the parlor with his crystal decanter of brandy. An hour later, he's slumped on the sofa, fast asleep and snoring like thunder. I pray tonight is no different.

Then Mrs. Jordan discovers Emma isn't primping for the dance. "Why aren't you getting dressed?"

"I'm not going," Emma tells her as we shell peas in the kitchen.

"Why not? Everyone will be there. What about your new gown?"

I wait for her to grimace, pat her lower belly, and feign the monthly inconvenience.

"Would Father allow Sarah to go too?"

"You know he wouldn't. Why do you ask?"

"If Sarah can't go, then I won't either."

I'm stunned. Emma is taking a stand on my behalf.

"Are you sure? What about your new gown?"

"I'm quite sure," Emma says with an assertiveness I've never heard before. I want to hug her.

"How can you toss all this away just to spare Sarah's feelings when she's a prisoner, for heaven's sake?" She gives me a peeved look as if it were my idea.

"I've made up my mind."

"You might not have another opportunity like this for a long time."

Emma gives her mother a defiant look.

"'Tis your loss," Mrs. Jordan says.

Supper is a simple affair of porridge and cornbread. In a futile attempt to please Mr. Jordan, I help serve it. True to form, he downs one glass of rum, and Emma is right there to refill it to the rim. Now it's just a matter of time.

But he doesn't go to the parlor after draining the second glass. He takes down his musket, lays it on the kitchen table and carefully oils all the moving parts. But why? And why now? I'm sweating with worry until he takes up Emma's offer of some brandy in the parlor.

A half hour later I hear the familiar snoring, and I creep out to meet Emma in the kitchen. "I was touched by what you told your mother, that you would do this for me."

"Don't get all sappy. I just realized there are no men worth getting fancied up for in this dismal town."

It's nearly 9 o'clock when we slip out the front door and take the moonlit path through the woods.

"We must be a sight," I say, hoping to keep Emma in good cheer. I carry Seth's bow with the arrows tucked into an over-the-shoulder quiver. Earlier, I carefully wrapped a snippet of fabric around each arrow just below the flint point, tying the strips with strands of leather. In a small burlap sack that swings at my side, I've stashed one of Mother's medical bottles that I've filled with turpentine.

I know Emma's worried we'll encounter someone and so am I. I already told her—and myself—that almost everyone in town will be at the ball, and the rest are, like Mr. Jordan, dead drunk or asleep. Still, we stop occasionally amidst the tall pines to listen for anyone following us.

Emma carries her mother's straw basket with one hand and a small, covered bucket of glowing embers with the other as she steps gingerly over the rocks and tree roots.

"I never should have let you talk me into this," she says. "I'll spend the rest of my life in jail if Father doesn't end it for me sooner."

I try to distract her. "What did you pack for Thomas's supper?"

"A turkey leg, a hunk of corn bread and some cider. Last night I brought him bread pudding and a nip of Father's brandy I snitched from his cabinet."

I laugh uneasily. I still haven't told her everything about tonight—my plan to slip away, perhaps forever, in the blast's chaotic aftermath. I feel like such a coward, and I'm running out of time.

As we approach the town, we walk silently. I hear music pouring out of the Essex Tavern. The fiddler squeaks out "Kitty, Will You Marry Me?" and dancers pound the boards like horses racing down a track. For a moment I imagine myself on Samuel's arm skittering across the crowded dance floor.

"I see Monsieur Chevalier through the window," Emma says. Even from afar I can make out his curled wig, red velvet waistcoat and white silk stockings as he gestures wildly for the dancers to link arms.

I tear myself away and drag Emma with me. The pastor's burned-out house is near the green, and his barn sits well behind, next to a field that has lain fallow since he left. I draw Emma into a thicket and press my finger to my lips.

"We've got to find a branch with thorns sharp enough to bloody up your arms and face."

"Not my face!"

"All right!" I scour the ground, finally finding what I need. "This will do. Come here."

Emma is a hair away from changing her mind and turning back home.

"I'll do it fast, so it won't hurt as much. Don't scream—bite your tongue if you have to." I draw back the branch. But she grabs my arm.

"I'll do it!"

Before I can resist, she whips the branch against her own arm, causing a tiny scratch.

"This will have to do," she insists.

I was afraid of this. Before she backs away, I pull a small bundle from my bag and smear bloody chicken innards on her face and neck. It stinks, and she's somewhere between gagging and screaming.

"It's from last night's dinner," I explain.

"That's revolting…how could you…"

"Head for the brush," I command. "I'll be behind that big cedar tree on the rise, where I can get a good shot."

Emma looks terrified.

I catch her arm for one last second. "Thank you. I'll never forget this."

"I won't let you."

I hurry up the slope. Yanking an arrow from the quiver, I dribble turpentine on the cloth at the tip. My hand shakes, but I manage to do the same with the other two arrows.

I fit an arrow's notched end into the taut bowstring, then draw it back to the corner of my eye and take aim. I can just make out Thomas leaning alone against the barn, his musket beside him. Against the moonlight, I clearly see my target, the old barn's thatched roof.

I relax the bowstring and wait for Emma's cue. My heart pounds wildly. Why won't my hands hold steady like they did in the backyard with Seth? It's been so long since I've shot an arrow. How could I think it would be easy now?

Emma's scream is so loud and real I nearly drop the bow. "Heeeeelp, help! A bear! Thomas, help me! Come quick!"

A second later, Tom grabs his gun and dashes away from the barn. "Emma, I'm coming!"

I dip the arrow into the embers and the soaked cloth flares up. With the arrow in place, I quickly pull back the bowstring, but the flame blinds me. I can't see the barn or anything else. In a panic, I let go anyway, and the arrow lands well short of the barn, fizzling out in the dirt.

Thomas's voice booms out of the darkness. "Emma, where are you?"

"Here," Emma moans. "I scared him away but I fell."

I grab the second arrow, and it too lands short of the barn.

I have one arrow left. Pulling back, I aim higher this time, way above my target. *Dear God, if you're there, please show me.* I let go, and the arrow flies in a high arc, lodging with a thunk in the tinder-dry roof.

I hold my breath, but nothing happens. I failed again and feel a wail of despair starting to rise in my throat. Then a flicker of light catches my eye. It becomes a flame as I watch in awe.

The flame spreads quickly to the rest of the roof. Finally, a bang erupts from inside the barn. Then another bang and a series of loud pops. Then a monstrous explosion throws me to the ground. For a second, I think I've been shot, but I pull myself up in time to see a huge fireball burst from the barn. As I crouch on the ground, embers and scraps of wood rain down.

Where are Emma and Thomas? *What have I done?*

I lay trembling, my ears ringing so loud that I hear nothing else. Then the ground shakes with another explosion and a second fireball shoots into the sky. Waves of heat swirl over me.

What if Emma and Thomas were too close to escape? The smoke makes it impossible to see and breathe. Where are they?

Gasping for air, I sprawl on the ground as a swarm of soldiers run from the green toward the barn, followed by dancers in fancy dress from the tavern. When I stand to flee, I wobble uncontrollably before bolting for the old trail through the woods.

I hear men shouting and I think Thomas is one of them. But what happened to Emma, I can't pretend to know, and it rips into my gut as nothing in my life ever has before.

No one was supposed to be hurt. And I pray to the God I really don't worship that I haven't lit the whole town ablaze.

Glancing back, I hope for a glimpse of Emma. A crowd surges down the road to watch the flames leap above the treetops, lighting the sky in an eerie wash of orange and red. Terrified, I can scarcely believe it's all my doing.

I hurry back through the woods, finally climbing over the rock wall that borders the Jordans' property.

I'm careful not to make a sound but suddenly, a familiar voice calls out:

"Sarah! Over here. My God, what a sight!"

Mr. Bascomb appears out of nowhere startling me. "I have the wagon all set to go." Mother is there, clutching Benjamin.

"Are you all right, child?"

"Yes, I'm fine." I'm not exactly fine, but I breathlessly give them both a quick version of the destruction I've wrought. My heart is beating so fast I'm gulping air, my head aches and the ringing in my ears makes me feel queasy. Worst of all, I don't even know whether Emma's dead or alive.

"You fool! What possessed you to do such a thing?" How quickly Mother's mood changes from relief to anger.

"I didn't want Samuel to die," I choke out. By now I'm a blubbering mess. "Mother, there was going to be a big battle over the ammunition and the cannons. Samuel was sure to die. Maybe Tom too, and others."

Mothers can mete out their worst punishments with silence, and mine is no exception. Her eyes are full of loathing. "I don't know who you are anymore."

I couldn't possibly feel worse until Emma, still bloodied, emerges from the path, panting.

"Where are you going? Are you running away? You are, aren't you!"

I'm thrilled she's alive, but deeply ashamed of my own cowardice.

"You weren't going to tell me about this part, were you," she says accusingly.

"I was," I lie sheepishly. "I was going to tell you... now."

"No, you weren't. You were going to sneak away in the night without saying a word to me. And after what I did for you tonight.

Do you know I actually did trip and gash my arm? This blood is real! I could have been killed in those explosions. How could you do that to your best friend?"

"I wanted to tell you," I said. "I just didn't have the courage. I thought you would hate me."

Emma scowls. "I do hate you. I don't even know where you're going, and I don't want to know."

I'm drowning in guilt, and I hate myself far more than Emma does. "I should have told you. I'm sorry. We're going to New York to see my father, God willing the pox doesn't take him first. I promise I'll write to you."

"Don't bother. I won't read it."

CHAPTER 37

Mr. Bascomb guides his wagon onto the dirt road and jolts the horse into a trot. We're in the back, concealed by bushels of corn and dusty old horse blankets. As the wheels bump over the ruts, tears stream down my face. Mother looks terrified as she tries to calm a wailing Benjamin.

Another explosion from the direction of Rev. Evans's barn startles us. I never expected such destruction. I thought...I don't know what I thought.

Mr. Bascomb snaps the reins and the horse presses ahead faster. "With any luck at all, we'll be out of Essex before they realize you're missing," he shouts. "I can take you only as far as Greenfield. A trusted farmer will keep you overnight and help you as much as he's able. After that, you'll have to find a way to New York."

I can't answer. My throat feels tight as I choke back sobs. I wish I could take back what I've done. I didn't want to hurt Emma. I'm ashamed of what I asked—really demanded—of her. I'm as selfish as she said.

As we rumble away from Essex, I remember how exhilarated I imagined I'd feel if it worked. It *did* work, but now I feel only sadness, panic, and a sick dread, knowing I can't take any of it back. I meddled in something far bigger than myself. Why wasn't I content to follow in Mother's footsteps, to bake pies and deliver babies?

For what feels like an hour, Mr. Bascomb doesn't say a word.

There's still one worry about this kind man that's nagged me since I saw Mr. Jordan welcome him into his study. When we're out of town, I throw off the sweltering blanket.

"I can't breathe," I tell him.

"Sit up here with me, unless we run into trouble."

I move up and breathe in the clear air.

"There's something I don't understand."

"What's that?"

"How can you be so chummy with Mr. Jordan?"

"He's my friend. Just like Silas Spooner."

"But you're not a rebel. You're a loyalist, just like my father."

He chuckles, and it surprises me. "I'm a businessman and a family man. That means more to me than anything."

"You mean ...you're not a loyalist?" Suddenly, my worst fears take hold. "Are you taking us straight to the rebels? Did I fall into a trap?"

He laughs. "No, of course not. I want to help you."

"Why?"

"Your father is my friend too. More than anything I want the fighting to stop," he says. "I want my store to prosper. I want to see people—loyalists or rebels, doesn't matter—line up to buy flour and buttons, and even tea. I don't want to see blood running in the streets."

For some reason, I believe him.

The wagon lurches and rumbles at a good clip along the road in the moonlight. But finally he eases up on the horse when we reach the wide, rushing Connecticut River.

"This is where we head south toward New York on a less traveled road," he says.

I'm so deep in worry that I don't answer.

"Are you all right, Sarah?" he asks as he reins the horse to an easy walk.

I can't bring myself to tell him how miserable I am, how I wish I could relive the last day.

"I don't know." My voice cracks on the last word.

"You'll be judged harshly by both sides," he says. "It was a crazy thing to do, but if you want my opinion, your heart was in the right place, or I wouldn't be here. You thought you could save lives, and you probably did. Don't know if it'll work in the long run but today, it did."

I relax slightly. If I tell him I'm no hero, it'll sound just like what heroes are supposed to say.

"But you've put yourself in awful danger. You and your mother are fugitives. The rebels will scour the woods to find you. They're desperate to get to your father."

"In New York, they'll be less likely to find me. Mother and I just need to get there. God willing, Father is still alive. He'll know what to do."

In truth, I never thought beyond firing the flaming arrow. I never considered the consequences and where we might end up.

We ride silently for hours on a road so narrow that the treetops touch overhead. We pass no one on the road, and my stomach settles down. Soon it's hunger pangs I feel. Soon I'm consumed by visions of apple pie and cheese. We've been on the road for six hours with barely a bite to eat.

Suddenly, Mr. Bascomb jerks the reins hard and the wagon stops abruptly.

"Quiet!"

Mother awakens. "What's wrong?"

"Shhhh!" Mr. Bascomb peers behind us at the dark road. "Don't let that baby make a sound!"

I tighten the hood of my cloak around my face and wait for an anguishing minute as we sit perfectly still.

"I thought I heard a horse," he whispers. "I think we're being followed."

It's so still not even the crickets are chirping. Only an occasional breeze rustles the treetops.

"Maybe it was nothing," he says, flicking the reins. The horse lurches forward.

Now every sound alerts me. Did someone catch up to us? Certainly someone on horseback can go faster than this creaky old wagon.

"Another few miles to Greenfield," he says. "Mr. and Mrs. Pratt will help you. It'll be dawn then, and I must hurry back to Essex before anyone questions my whereabouts."

The thought of losing Mr. Bascomb saddens me. He's become a

trusted friend who risked his life for my family. I want to tell him what I feel but nothing comes to me. Finally I blurt it out.

"Mr. Bascomb?"

"Yes? What is it, Sarah?"

"I haven't the words to thank you properly for what you did."

"Only writers think everything requires words."

A small, ramshackle farmhouse comes into view and Mr. Bascomb reins the horse to a stop. He exchanges a few words with a farmer already up and about his chores. As Mother hands Benjamin to me, she brushes corn husks from her clothing. I wish Mr. Bascomb a safe journey home.

"Goodbye, Sarah," he tells me. "God be with you."

———————

As the sun rises, Mother and I are gulping porridge at the kitchen table. Never has mush tasted this good, and I help myself to seconds. Mr. Pratt looks tough as nails, though he's old, maybe 60. Short and wiry, he moves like a much younger man.

"I have just one horse I can let you take," he says. "I sold my wagon to the last family that came through here, desperate to get to New York. Old Cyrus isn't fit for carrying the two of you and the baby, but I could let you have him for 7 pounds."

My heart sinks. We fled Essex with less than 4 pounds, the money Father hid for us.

"Mr. Pratt, you've been too kind for words, but we can't pay you anything," Mother says.

"I surely can't let you have the nag for nothing. We need to buy supplies."

"Could we take the horse with a solemn promise to pay you back later?" I ask.

"Do you take me for a fool?" His earlier hospitality is gone.

"It's no use, Sarah. Even if we had the money, we can't all three fit on the horse." Mother puts her face in her hands and begins to cry softly. It's not like her, which tells me how exhausted and beyond hope she is.

"I got no room for charity," he says. "I work my farm without the help of a hired hand. My wife's crippled with the gout. Poor thing suffers so with pain that she spends most of her time in bed. I've got no time or patience for this blasted war."

Mother stops sniffling. "Perhaps I can help your wife. I've helped others lame with the gout."

I want to tell her to forget her foul potions, balms and teas. We don't have time. But Mr. Pratt smiles for the first time since our arrival. "That's most kind of you, Mrs. Barrett."

I grudgingly accept this unscheduled delay, not that I have a choice. Then a plan starts taking shape in my mind, one Mother will surely put down as dangerous and foolish. And I have to admit it's both. But we have nothing to lose.

"Mr. Pratt, my mother is the finest midwife in New Hampshire," I say. "She's better at delivering babies than the doctor. She can cure all kinds of ailments."

"Sarah, hush." Mother looks embarrassed.

"It's true. Everybody says so. She's very clever with herbs and brews. And she's best known for saving people from the smallpox."

Mr. Pratt's eyes perk up. "Is that a fact?"

"People pay her handsomely for her skills. Mother, remember the man who gave you a hog, just for relieving his arthritis?"

She gives me a blank look but nods.

"I'd be much obliged if you could see to my Mildred," Mr. Pratt says.

"Of course I would," Mother says.

"Of course, she doesn't treat her patients for free," I add.

Mother gives me a stern look, the one that says I've once again overstepped the bounds of polite conversation. "Mr. Pratt, I only ask people for what they can pay."

He scowls at me. "I see what you're up to, young lady. You drive an impossible bargain."

He sips his cider silently. Have I made things worse?

Finally, he speaks to Mother. "Madam, you may have the horse on the condition you tend my wife for two weeks. That should be time enough to see if your potions do any good."

"But Mr. Pratt," she says, "we must leave here as soon as possible. Two weeks—"

"Mother, it's all right." I see a way out of our predicament. "I'll go to New York alone. The horse can carry but one of us, and it should be me. I'm the one they'll want for destroying all their weaponry."

"No, I won't hear of it! We stay together. We're a family. You're only 16, too young to go off on your own. How would you even find your way?"

I ignore her objections. "But Mrs. Pratt needs you. You'll be safe here, you and little Benjamin, won't she, Mr. Pratt? I can come back for you later. Perhaps Father will come too."

"Sarah, you know how sickly he was with the pox. He's likely passed by now."

"No, I don't believe it," I insist. "The sooner I get to New York, the sooner we'll know."

I can tell Mother is too exhausted to hold her ground. "A young girl alone on a horse, traveling a great distance—surely, you'll arouse suspicion. It's too dangerous. And what do you know about horses?"

She's right. I know next to nothing, but I ignore that little fact and push on. "I have it all figured out. I'll dress like a boy. No one will know."

Both Mother and Mr. Pratt look at me as if I said I'm flying to the moon on the back of a turtle.

Mr. Pratt even twitches a little smile.

"Maybe Mr. Pratt has some breeches and a shirt I can wear," I say. "And a hat."

Mother is unconvinced. She tells me I'm insane.

"But this is our best option. I've already decided I'll go."

Mother starts to open her mouth but looks too worn to put up a fight.

Mr. Pratt stands up suddenly. "I'll find some clothes and such for you. Won't be much better than rags. And you'll surely need a map." He seems eager to be rid of me. I don't care. The sooner I leave, the better.

"Hurry! Oh, I'll also need a roll of bandage too."

"What?" He scowls, and I scowl back harder. "In case of injury." He goes off muttering and returns minutes later with the goods.

In the back room, I strip off my dress, petticoat, shift and stockings. I gaze at myself and feel a flush of embarrassment. Maybe this *is* lunacy. I wrap the bandage roll tight around my chest and tie a knot. My breasts flatten out like two pancakes. Almost. I put on Mr. Pratt's old, scratchy linen shirt and scrutinize myself. There's barely a rise where my breasts are. For once I'm glad I'm not blessed with Emma's mountainous bosom.

I slip on the old, patched breeches. It all feels so strange and uncomfortable, dressing in men's clothing. My chest already hurts from the tight bandage. I stuff my hair under the dusty old cap Mr. Pratt gave me.

Mustering my courage, I walk back into the kitchen.

"You still look like a girl," Mother says. Two long ringlets have slipped out from under my cap. "You can't hide all that hair. Give up this ridiculous plan and get out of those clothes."

I storm to the back room, embarrassed and frustrated. Mrs. Pratt's sewing lay on the table, along with a needle, thread and scissors. Without a second thought, I grab the scissors and yank off the cap, sending my auburn curls nearly down to my waist. Fighting tears, I pull my hair back in a ponytail. In one quick, sudden move I lop it off. What's left falls to my chin. I jam on the hat and storm back into the kitchen.

"Now do I look like a boy?"

"Oh, dear God, what have you done," Mother shrieks. "Your hair!"

I can't hold back the tears, and that infuriates me more. But I stand there defiantly.

"You were stubborn when you were four and you haven't changed all that much," Mother says wistfully. "I can see there's no changing your mind. Go, then. Go quickly. Don't forget to come back for me."

"Mother, I promise I'll send word when I arrive." I give her and Benjamin a quick hug and hurry outside to find Mr. Pratt hoisting a battered saddle onto the horse. I don't know who will give out first—me or Cyrus.

The farmer hands me a map he's drawn himself. "Stay close to the river. And watch out for rattlesnakes."

CHAPTER 38

C YRUS IS OLD AND sway-backed, and though I push him as hard as I can, the best he can do is a slow shuffle. The road follows the river south, and as the day wears on I encounter few people along the way. I tip my cap and nod, hoping they aren't curious.

Just in case, I make up a story about who I am, and why I'm on the road. My name is Matthew Tipton, and I'm headed for New York to bring back a supply of tobacco seed for the family farm. Using the lowest voice I can squeeze out, I practice my story over and over.

I ride for hours, passing through a few small towns. It's all strange and new and exciting, but I don't dare stop and look around. Finally, I've escaped Essex. It's what I wanted, but not this way. I have only a few coins in my pocket. And I look (I hope) like a boy in ill-fitting clothes. Will Samuel ever want to kiss me again? Will Emma ever talk to me again?

When I finally slide off the horse near Springfield, the insides of my thighs and calves are so chafed from the woolen breeches that I cry out. Every step torturous, I walk like a crab, leading Cyrus down an embankment to a mossy spot beside from the Connecticut River.

I ease myself down onto the ground, my entire body screaming. Why did I insist on doing this? What was I thinking? That it would be as easy as riding Lucky into Essex from the farm? I take off the cap and fling it on the ground. My hair falls into my eyes, another reminder of what I've done so hastily. It will take a year to grow back. I've never felt so miserable and ugly and alone.

I feed Cyrus some of the grain Mr. Pratt gave me and rub him down with a wet rag. Then I do what I've been dreading. From my knapsack, I take out the hog grease Mr. Pratt assured me would relieve any ills I or the horse suffer. Opening the linen pouch, a putrid odor greets me. Before I can change my mind, I drop my breeches and smear a fingerful on the red welts on my legs. Though it soothes the pain, it's the final humiliation.

After eating a hunk of bacon, a wedge of cheese and stale bread, I feel better. At dusk I spread the horse blanket on the moss for bedding. Building a fire is out of the question—it might draw attention. I listen for every little sound, wishing Mr. Pratt had kept his rattlesnake warning to himself.

Thankfully, it's a warm night. The rushing water lulls me into an exhausted sleep, but the mosquitos buzz mercilessly. I wake up flailing at them like someone gone mad. Isn't it enough that I stink like a hog? But to be devoured by mosquitos too? Sleep is impossible. I sit up and look at the sky, bright with stars. Bats swoop and dive over the water.

It's then that I see the flicker of what looks like a campfire about a mile upriver. Could be a trapper or a fisherman—or a rebel patrol. I listen: Nothing.

Just as I finally doze off, a horse whinny jolts me awake. It comes from the direction of the campfire. Now I'm certain it's a whole regiment dispatched to find me. I draw the blanket tighter. Will I hang for what I've done?

Before sunrise, I saddle the horse as best I can and find my way back up to the road. As I mount up, pain shoots through my chafed legs. I have no choice but to forge ahead—and stay ahead of whoever is behind me.

It's such a clear, starry night that it's not hard to make out the road. But it's also clear that Cyrus is in no mood to proceed. A kick to the ribs does nothing but nudge him to the roadside, where he chomps on some grass.

"You lazy beast!" I jab him again and again, until I remember the exhausted, bloodied horse that galloped into Essex that day after the Lexington and Concord battles. I reach down and pet him, stroking the gray hairs above his eyes.

"Come on old boy, we have to go," I plead. "Do this for me, and I'll give you an apple." I don't even have an apple, that's how low I've sunk—making empty promises to a cranky horse. After a few moments I flick the reins and he lumbers down the road.

The air is cool, and I pass no one. What would Father say about what I did back in Essex? I imagine him praising my ingenuity, skill, and bravery. But then I see him pounding his fist on the dinner table and denouncing my lunacy. One thing is certain: Once he calmed down, he would help me out of the mess I'm in. On the other hand, he could well be dead of the pox by now, just as Mother fears.

By dawn I've covered enough ground that I allow myself a break. At the river's edge I refill my canteen and sit down on a grassy spot. The hog grease has calmed my sore thighs some, but my whole body aches with fatigue. I stretch out, promising myself just a few minutes rest. The grass feels so good. A soft breeze keeps the mosquitos at bay. Just a couple of minutes.

I wake with a start at the sound of sails flapping on a boat cruising down the river with a load of lumber. Judging by the sun, I've slept an hour or two. *You idiot! Those hours were crucial.* I grab the reins and hoist myself onto Cyrus who ambles back to the road. We seem to have struck an agreement on who's in control.

About noon I stop and fetch the last scrap of cornbread and bacon from the knapsack. Looking behind me, I see a cloud of dust and hope it's just another rider in a hurry to get to New York, and not a rebel posse. I put the food away and prod Cyrus into a trot—a near impossible feat.

After a while, my back aches from Cyrus's barely bone-jarring pace. And my stomach growls. My own bed, my own quilt, my diary, my hair—I so miss it all. Will I ever see Emma to give her the proper apology I keep rehearsing? Just remembering Samuel's touch makes me sad.

I keep practicing my "Good day to you" in a husky, deep-throated voice that likely will fool no one.

I stop only for a swig of water, but when I hear a galloping horse, I panic and kick Cyrus mercilessly. Something tells me to ride like the devil and hang on as best I can.

Suddenly, a tree branch comes out of nowhere, and I don't have time to duck. It whacks my forehead and sends me flying. I land on my face and pain rages through my head. I spit out a mouthful of blood and dirt.

I'm dizzy and confused. The last thing I see before everything goes black is Cyrus rearing back and neighing like his saddle was on fire.

"Boy! Boy! Are you all right?"

I open my eyes and try to make sense of what I see: a young man in dusty clothes hovering over me with a canteen.

"Take a drink," he orders.

My hands shake as I put it to my lips.

"You took quite a spill. Lucky your horse didn't run off," he says. "What's your name?"

My rattled brain searches for my alias. "Matthew...Matthew Tipton. New York...tobacco seed." I try to get up but my head spins.

"Stay put for a spell," he says. "I'm Calvin Hopkins, postal rider. Come from the north country, on my way to New York."

I'm suddenly alert. What does he know? Can he see through my ridiculous disguise?

"How old are you, boy?"

I feel my face redden. "I'm 14," I lie, trying to lower my voice. "My father has a tobacco farm near Springfield. He needs seed."

He eyes me suspiciously. "Mighty young for such a mission. Why were you in such a hurry? Your father that desperate for seed?"

I feel my throat tighten, as I search for a plausible reason. "Thought you were chasing me. Didn't know if you were friend or foe."

"Fair enough. These are dangerous times. Hell of a commotion up north in New Hampshire. Have you heard?"

I shake my head.

"Someone blew up the patriots' stockpile of guns and ammunition in Essex. Went up in a huge explosion. A miracle no one died."

I gasp with feigned surprise, trying to gauge which side he's on. "Do they know who..."

"No, but probably the damned British."

"Damned shame," I say, hoping I sound manly.

I try to stand, and my cap falls off, revealing my mess of short red curls.

"Let me help you," he says. I take his hand and he pulls me up. "You are slight for a lad of 14. Are you sure you're fit to ride?"

He's smiling now, and I suspect he sees through my ruse. That gives me pause. What else does he know that he's not telling me? Have my breasts escaped the constricting bandages?

"I'm fine. Thank you for your help," I say cautiously.

"I'd best be on my way," he says. "I have much ground to cover quickly." For the first time, I notice his horse loaded down with saddlebags full of mail on either side.

"Safe travels… Matthew," he says with a peculiar grin. "And go easy on that old nag."

EPILOGUE

September 10, 1776

Dear Diary,

Working at Jonah Livingston's New York Loyal Gazette *isn't much better than involuntary servitude. The cranky old goat thinks I'm soft in the head, full of grandiose ideas. I want to write the news, but he told me that was a "preposterous" undertaking for a woman. Instead, he has me taking advertisements—that is, when I'm not cleaning the printing press with stinking horse piss.*

"Girl! Where's that ad for Dr. Keyser's pills?" Jonah bellows for the third time.

"The one that claims to cure 'a fashionable disease' that can't be mentioned by name?" I ask without cracking a smile.

"I don't need your sass, girl," he mutters, searching for his glasses, which teeter on top of his bald head.

"Jonah, it's right in front of you." I call him by his first name just to rile him.

"Insolence!" he rumbles. "If it weren't for your father, God rest his soul—"

"Why don't you visit Hazen's Coffeehouse?" I suggest. "A biscuit might sweeten your disposition." And give me some much-desired solitude.

Finally, he leaves, slamming the door. Finally, a moment to myself. All the ads are in place, ready to print when he returns. The furrier with his new shipment of ermine muffs, the jeweler moving to a new location, the saddle maker looking for his runaway slave, the brewer touting his Eden beer, the tavern owner offering the finest ale and fried oysters in the "neatest manner." All of them are set. Almost.

The last one offers the services of an experienced midwife. With Mother, little Benjamin, and me crammed into a flat, she is desperate for work. I set the type quickly: *Midwife with years of birthing experience. Skilled for even the most troublesome births. Excellent knowledge of herbal remedies for gout and other afflictions. Ask for Destinatus at this printing establishment.*

A week later Jonah struts into the *Loyal Gazette* after a stop at Hazen's and a chat with New York's bigwigs.

"They're all abuzz about my commentary predicting that this little rebellion will be over by Christmas," he gloats. "I think this calls for a new velvet waistcoat. I'll be at the tailor's shop being measured, if anyone important inquires."

"Make sure it's big enough to accommodate your impressive girth," I say, holding back a smirk.

"My girth is none of your concern, girl. Now get back to work before I fire you." I'm not worried. He threatens to fire me nearly every week.

With Jonah out of my hair, I have time to study the two responses to Mother's advertisement—both of them ladies nearly due to give birth. Good! This will bring in much needed money, so we can eat something other than Mother's vile cabbage soup.

I'm in my leather apron scrubbing the press when I hear a man up front talking to one of Jonah's dimwitted apprentices.

"I've come about the advertisement for a midwife."

The voice startles me, and I race to the front of the shop.

"Samuel!"

"Sarah?" He scans my dirty apron and my ink-stained hands.

"I didn't know you were here in New York until I happened to see the newspaper ad placed by a certain someone called Destinatus."

He has the biggest smile I've ever seen on his serious face.

"I didn't know if you were...alive," I say, shocked to see him.

"I'm very much alive." He takes my hand and pulls me in close. "I've missed you so." He tilts my head upward and his lips brush mine. I feel a tingle, and I don't even care if the apprentice is watching.

Last I saw him he was playing a drunken beggar—a ploy to keep an eye on the patriots and avoid the noose. Now he's elegantly attired, a vision in silk stockings and powdered wig.

"I'm an apprentice at the law firm of Stoneham, Delancey, and Winston across town," he says with a bit of a swagger. "They work primarily for the British. And your father—?"

"He died of the pox before I could see him one last time."

"I'm so sorry. Please give your mother my condolences."

"Father knew Mr. Livingston, the *Loyal Gazette's* owner. That's why I'm here."

"Perhaps we can do something about that," he says, eying my disheveled appearance.

"No, I like it here. One day I'll write the news, once I convince the owner I have half a brain."

He looks skeptical but manages to keep his mouth shut.

"I will. You'll see."

"Sarah Barrett, I don't doubt for a second that you believe that."

I take it as a compliment, though I'm not sure it was intended that way.

"And your mother?"

"She's here in New York with little Benjamin."

"And Emma?"

"I got a letter through to her, and she wrote back that she's teaching school." I don't mention my lavish—and sincere—apology to her for running off, nor how I tempted her to move here because of the abundance of young men in New York.

We stand silently for a moment just looking into each other's eyes. I know it will come up, and finally it's Samuel who brings it up.

"I expect you know someone blew up the munitions in Essex

the night you escaped."

"Yes, I know." I continue to look straight at him.

"It's mighty peculiar," he says. "No one knows for sure what happened. It wasn't the British, though the rebels blamed us. They found a couple of arrows and now they think it was Indians, but I'm not so sure. What do you think?"

"I don't expect we'll ever know," I say.

I glance up at him and see the corners of his mouth rise slightly. His eyes hold a hint of amusement.

"Seth was a fine archer, was he not?" Samuel muses.

"That he was," I say. "That he was."

AUTHOR'S NOTE

I GREW UP IN Keene, New Hampshire, in a rambling frame house built just a few years after the American Revolution. From my living room I could see the tavern where 29 Minutemen gathered before marching off to Lexington at the outbreak of the war.

I was immersed in history. My father loved everything about the colonial era—the furniture, the guns, the clocks, the bedwarmers. One time he took me to a cave where a loyalist, hounded out of town by rebels, hid during the war.

All of that stayed with me on some deep, personal level and inspired *Outcasts of Essex*. Though fictional, it's rooted in history and backed by extensive research.

The Revolution was not universally supported by the colonists. In fact, historians estimate that 15 to 20 percent opposed it and many others didn't feel compelled to choose a side. Some loyalists lost their homes and businesses, as well as their right to travel and possess arms. Some were thrown in jail. The war split families, just as it did with my protagonist, Sarah.

In the novel, a loyalist pastor is routed from his pulpit and brutally tarred and feathered. That was the real fate of British-leaning colonists like Boston customs officer John Malcom, who was mockingly paraded through the city after suffering severe burns from the hot tar. Many loyalists fled the colonies for Canada or England.

The Committees of Safety existed throughout the colonies,

replacing British regulations with their own as the war gathered steam. The committees enforced the boycott on British goods, supported George Washington's troops, routed out British sympathizers, and called for men to take an oath declaring allegiance to the patriots. In my novel, Sarah's loyalist father refuses to take the oath and winds up in jail.

Smallpox was rampant and deadly during the Revolution, just as it was in my fictitious town of Essex. The crude form of inoculation used in Essex was introduced to the colonies in the 18th century and was highly controversial. In some places, it was banned; many feared it would merely spread the disease, though there was growing evidence it eased the symptoms and would provide long-term immunity. Early in the war, Washington opposed inoculation, and smallpox devastated American troops. Eventually he gave in, ordering it for his men. Some historians credit his decision with helping to win the war.

The assassination attempt on George Washington, as told in *Outcasts of Essex*, really did happen. Thomas Hickey, a member of the general's elite Life Guard, was implicated and died by hanging before a crowd of 20,000, according to historians. New York's mayor and governor were also implicated in the widespread plot, which called for assassinating some of Washington's underlings and destroying a cache of rebel weapons.

While no major battles were fought in New Hampshire, the colony dispatched Minutemen at the start of the war and supplied regiments for battles throughout the seven-year conflict.

While *Outcasts of Essex* climaxes with a spectacular explosion at an armory, the incident was purely an imagined one. I was inspired by a much calmer 1774 episode in Portsmouth, N.H., when about 400 residents stormed Fort William and Mary and easily seized a cache of guns and ammunition from the lightly guarded British outpost.

However, one of the novelist's joys is inventing alternative endings. In my novel, Sarah blows up her town's armory with a flaming arrow, preventing either side from using its vast stockpile of ammunition in war. It was a confused, risky, heartfelt, perhaps noble gesture – and one that would bring her unimagined consequences for years to come.

ACKNOWLEDGMENTS

I WANT TO THANK my husband Steve Chawkins for his superb editing skills. He has been my rock, my sounding board, my cheerleader from the start, encouraging my daily trips down the rabbit holes of Revolutionary War history.

I also want to thank all the friends and colleagues who took the time to read and comment on Sarah's story along the way: Stephanie Hoops, Colleen Cason, Neva Felino, Brenda Loree, and Shelba Robison, to name but a few. Your thoughtful insights were a huge help.

Finally, thank you to David Ross and Kelly Huddleston at Open Books for believing in this story and presenting it to readers so beautifully.